I'm doing this for you, James.

I slipped the card key into the lock and the hotel door opened. I closed it behind me. Looking around the room I saw it was a spacious suite done in rich eggplant purple and cream colors, with a sitting area and a sumptuous bedroom.

I could see the back of Damon's head. He was seated in an armchair, looking out the window. His suit jacket and tie were draped over the back of the chair.

I took off my clothes and folded them into a neat pile as instructed. When I had nothing on, I dropped to the velvet-soft carpet and crawled over to him.

Seconds ticked by. I figured that was part of the test, too. We'd see which one of us got impatient first.

He did. "Please me," he said.

I looked up. "Excuse me?"

His expression was stern. "Did you not hear me? I said please me."

I blinked at him for a few more seconds, trying to think of what to do. "I don't know you well enough to know what pleases you."

"Then it is your job to guess, and find out."

SLOW SEDUCTION

CECILIA TAN

FOREVER

NEW YORK   BOSTON

Forever
Hachette Book Group
237 Park Avenue
New York, NY 10017

www.HachetteBookGroup.com

Printed in the United States of America

RRD-C

First Edition: January 2014
10 9 8 7 6 5 4 3 2 1

Forever is an imprint of Grand Central Publishing.
The Forever name and logo are trademarks of Hachette Book Group, Inc.

The Hachette Speakers Bureau provides a wide range of authors for speaking events. To find out more, go to www.hachettespeakersbureau.com or call (866) 376-6591.

The publisher is not responsible for websites (or their content) that are not owned by the publisher.

Library of Congress Control Number: 2013949886

*For everyone who fills my life
with love and art—you know
who you are.*

Love is art.

Love is the greatest pleasure of all.

Contents

Acknowledgments

Thanks go to Lori Perkins, my tireless agent, who always believed that someday my BDSM fantasies would be publishable, once the rest of the world caught up to me. Lori, thanks for being so patient and for being right!

I should also thank two real-life glass artists. One, Josh Simpson, is mentioned in the story as the man who makes miniature planets and hides them all around the world for future archaeologists to find. The other is the one whose work inspired me to imagine James's "Great Wave" sculpture in *Slow Seduction*: Paedra Bramhall. In 2001 or so I saw an installation of her work that represented the female womb, which included immense jagged stalactites of red glass.

Thanks to the New England Leather Alliance (nelaonline. org) for carrying the torch of BDSM community education. They're the *opposite* of a secret society, and I recommend anyone who wants to know more about BDSM to contact them or join!

And apologies to Tate Britain. The pre-Raphaelite exhibition really happened, but everything else about the museum is the invention of my fevered imagination.

SLOW
SEDUCTION

One

Break the Sky in Two

I stepped off the plane in London, already tired and sleep deprived. By the time I got through customs it was even worse. Martindale had said I should tell them I was there on vacation and not to mention work, but the customs agent seemed so friendly, inquiring about my visit, it hadn't occurred to me it was anything more than idle chitchat. In the course of the conversation I mentioned I was looking forward to the show at the Tate. His questions got more and more pointed until I finally had to say I was there for a job interview—just an interview!—and that if I got a job, the Tate would be handling the paperwork. He glowered at me after that and grumbled about letting me in. I guess there was a terrible glut of art historians looking for work in the UK if they were out to protect their jobs so fiercely. Ha.

Either way, it was a lie. I wasn't there for an interview. I had a job waiting for me. Reginald Martindale, the museum curator James had introduced me to, wanted me as a tour guide for special groups through the pre-Raphaelite exhibit they were opening in a week. Only a temporary job, but it was still a job of sorts, as well as a good excuse to leave New York.

I still didn't have my degree. After I'd reported my thesis advisor for sexual harassment, all hell had broken loose. I told the truth: he'd said he'd approve my dissertation if I granted him sexual favors. He lied and said that I was the one who came on to him, trying to get him to pass me in exchange for favors instead of rewriting my thesis. The full inquest period was sixty days, which made me miss graduation anyway. At this point my thesis draft was in the hands of the department for evaluation, and Renault was being forced to take academic leave until the inquest was over. I wasn't hopeful about the thesis. It was a first draft—I'd expected to work on it after he read it—and I knew I had cut corners in it. On top of that, he had friends and allies in the department and the dean's office who defended him and didn't believe me. Some had called for a misconduct investigation of me. Others had called me a slut.

Right now, I had done all I could do, and had taken all I could take. It was a good time to get away from school for a while.

As soon as I got through customs, I sat down on a bench with my suitcase and texted a number I'd memorized. *I told a lie today, but it was sort of a necessary one. You know I try not to tell them at all, but it was a customs officer at Heathrow giving me "the what for." I was afraid he'd send me right back to New York City. I'm in London.*

When I sent the text, it made a pleasant whooshing sound, as if it were flying through the ether directly to James's ear.

James Byron LeStrange. I had no idea if I would ever see

him again. I clung to a few ragged hopes that I would. For one, the phone he had given me kept working. Someone was still paying for it. Maybe he hadn't even noticed, in his vast riches, that the account was still being paid? Would international roaming charges finally be the thing that brought the phone to his attention and made him cut it off? I clung to the slim hope that the phone's continued life was a sign, a crack in an otherwise closed door. I had hurt him badly the last time we saw each other. I knew that now. And yet in the months that had passed since that fateful night, I had not stopped loving him.

I sent him a text every time I told a lie. Sticking to the rules. Being a good girl. Even if Stefan, his driver, was the only person who saw the texts, since he was the last person with that phone, I hoped he'd relay the messages. The texts never bounced, anyway. And Stefan knew all about me and how James had abandoned me, so I didn't mind him seeing the messages if he still had the phone in his possession.

I hoped they weren't breaking Stefan's heart. He was a nice guy and a friend when I needed one.

I figured out how to get a transit card and then caught the Underground to King's Cross, where I had booked two nights in a cheap hotel with shared bathrooms. The place was barely a step above a hostel, but at least I would have a private sleeping room.

It was the beginning of June. I hadn't seen James since the beginning of April.

The clerk at the hotel was a young Indian man, unfailingly polite, with his shirt buttoned all the way up the collar but not wearing a tie. He explained what time breakfast was, apologized that the water pressure in the shower was not very good, and handed me a card with the Wi-Fi password on it. When I got up to my room, I found it was so small the door didn't open all the way and I literally could not get in without crawling across the bed.

The window was open and I could see the towers of St. Pancras train station at the end of the block.

I turned on my phone again and found the hotel's Wi-Fi signal. Well, that was one way to avoid huge roaming charges.

I texted: *I got called a slut and a whore for reporting sexual harassment at the hands of my thesis advisor. Yet when I rode naked in the back of a limousine and screamed from orgasm as we drove through the streets, I was cherished and praised. I know which world I'd rather live in.*

The next morning I made my way to Martindale's office, which was in an unassuming building a few blocks from the actual museum. Here's where I confess I told another lie. I had told Martindale I was coming for the job. It was true that I had jumped at the chance to see this major exhibit of one hundred and fifty paintings and to get out of New York. But I had one more ulterior motive. I was there to pump him for information about James. Rumors were swirling through the Lord Lightning fan community that he was in England and that he might not be retired after all. If he was here, maybe I had a chance. And if Martindale knew anything, maybe that furthered my chances.

I had to find out.

I was in my best clothes, a cream-colored interview suit, rumpled from being crammed in my bag on a transatlantic flight. Martindale was polite and didn't mention the wrinkles. He sat behind a desk strewn with *objets d'art,* and I recognized a paperweight as James's work. I waited until we had gone through all the formalities and I'd given him the briefest sketch of how strife in the art history department had led to my leaving the university without my degree in hand.

"You think you'll have it eventually?" he asked.

"It's mostly a matter of paperwork," I said. At least, that was what I hoped. "I may have to go back to defend, if they'll let me. It's very political."

"Well, I certainly understand how political both the art world and the university system can be. For what it's worth, I thought your doctoral dissertation to be top notch. You wouldn't be here if I didn't."

"Thank you." I blushed a little from the praise. "I have a favor to ask, though, if I could?"

"Of course, my dear. What is it?"

"Our mutual friend, the man who introduced us...I've...fallen out of touch with him. I would love to at least know how he's doing. If that's not too much to ask."

Martindale folded his hands on his stomach. "Yes, the enigmatic J. B. Lester. Well, you know, he can be a bit of a recluse."

"I know."

"He's been *impossible* to reach lately. And he owes me a piece."

"Oh," I said, since I didn't know what else to say.

He stared at his hands for a long moment. "It's funny you should ask about him today, as I did get a small package in this morning's post. It contained no letter, no explanation, just some photographs."

"Photographs? You mean, like actually printed on photo paper?"

He barked with laughter. "Yes, dear, actual photos. Take a look and tell me if you think they look like his work."

He handed me the envelope, and I shook out a small stack of four or five pictures. My breath caught the moment I saw them. I had no doubt they were from him.

The pictures were of a shoe. A slipper. A glass slipper.

Martindale took me to tea. We rode the Underground not very far and came up in yet another bustling aboveground train station, and then walked to a hotel a few blocks over. There were signs everywhere pointing tourists to Buckingham Palace.

"Indeed, now you can say you've been to tea at the one and only Buckingham Palace . . . *Hotel,*" he said with an impish twinkle in his eye as we sat down to a luxurious meal that was like having a tiny bit of lunch followed by copious desserts. And pot after pot of tea. He said it was his custom to not only take new hires here, but also anyone visiting from the U.S., to help them get over jet lag. Several pots of heavily caffeinated tea later, I certainly didn't feel sleepy.

When we parted, he handed me a pass to get into the museum in the morning. "I expect to have a group of donors for you to show around Wednesday afternoon, so you have a few days to get to know the exhibit," he said. "I meant to bring a copy of the catalog with me for you as well, but you'll have to pick that up tomorrow when I'll have your badge ready. Forgive an old man for growing forgetful!"

"Oh, tomorrow would be great," I told him. "I really look forward to it. I can't thank you enough."

We went our separate ways at the Underground, and I felt like I'd just spent the afternoon with a long-lost uncle.

When I got back to my almost-hostel, I logged on and checked in with Becky. My apartment-mate back in New York was online, as usual; I could see her chat avatar when I opened up the laptop she was lending me. I pinged her and immediately the video chat window on the screen opened and I could see her wide grin, the wall of her bedroom behind her and the corner of a Lord Lightning poster.

"You made it!" she said. Her hand showed up as a sketchy blur as she waved hello to me. Her long black hair was loose around her face and, even with the low-resolution video, I could see she had the smudges of last night's eyeliner under her eyes. "You're there!"

"I'm here. I'm at this ridiculous little hotel. I mean, really little! Can you see the room behind me? It's like I'm in a closet. I can't afford to stay here very long, though. I'll have to move to a hostel or find someone who will lend me a spare room or something."

"I told you Paulina and Michel offered, right?"

"You did." They were friends of Becky's she'd never met but knew through an online Lord Lightning fan club. I was skeptical of going to live with total strangers for three months.

I must've looked as skeptical as I felt, because Becky said, "Oh, come on, Karina. Just meet them for coffee...or tea! They drink tea there, right? If you don't like them it's not like you made a commitment or anything. Maybe they'd have more advice about where to look or at least a reliable hostel. Some of the places I've seen on the Internet look so sketchy."

"You sound like my mother."

"But they *do!* Look, I can see Paulina's online right now.

Let me connect you and you two can talk to each other." She
was silent a moment, but I could see she was typing. Then
she said, "She can't get on audio or video right now, but she
says they'd totally love to have you over for tea tomorrow. I'm
sending you the address."

"All right, fine. Tell her I'll be there." I supposed she was
right. It couldn't hurt to at least meet them.

Becky typed on her keyboard for a few seconds more,
then looked up at me. "So, I should tell you that Professor
RantyPants was here today."

"What? You mean Renault?"

"Yes. He got drunk and came down here and pushed the
buzzer in the vestibule and then wouldn't believe I wasn't
you."

"Becks! That's terrible! That's . . . that's stalking!"

"Oh, I know. I had the campus police come and roust him,
and, well, I can't imagine that will look too good for his reputation."

"Holy shit, no, I wouldn't think so. Still, I'm scared for you."
And very glad that I wasn't there. "Why now, though? Why
didn't he do that when I first accused him?"

"Well, what he was saying didn't make much sense. I figured it was too much booze talking."

"Why? What did he say?"

"Aside from calling you every name in the book? This was
the weird part. He went on about how you got him banned
from the Crimson Glove Society."

"The what?" I asked. As I said it, my jet-lagged mind caught
up. Renault had been at the party James had taken me to.
He mentioned to me that if I accused Renault of sexual harassment, it would probably scuttle his chances to become a

member. James had never said the name of the group, but that had to be what it was about.

James never said a lot of things.

I hadn't told Becky that part, so James wasn't the only one guilty of not telling the whole story. I didn't want to go into that now. "Probably some exclusive club he wanted into," I said, "and didn't get because now he's got a black mark on his record." That was the truth, if not the whole truth. I decided I didn't want to talk about Renault anymore. Not when we could talk about James instead. Angry and hurt as I was, thinking about that night and James stirred my blood, reawakening the aroused longing I felt. "Now, I have news."

"News? What kind of news? About him?" When Becky said "him," she meant *him*. Yes, it was kind of weird that the man I was so desperately in love with, she worshipped as a pop idol, but at least I had someone I could talk to about him. No one else knew his secret.

"About him," I agreed. "You know the museum curator he introduced me to? The guy who convinced me to come here in the first place? He got some mystery photos in the mail."

"I love a good mystery!" Becky leaned in close and her eyes looked huge.

"They were of glass sculptures, and someone had sent them to Martindale. He suspected they were from him. I'm sure they were."

"What made you so sure?"

"Not only did it look like his work, but the sculptures are of glass slippers."

Becky gasped. "And you guys have that whole Cinderella thing going on. He's as obsessed with you as you are with him, Karina."

"Are you sure? What if he's obsessed with playing God to poor little girls? What if he wants to be Prince Charming but doesn't give a fuck who Cinderella is?"

"Rina, seriously, did he ever give you that impression?"

"No, but he also never gave me the impression he was going to run off and abandon me, either!" I'd spent a lot of time trying to figure out what was going through James's head since the night he had left me in the middle of a sex party for millionaires. Becky had helped, speculating and sympathizing. She listened to me cry and had heard these complaints from me before. "Maybe he's looking for *another* Cinderella."

"You don't know that," she insisted. "I think you have to keep looking for him. Was there a postmark on the photos?"

"Martindale said there was no return address."

"Yes, but do the envelopes there get stamped like they do here? Some clue as to where it was mailed from?"

"I don't know."

"Well, find out! Every clue helps when you're trying to solve a mystery, Rina. Seriously."

"I'm bad at this cloak-and-dagger stuff, Becks." I also didn't think it was going to be as simple as putting together a string of clues like some Agatha Christie novel. "I'll ask Martindale tomorrow."

"Don't look so down, Karina," she said. "It's a good sign. I know it is. The latest rumors are that he's in England. I'll see if I can find out anything more specific. I sent you those links for discussion boards and websites, didn't I?"

"You did. Thanks, Becky. I wish you were here." I looked around the room. "Except there wouldn't be space for another person in this closet."

She chuckled at my joke. "Maybe I'll come visit at the

break in July. Oh, speaking of which! Eek! I better get dressed. I'm supposed to be at class by two o'clock."

"Ooh, okay, I'll let you go." I wanted to hear about her class. She was teaching a summer session literature seminar and had been stressing majorly over it. I was sure I'd hear all about it later. "Bye, Becks."

"Bye, Rina. Don't forget! Tea with Paul and Michel tomorrow." She waved one last time and then her screen went dark when she closed her laptop.

The tiny room felt very empty then. I sent an e-mail to my sister, Jill, telling her about tea at the Buckingham Palace Hotel.

The sun was setting on this warm summer evening as I stared out of the open hotel window. The sky was alight with streaks of rose and magenta. The towers of the train station really looked more like a castle than a transit hub. Two children ran down the cobbled street toward the park, laughing, their father following behind, unhurried. I wanted to imagine that it was a castle, that I had come to a fairy-tale land, but reality was holding me in a very firm grip.

I sat back down on the bed. I wanted to walk around but I didn't know the neighborhood. Was it safe? Maybe it was at the moment, but once the sun went down, would it be? I remembered all the warnings my mother had given me, first when I went to college, then when I moved to New York City for grad school. Don't talk to strangers. Don't go out at night. Don't walk alone. They all applied suddenly. I was in a foreign country and out of my element.

The e-mail Becky had sent with the links to the LL fan sites beckoned me. Well, that would be one way to keep myself busy for a while . . .

I had avoided looking at the sites up until now. It was weird enough that the man I had fallen in love with, the man with whom I had done some of the most intimate and out-rageous sexual things, was secretly an international rock star, but it was even weirder to realize that millions of women, my own roommate included, spent their days lusting after him.

I clicked on the first link somewhat hesitantly. A fan site popped up, and a song of his began to play. Headings on the site beckoned me to sections: *News, Photo Gallery, Your Stories, Meetups.*

The *News* page appeared to be a mix of blog posts and links to news stories about anything and everything remotely related to Lord Lightning. Some guy who had once played guitar on one of his albums had a solo record out now, and so most of the recent articles were about him. The *Photo Gallery* contained promo photos, concert shots, and occa-sional fan photos where people had uploaded pictures of themselves meeting him. Most of them were women, grin-ning wide-eyed in excitement and disbelief at standing next to their idol. None of those were more recent than several months ago, the last time he appeared.

The night we met.

I had to stop looking at the pictures. He always appeared wearing a mask or so heavily made up he was unrecogniz-able, but the comments people left freaked me out a little. "So beautiful! The most beautiful man alive!" read one. "Yummy. I could nibble those abs like ears of corn," read another. Others were more graphic. It wasn't that I didn't agree with them, but the flare of jealousy I felt was so hot my cheeks burned. Jeal-ousy and arousal, too, triggered by the frank erotic thoughts these fans had about him, about the little bit of skin he showed in a photo shoot or the suggestive pose on an album cover. Some guys get up there, sing, and get famous, I know that. But Lord Lightning wasn't just a musician. He was a Sex Symbol with a capital S. He was *made* of sex.

The *Your Stories* section was even worse. One section was meant to be true stories like "The Day I Met Lord Lightning for Winning a Radio Contest," but there were only a few postings there. The fiction section, on the other hand, was huge, with thousands of stories. And I couldn't help but notice that many of them were rated "R" or "X," like movies.

One of them, entitled "Limo Ride," caught my eye. I couldn't help myself. Against my better judgment, my curiosity got the better of me, and I clicked on it.

Ever since the day I became my lord's personal makeup and costume artist, my life has never been the same. I'll never forget the day we were on our way to a public appearance. He'd chosen spandex to show off his incredibly well-toned body. I was in the best shape of my life, too, since he had me join him for workouts with his personal trainer. I knew every inch of his body, of course, since it was my job to fit him for costumes, and as you know, many of them fit him perfectly. When I say every inch, of course I also mean every inch of the magnificence of his love rod. Even flaccid, it was one of his most prominent and desirable features, and I was forever designing clothes to accentuate that delicious moose knuckle.

But of course when not flaccid it could be a problem. A very embarrassing problem, not to mention it would ruin the line of the costume. So taking care of that became my job, too. So there we were in the limousine, from which he would emerge into a thousand camera flashbulbs and videos. "Caramel," he said to me, gesturing to the raging boner so prominent that the reddened tip protruded from under his waistband, "this is a problem. Fix it."

"Right away, my lord," I said, pulling the boner free with one hand and then straddling him. I never wore underwear anymore under my skirts, not when this kind of "problem" was prone to pop up a few times a day.

"The problem," he growled into my ear as he thrust hard into me, "is that you are so damn sexy, I can't help but get hard every time you're near."

"So, fire me," I said, squeezing him with my love muscles.

"Not on your life," he said, thrusting harder and deeper. "I can't live without you."

I couldn't read any more of it. For one thing, it was ridiculous and laughable, but on the other hand, I found myself turned on by it at the same time. *Oh my God*, I thought, *these are the kinds of fantasies these women have about him every day.*

I couldn't really be offended by it. After all, they had no idea what he was really like. Everyone wants to think there's something perfect out there, or some*one.*

Sometimes it's not a fantasy, though. I had my Prince Charming and I fucked things up. I drove him away.

I slept uneasily that night, disturbed equally by jet lag and longing.

Two

You Wouldn't Believe
What I've Been Through

Rain was coming down as I hoofed it through the crowds of morning commuters to the Underground. London was different from New York, but in a few ways, at least, they were the same: tons of people catching the subway to get to work; a plethora of small shops where one could pick up bottled water, candy, and newspapers; and guys selling cheap umbrellas on the street the moment the rain started to fall. I bought a black one so I wouldn't arrive at the museum looking like a drowned rat.

I managed to get there before the doors opened. There was a line outside the building of perhaps a hundred people standing in the rain, some of them holding newspapers over their heads while they waited to get in. I listened to them chatting. Some conversations were about the rain, some about how the museum was undergoing renovation. The wait was only a few minutes; then the glass doors were opened—I didn't see by whom—and in we went.

Everything that wasn't under renovation was up a flight of

stairs from the ticket lobby. I traded in the pass Martindale had given me and followed the crowd upward. There seemed to be a series of galleries arranged chronologically and a wide central atrium that had numerous modern and contemporary pieces in it. That surprised me, since I had thought all the modern stuff was at the Tate Modern, a completely different museum. But apparently Tate Britain had its share.

Across the atrium I was arrested by the brazen, disdainful stare of Rossetti's "Astarte." It was like being sneered at by the most popular girl at school—I hated that painting and didn't think it deserved the attention it got, but at the same time, seeing it was like seeing a face I knew in a sea of strangers. My homesickness lifted a little. Astarte was even bigger than she was in the actual painting because she was on a fifteen-foot-tall banner showing the way to the special pre-Raphaelite exhibit. I hurried over to her and saw the entrance.

There was a queue set up with zigzagging ropes, but no one was in line to get in. I nearly rushed straight through, but stopped when I saw there was a large canvas hanging right there where anyone waiting would have had something to look at. It was odd that this one painting was the only one outside the gallery, but it was even odder that it was unfinished. The trees were very detailed, but the people in the painting looked more like statues or ghosts, barely sketched in and lacking features. I moved closer to read the information plaque next to it.

Burne-Jones! The painting was by the same artist who had done *King Cophetua and the Beggar Maid,* my favorite painting of all time. This was apparently a scene of Tristran and Iseult, the lovers in the King Arthur legends. I didn't know King Arthur that well. There appeared to be one couple in the center of the painting and then a handful of other people around them in various poses of angst.

A young man in a suit with sleeves slightly too short and hair in need of combing came up beside me. "Fascinating, isn't it?" he said, sounding like a BBC announcer.

"Yes. Why was it left unfinished?" I asked, looking at the painting instead of at him.

"I don't know the entire story. I'm no expert, but the canvas was recently found. Publicity about the exhibition made the collector who had it wonder about it, and voila, turns out it was a hitherto unknown piece. They say Burne-Jones was trying to work out his conflicted feelings about being torn between his wife and mistress. He never did figure it out, so never could finish the painting."

"Wow. Well, that explains why these folks look so unhappy."

"Amazing, isn't it? He didn't even paint their faces and you can see their emotions just from the posture. I'm Tristan, by the way." He held out his hand.

I took a better look at him. He had pasty skin, and his brown hair was the same color as his suit. I must have hesitated a little too long while wondering if he often tried to pick up girls at the art museum, because then he went on. "You're Karina, right? If you're not, my apologies. I'm looking for an American girl who matches your description."

"Oh! Yes, I'm Karina!" I shook his hand. "Sorry! I wasn't expecting to be meeting anyone."

"Perfect! Great!" When we shook hands, he pumped my hand up and down before letting go. "I'm Martindale's summer intern. I'm actually on an errand for him right now, but when I saw you, I thought, could that be her? Best find out!

And so, voila, here you are. So nice to meet you. Have you been through the exhibition yet?"

"No. I've only been here a few minutes."

"Oh, you'll love it. It's fantastic. Such an honor to work on. And Mr. Martindale is a genius. You must tell me what you think of all the paintings—!" He paused for a breath and seemed to catch himself. "Ah. I must be going. But on my way back I'll try to catch up with you."

"Thank you . . . Tristan."

"Yes, that's my name! Just like in the painting! See, now you'll never forget it!" He beamed and shook my hand again and then hurried off. I felt rather like I'd just met the art-world version of a big, energetic puppy.

I looked at the unfinished painting for a few more minutes and then turned away from its vision of angst, confusion, and unfulfilled love to enter the main exhibition.

Seven rooms of pre-Raphaelite art awaited me. A smattering of sculpture or other pieces of art sat here and there in the middle of the floor, and the rest was paintings. I made my way through slowly, savoring the view. The museum was still not very crowded, and although more people were starting to filter in, I was ahead of most of them.

So many of these paintings I had analyzed in detail in my thesis. Seeing them in person, though, was completely different from seeing them in a book or even in a high-quality scan online. There was so much richness lost in a photograph or scan. And the details! I felt almost foolish for analyzing them when there were so many I had never seen in person.

By far, though, the painting that had the most hidden detail was good-old *King Cophetua*. As I made my way through the exhibit, I wondered at the fact that I didn't see very much by Edward Burne-Jones at all. Then a few small pieces came along, including a portrait of his mistress, and then in the next room, one of his wife.

But almost all of his works were in the very last room because, of course, these kinds of art exhibits are always arranged to save the best for last.

I got goose bumps when I saw *King Cophetua.* My entire body tingled and I felt almost like I was floating as I crossed the large room to stand in front of it. Unlike Astarte, with her sour expression and carefully posed fingers, the Beggar Maid had wide, welcoming eyes, inviting all to gaze up at her as adoringly as the king at her feet.

Though I'd studied the painting, I had no idea how huge it was. The canvas was ten feet tall, making the figures in it life-size. The other thing you don't see in the books is the frame, an ornate, sturdy, gilt thing that was like a throne. A foot wide itself, it made the whole painting almost as tall as the ceiling in the gallery.

Looking at it, I could imagine the painter so struck by the beauty of the women in his life that he was transfixed, and he painted this subject of the transfixed king who has set his lance aside and taken off his helm so that he can gaze unabashedly at the beauty before him. And that's the experience that I had seeing the painting, as did others there in the gallery. Some had to sit down, like the king, so they could keep looking without distraction. Eventually I sat down, too, on the low bench in the center of the room, which put me somewhat far from the painting, but the pull of it was no less powerful for being farther away.

Amazing.

"Quite a sight," said a voice to my left.

"Oh! Tristan!" I was startled. "How long have you been sitting there?"

"A few minutes," he said with a big grin. "But that's all right. The view is quite engaging!"

"Hah." I got the feeling he had been staring at me instead of the paintings, but his flirting didn't bother me. He seemed genuinely nice.

"You've been in here for hours," he said. "Fancy some lunch? I'll buy."

As soon as he mentioned food, the breakfast I had eaten at the hotel seemed very long ago. "I could eat."

"Come on, then. Gift shop first, though."

Through the doors we came out of the exhibition and into the special gift shop dedicated to the pre-Raphaelites. I didn't need a Rossetti refrigerator magnet or a scarf with a pattern of the flowers from one of the paintings, but Tristan marched up to the counter with a copy of the exhibition's catalog, saying something to the cashiers about how Mr. Martindale had approved him taking one for me and being very self-important about it. The two cashiers never said a word. One was older and she gave him a skeptical look, while the younger one giggled a little.

Tristan handed the catalog to me as we walked through the museum's hallways. "Here you go. You'll be needing that," he said. He led me to a different exit from the one I had come in through.

The book was quite heavy even though it was the paperback edition. I held it to my chest as we walked to the doorway.

"Oh! I left my umbrella at the other entrance," I said, as soon as I realized it was missing.

"No matter. It's barely a drizzle and we're not going far," he said.

"I don't think I should get this wet, though." I held up the glossy art book.

"Ah, yes. You may be right. Hmm. Well." He took off his jacket and held it by the shoulders. "Will this do, then?"

"Oh, Tristan, you don't have to—"

"Sure, I do. Come on." He stepped out and I followed him. I ducked my head and hid the book against my chest as best I could, and we half-walked, half-ran to a café I had passed on my way from the Underground. It started to shower a bit harder moments before we reached the door, and we hurried inside, a bit breathless.

We got a table near the back, away from the door, and I glanced at the menu. It didn't look all that different from a lot of cafés in New York. Soup, sandwiches, and some hot entrées. "Ooh, shepherd's pie. I love that."

"You're not going to have a sandwich?" he asked, puzzled.

"I'm in England, I want to eat something English," I said. "Is that so strange?"

"It's just that I'd always heard Americans loved sandwiches." He rubbed his chin. "And I thought you might like to go somewhere that would remind you of home."

"Aw, that's sweet, Tristan. But I really do think I'll have the shepherd's pie. Or maybe the Cornish pasty?" I pronounced it like "pastry" but without the "r."

"That's *pass-tee*," he said, correcting me. "It's the English version of the em-pana-dana."

Now he really was making me laugh. "That's empa-*nah*-da," I said, correcting him back.

"Ah, well, I never was any good at Spanish. I had to play

Don Quixote in a school play once. Talk about a complete debacle." He closed his menu. "Well, I am going to get a sandwich myself." He waved to get the waitress's attention.

We placed our orders and then went back to small talk, which Tristan was a champion at. The weather, things to see in London, movies—he had a seemingly endless supply of topics to chat about. The shepherd's pie was very tasty.

I paged through the catalog a little while he visited the men's room. Having now seen the paintings in real life, I thought the photos looked flat and lifeless.

We made our way back to the museum together, but he went quickly back to work, while I headed to the exhibit for another look. I'd soon be leading tours, I reminded myself.

I got caught up in staring at the paintings of Burne-Jones again. One series of his was of Perseus and Andromeda. Was Perseus's armor the same as Cophetua's? Both appeared to be made from layers of black leather with spikes and swoops on it, fanciful and not at all historically accurate. That made me wonder.

Fortunately I didn't stare at the art so long that I was late to tea, though it was close. Martindale saved me by showing up with my employee badge.

"Here you are. Very official," he said, handing me the engraved name tag, which I pinned to my sweater. "And I see Tristan got you a copy of the catalog. Very good. Turns out the first group I'd like you to show around will be during off hours, tomorrow night."

"That sounds exciting." I hoped I could find a way to iron my clothes before then. "Um, could I ask you a question, though?"

"Of course."

"Not about the exhibit. I mean, about our mutual friend."

We were standing in the middle of the final gallery, in front of Andromeda and Perseus. I felt I was being very cool and casual about it, though even bringing up the subject of James made my heartbeat race.

"Oh?"

"Yes. I was wondering, those photos, was there any indication on the envelope where they'd been mailed from?"

"There was no return address." He frowned, knowing he'd told me this the day before.

"But was there a postmark?"

He thought for a moment. "Perhaps there was. Meet me at my office tomorrow at closing time and we can examine it then. If you think that will help you to locate him, well, I am entirely in support of that idea."

I left after that and went to meet Becky's friends Paulina and Michel.

I arrived at their flat and spent a few moments searching for a doorbell. Their doorway was at the side of a small café, but the café was closed and the windows papered over as if it were under construction. The flat was on the floors above, and once I finally found the bell, Paulina came down the stairs to greet me.

I don't know what I was expecting. I guess maybe people more like Becky. But Paulina and Michel were a little older and more reserved than I'd been guessing. They looked to be in their forties, or maybe even fifties. Paulina was a tall Russian woman with streaks of red, blond, and gray hair, all of it piled atop her head, and there was a streak of flour across her forehead. "Karina. Are you Karina? Come in, come in! I'm just baking us some things for tea. Excuse my mess!" She gestured for me to follow her up the stairs.

At the top of the staircase was a short, dark-haired man, almost exactly my height, with round wire-rimmed glasses perched on his nose. He took my hand and kissed it. "Welcome. I am Michel, but my friends call me Misha."

"Nice to meet you," I said. I looked past him to the parlor behind, though, and added, "Oh." Every inch of the walls was covered with art, some of it sculpture, some paintings in frames, some that looked painted or attached directly to the wall. There was a fireplace and a large mantelpiece, and the furniture was placed among sculptures and shelves covered with books and knickknacks and things, a glorious riot of color and clutter.

Amid the chaos sat two red velvet chairs with claw feet and a love seat that faced the fireplace with a coffee table in the center. Or, a tea table, I supposed. Pots and cups and china as mismatched and eclectic as the decor waited on a tray.

"You two sit down," Paulina said. "The scones are about to come out of the oven."

She went through a doorway into the kitchen, and I followed Misha to the chairs. Something smelled sweet and delicious. I took a seat and Misha poured tea into my cup. On the table were a few slices of finger sandwiches and what looked like chocolate cookies. Now that I was sitting down in front of it, I could see the large painting above the mantel was a portrait of the two of them, only it looked like they had swapped clothes before posing. Interesting. The likeness of the painting to their faces was striking.

"So what brings you to London? Becky said something about a summer job?" Misha asked me.

"Yes, I'm helping out with this pre-Raphaelite exhibit at the Tate Britain," I said. "I get to give my first tour tomorrow."

"And you are an expert on the pre-Raphs?" His accent was French and yet he clearly didn't struggle with English at all.

"I wrote my dissertation on them." I added a lump of sugar to my cup and stirred. "And I happened to meet one of the curators from the museum, and one thing led to another."

"Lucky girl," he said, and it sounded like *lucky gull.*

Paulina emerged with scones still hot from the oven on a tray. For a few minutes then we were all too occupied with breaking open the delicious baked goods, slathering them with butter, and eating them to have decent conversation. It was one of the most fantastic things I had ever tasted. Better than the ones at the Buckingham Palace Hotel.

Paulina smiled indulgently when we all finally slowed down and sat back. "Some folks call our place the House of Indulgence," she said.

"And they're not wrong!" Michel chimed in, licking crumbs from one of his fingers. "Now, where were we? Becky was telling us you're looking for a place to live."

"Yes. Just for the summer," I began. "I'm supposed to go back to school to finish up my doctorate."

"And you're poor as a church mouse?" Paulina guessed, or maybe Becks had told her.

"Pretty much. The thing at the Tate is sort of off the books. I'm getting paid under the table."

"Oh, now *that* is intriguing," Paulina said, leaning closer to me. "The art world has its mysteries, though, doesn't it?"

Does it ever, I thought, wondering if they were familiar with J. B. Lester as well as Lord Lightning. But I couldn't tell them of the connection if they were. As far as I knew, Becky and I were the only people who knew that the glass sculp-

ture artist and the rock star were the same person. "You two
seem very . . . arty."

"We dabble," Paulina said with a shrug. "All of our friends
are artists of some kind."

"I can't help but admire the painting. Did a friend do it?"

"Oh, yes. Fantastic, isn't it? Our showpiece." Paulina gestured toward the mantelpiece. "Truth be told, we're trying to
turn the space downstairs into a gallery. But the money's a
trickle and there's a lot of work still to do . . ." She trailed off,
looking into her teacup. Then she and Michel shared a look.

Michel spoke next. "As we told Becky, we do have a room
upstairs, currently storage, and one of our goals is to get it
cleaned out. We'd be very happy to offer you the room in exchange for your help cleaning it and working on the gallery
downstairs."

It took a moment for what he said to sink in. "Wait, you
mean work instead of paying rent?"

"Yes." He smiled a knowing smile.

"That's a great idea! But, well, maybe I should see this
room so I know what I'm getting myself into?"

"Fair enough," Paulina said. "We may as well go upstairs
and have a look, then."

She led the way, I followed, and Michel brought up the
rear. He pointed out the door to his own studio, and then
we went up another set of stairs. Paulina's studio was toward
the front. She let me look in for a moment and I saw various
canvases in various states of half-finished. From there we
went toward the back of the building. She pushed open the
wooden door at the end of the hall, and it swung open into
the room.

The space for the door to open was the only fully clear

space on the floor. Everywhere else there were towering piles of books, including on what looked to be a small, low bed, the table beside it, and the dresser against the wall. A lot of books. But not so many that I couldn't imagine what the room would be like when they were neatly arranged on shelves. The window on the back wall was set high up, above the shelves and almost to the ceiling.

"Ideally," Paulina said, "we'd get some shelves and things set up downstairs in the lounge area, and a lot of these could move down there. But we haven't got that far yet."

"I think I can handle it." The late-afternoon light came through the small window that faced the back alley. It would be a charming, cozy room once the books were tamed.

"Excellent! Paul, let's break out some champagne to celebrate," Michel said. "Welcome to the ArtiWorks!"

Paulina chuckled. "You'll soon learn that Misha will use any excuse to open a bottle of champagne. Thankfully we can buy it in half bottles now."

"ArtiWorks?" I asked as we went back downstairs. "I thought this was the House of Indulgence?"

Michel chuckled. "The name of the new gallery, that is, if we can ever get it finished and opened," he explained, as he popped open a small bottle and poured for us. The bubbles tickled my nose.

"So are you also a Lord Lightning follower?" Paulina asked, while we were sipping.

"Not exactly," I said, not sure how much to say.

"Becky told us you are trying to find him," she continued. "But that's all she said."

"Yes. I . . ." I trailed off, not sure what to say.

"You don't have to tell us anything," Michel said quickly.

"We are nosy people. I can tell you that we sometimes hear about his whereabouts. So there is that."

I couldn't help but ask. "Have you heard anything lately?"

They both shook their heads. Paulina poured me some fresh tea. "We've heard he's in England," she said with some disappointment in her voice. "Usually we know more, but not this time."

It was a tenuous lead, but at least it was a lead. I felt a flare of hope. They seemed like such nice people. I looked up at the painting. They were both smiling in the portrait and they looked much younger, but sometimes portrait painters made their subjects look better in paint. "How long ago was the portrait done?"

"Oh, years ago," Paulina said. "Although it was based on a photo even older, taken when we were still working at the university. Where is that one, Misha?"

"Oh, here." He got up from his chair and went to a shelf that was crowded with photos in frames. He pulled one out and brought it to show me. "The painter of course didn't put in all the students, just us."

My breath caught and my throat felt like it was closing. The photo showed a group of people, Paulina and Michel in the center, looking young in their swapped clothes, but there were a few others in the shot. One of them was a tall man who had moved his head at the moment the picture was taken, so his face was blurred. One couldn't be sure of his features, but his posture, his frame, the set of his shoulders . . .

It looked like James. It had to be him.

The two of them seemed to be holding their breaths, too. I tried to think of what to say.

Paulina took the frame gently from my hands.

"We miss him, too," was all she said, before she put it back among the crowd of others, obscuring it again.

"When will you move in?" Michel asked.

My head was still spinning from the sudden revelation that these two were something more than fans, that they knew what he looked like without a mask, that they *knew* him. At least they had known him years ago. It seemed that he was hiding from them, too. "Well, I guess I should try to get the bed and dresser cleared off before I attempt to," I said, trying to bring my mind back to the task at hand.

"No time like the present," Paulina chirped, looking hopeful.

"I'll help, if you like," Michel offered.

"No, no, I'll get started. There isn't room in there for more than one person anyway," I said. "I'll go get my stuff from the hotel a bit later."

"I need to go out in a bit anyway," Paulina said. "I'll come with you to help move your things."

"I don't have that much stuff." I couldn't help but grin, though. "Just one suitcase and a computer bag. But I wouldn't mind company."

"That's settled then. I'll come up and see how your progress is going in a few hours," she said. "Misha, the dishes are yours."

"Yes, dear," he said with a sigh. "She's a fantastic cook, you know, but this is the price she exacts. When she cooks, I clean."

He went into the kitchen, and I went upstairs, while Paulina settled by the fireplace with a book, sipping what was left of the tea. If I hadn't been sure before, now I was quite convinced that I was in for an interesting summer.

Three

Too Cool to Fool

It was a good thing I wasn't supposed to give that tour until the evening. Jet lag kept me up all night, though at least I put it to good use reading the catalog, and then I slept through the morning. When I woke up in the early afternoon, at first I couldn't remember where I was, and the tiny bed surrounded by books seemed like something out of a dream. Then I remembered Paulina and Michel and our late-evening run to the hotel to get my things. The clerk seemed very skeptical of me checking out at eleven o'clock at night, as if the two of them were some kind of disreputable characters who might be kidnapping me.

Maybe they were, artists kidnapping me off to art fairyland.

After I woke up, Paulina made me breakfast and helped me iron my blazer so I would look presentable. I had bought the jacket to wear to job interviews, and once the wrinkles were out of it, I looked sharp and smart, I thought.

Martindale thought so, too. "Ah, you look perfect," he said

as he ushered me into his office. "Thank you for being will-ing to do this after hours."

"Oh, of course, whatever you need," I said.

"Many of the donors have no difficulty passing through the crowds, but there are some who prefer not to appear in such public venues. Tonight's guest is in that category. We should meet his party shortly. But before they arrive, let's look at that package again."

He sat behind his desk and took out James's photographs, still in the same envelope they had been mailed in. He passed the small item to me.

It didn't have a postmark on it, but instead of stamps it had a label that had clearly been generated at the post office for the correct postage amount. The label had various numbers and letters on it. "Do you know what these mean? Could they be used to track the package?"

He peered across the desk where I was holding up the en-velope. "I don't rightly know."

"Do you think we could look it up on the Internet?"

"I don't know. Could we?" He turned toward the computer stand to one side of his desk, where a monitor and keyboard sat idle. "I admit I don't know how to do much with this other than answer my e-mail."

"Can I give it a try?"

"Please. Let's switch chairs." He got up and ceded his chair to me with a little bow.

The computer was on and the screen lit up as I jiggled the mouse. It wasn't difficult to open a Web browser and I started to search. The Royal Mail website talked about the switch from postage to metered labels, which meant whoever mailed the package had gone to a mail counter to post it. That was a start. But I couldn't find a directory that explained what the label codes were, only a tantalizing bit about how the codes were unique to each mailing branch.

"Well," I told Martindale, "this would tell us where it was mailed from, if we could find out what the actual codes were. That doesn't seem to be on the website."

"Perhaps the police?" he suggested. "This seems the sort of thing they would be keenly interested in."

"I'm betting if I keep digging I'll find it," I said.

"Well, best to continue it later. It's nearly time for our appointment."

I turned off the monitor and handed him back the photos, but he demurred. "Why don't you hang on to them for a while?"

I slipped the envelope into my purse.

We took the short walk from the office building to the museum. The weather was lovely, cooling a little as the afternoon turned to evening, and there was a breeze from the direction of the river.

As we approached the back entrance, the driver got out of a limousine sitting at the curb, and I thought instantly of Stefan.

A moment later the driver had opened the passenger door, and a man in a sleek-looking suit with artfully tossed black hair stepped out. He was runway-model gorgeous, with the flat, disdainful look in his eye you see on the covers of magazines. Two women, one blonde and one brunette, with the same look about them followed.

I did a double take when Martindale led me right to them. I had been expecting rich art donors to be older, more like Martindale himself.

Instead, the man reminded me of James, and the two statuesque women of Lucinda, with their cool beauty. I had only met her once, at that kinky party, but she had made an impression, poised and sexy, like so many of the people there. Self-possessed and confident, yet exuding a sort of erotic vibe—or maybe at this point for me that kind of self-possession *was* an erotic vibe. That was James all over, completely in control, knowing that he turned heads and left people drooling in his wake. That cool exterior hid a passionate, wicked core. I remembered the exacting efficiency with which he tied me up with ropes as well as the way he had trembled against me, barely able to stop himself from fucking me before I was ready...

Martindale brought me back to reality. "Mr. Damon George, this is Karina Casper. She'll be showing you around the exhibit."

"Pleased to make your acquaintance, Ms. Casper." The man took my hand briefly.

Martindale seemed to be waiting for him to introduce his companions, but he said nothing about them and they hung back, silent. Martindale cleared his throat. "Yes, well, let's go in."

A security guard met us at the doors to allow us inside. Martindale then led us through the back-entrance access hallways I had not been in before and into the galleries. The two women were wearing heels that seemed impossibly high, and we walked somewhat slowly, the sounds of their heels and our shoes loud in the empty museum.

"Pardon the dust from the construction," he said, as we went past one of the areas where the major renovations were taking place.

"Why should I mind it?" Damon George said. "I'm paying for a lot of it, aren't I?"

"Ha-ha, true," Martindale agreed. "Now, here we are. I'll leave you in Ms. Casper's hands. Karina, when you're done, pick up the phone here to let security know."

"Yes, Mr. Martindale," I said, wondering if I should curtsy. I didn't. He gave me a little wave good-bye and then left.

The lights were already on full brightness as we stepped into the first gallery.

I took a deep breath, preparing to launch into a speech about the founding of the Pre-Raphaelite Brotherhood, but he stopped me before I could start.

"Karina Casper," he said. "May I call you Karina? You can call me Damon instead of Mr. George."

"Um, sure." I tried to guess his age. Thirty, maybe? "Is there something in particular you want to know about the Pre-Raphaelites?"

"Perhaps. Or perhaps I merely wish to commune with the art." He clucked his tongue and walked down the first row of paintings, the two women trailing behind him like obedient pets.

Given that they reminded me of the people I'd seen and met at that kinky ball, I wondered if they were under an order of silence.

Maybe I was too after that comment about communing with the art. He was clearly as arrogant as they came. I reminded myself that he was a major donor and kissing his ass was my job.

So I followed along like one of his pets. He said nothing until we came to the famous image of Ophelia drowning herself. "Surely you see that this painting is about violence against women," he said. "How dare they show it in public?"

I nearly rose to the bait, except that it was so obvious he was saying something outrageous to get a rise out of me, and I didn't want to give him that satisfaction. "Our mission is to preserve and display the art," I said in my best tour guide voice. "Not to condone any particular interpretation of it. Any work of great art will have multiple interpretations. In fact, I'd say the greater the art, the more interpretations there will be."

He sniggered. "Very politically correct, my dear."

What wouldn't have been politic would be to say what I was really thinking, which is that I didn't give a damn what his opinions were on art. Or anything. Arrogant prick. But I gave him my "waitress" smile and we moved on. He didn't linger over many of the paintings, skimming along until we came to the final gallery.

"Now, here are the really sexy ones," he said, opening his arms wide as if he were going to give the nudes of An-dromeda a hug.

I should have known those would be his favorite paintings. Andromeda was the only nude in the whole exhibit. Depicted in three large paintings by Burne-Jones, Andromeda is rescued by Perseus from the sea serpent that is about to eat her. In the first, there's a kind of love-at-first-sight moment, where she's naked against the rocks and he takes off his helmet to look at her. In the second, we see her back turned while Perseus wrestles with the black coils of the sea serpent. In the last, she is clothed and they are bending over a font together so Perseus may show her the head of Medusa in the reflection.

It struck me suddenly that Andromeda's dress in the final painting was strikingly similar to the one worn by the Beggar Maid. I stepped closer to examine it.

"You have it backward, you know," Damon said, stepping

close and talking quietly into my ear, the way you would if the gallery were crowded with people. Since it wasn't, I stepped aside, but he kept going. "You read it right to left, but the real story is the other direction."

"What are you talking about?" I frowned, wondering what nonsense he was spouting this time. Was he trying to get a rise out of me again? "It follows the mythical tale."

"Ah, but that's the thing. You're supposed to see it as the great and mighty Perseus is tamed and domesticated by the beautiful girl. The first thing he does? Uncover his head, then cut off the head of a snake, and then in the end show her how safe and tame the snake-head of Medusa is. In other words, he emasculates himself for her—the snake, the head, and the sword all being phallic symbols."

"So? That's still reading it left to right."

"I know. That was the acceptable story to Victorians. But the real story is the other way. It's that he begins tame, fools her into thinking he's safe, and by the end is about to put his helmet on and ravish her."

"That's ridiculous."

"Ancient Greek was read from right to left, not left to right," he said smugly.

I racked my brain, trying to remember everything I knew about the paintings. I was fairly sure that Burne-Jones had painted three or four more of Perseus, and if only I knew the dates I could probably prove him wrong, but since these hadn't figured into my thesis, I didn't know the dates off the top of my head. "How do you know so much about Greek culture anyway?"

He laughed and turned to face me in front of the painting. "Don't you think there's a resemblance?"

The crazy thing is, there was. He could have been Perseus come to life, but with a much more annoying smirk. I still didn't make the connection, though.

"George is anglicized from Georgiades," he said. "So let's just say...I know my Greek."

Fine. "A very interesting theory, Mr. Georgiades."

"Damon, please." His eyebrow arched with mischief, and I knew he was about to say something else designed to get a rise out of me. "I only enjoy formality with those I'm fucking."

I knew it. Well, if he thought he was going to shock me, he was wrong. "Is that why your companions don't speak?" I asked. "And don't have names?"

His grin widened with delight. "You're very perceptive, Karina! I wouldn't have guessed you for the type, but then...people never do. I suppose you went through the whole slap and tickle nightclub scene in New York?"

"No," I said coldly. "Not really."

"Hmm." He merely gave me a nod and then turned back to the painting behind him.

He snapped his fingers, and the two women fell into a sudden embrace, kissing each other. I took a step back.

"You're welcome to stay and watch, Karina, but if it's too much for you, all I ask for is, oh, about seven minutes of privacy."

"Are you kidding me? I can't leave you alone with these paintings!" That was a much more shocking idea than that he had two sex slaves following him around. Oh. It dawned on me then that he'd brought them to the gallery specifically to get off. No wonder he paid a huge sum to have a private, after-hours viewing of the art.

"Even if I promise we won't touch them?" At the word

touch, he rubbed the length of his cock through his trousers.

I wasn't about to let that distract me. "I'm sorry, Mr. George, but I don't know you well enough to trust your promise. Just because you're rich doesn't mean you're honorable."

He bowed his head. "All too true. I suppose you'll have to stay, then." Before I could argue further, he snapped his fingers again and said, "Present."

The two women disengaged instantly and struck poses with almost military precision, feet apart, hands behind their backs, thrusting their chests forward. Damon circled them, examining their bodies first with his eyes, then running his hands over the breasts of one, feeling the hardness of her nipples where they stood out against her blouse. He then ran his hand down the other one's mound and hiked up her skirt. From where I was standing behind them I couldn't quite see, but I was betting she had no panties on. She made a sound as—I guessed—he put his finger inside her.

"So ripe, so ready," he murmured, as he lifted his hand to her face. She licked his finger.

He stood facing me then, one hand up the skirt of each woman. They struggled to stay silent as he played with their privates. I remembered struggling like that, trying to hide the fact that James was getting me off under a restaurant table. Damon's grin was wicked, his eyes locked on me as he tormented and pleasured the two women. I couldn't help but try to guess what he was doing. When one of them stifled a yelp, had he pinched her clit? Put a second finger into her? When the other bent her knees to steady herself and caught her breath, was she close to coming? I could hear the wet sucking sound of one of his hands penetrating her over and over.

I tried not to move, but I wanted to press my own legs together and tamp down the arousal I was feeling at the sight.

Both women were barely staying balanced on their high heels as they shook with desire. I wondered if he was going to get them off right there in front of me.

No, he was crueler than that. He cleared his throat, pulled his hands free, and held them out for the women to lick clean. As their tongues went to work, he said, "We have scandalized Karina enough. I'll finish with you two in the car. To the ladies' washroom with you now. Neaten up, and *no touching each other.*"

He snapped his fingers again, and the two flushed, panting women straightened up, neatened their clothes, and then sauntered off toward the restroom, one of them smirking with glee.

Damon turned to me. "You look much more intrigued than scandalized, actually, Karina."

I tried to arrange a properly offended look on my face, but failed.

"Were you aroused by what you saw? Or by the idea of it?" he asked.

I was aroused by the memory of James touching me that way, I thought. That was all. "Mr. George," I said. "What are you getting at?"

He grinned. "So formal. I told you I only like to be formal with those I'm fucking. If I didn't know better, I'd say you were flirting with me."

He was infuriating. I was about to tell him to fuck off when he reached into his jacket. He pulled out a business card from the inner pocket, but that wasn't all. With the card was a red satin glove.

I stared at it. The Crimson Glove Society? Was that what

Renault had called the secret group of rich kinksters James was part of? James had told me they had started in the UK. Damon tucked the glove away and handed me the card.

All that was printed on it was a phone number. Déjà vu. It was exactly like the card James had given me once with his own number on the back.

I held the card between two fingers and sneered. "And I suppose you expect me to call you when I can't stand it any-more and need Daddy to come spank me?"

"Oh no, Karina. That's not my number. That's a much more intriguing proposition."

I looked at him skeptically.

He stuck his hands in his pockets and shrugged, as if trying to take his arrogance down a notch. "It's a private club here in London. I'm a recruiter of sorts."

"You recruit new members?"

He huffed a little laugh. "Not members. S-type trainees."

"S-types?"

"Slaves, servants, submissives," he said with a small smile. "There's a training program. The two women with me? They're trainees, nearly ready to graduate into full service at the club."

My mind raced. It was one more lead, one more thing that could take me to James. That night after he'd kicked me out, who did he turn to? Lucinda? Some other acquaintance at the party? And if he was here in England, which seemed certain to me, whether he was looking for a new Cinderella or trying to forget the old one, wouldn't the Crimson Glove Society be where he'd go?

I took a deep breath. "Are you inviting me to . . . to become a trainee?"

He seemed very serious now, very sober and unlike the cocky playboy he had been. "I am inviting you to entertain the idea. If you'd like to talk with these two about their experiences, I'll give them permission to. If you are interested after that, I will sponsor you for training."

"And if I call this number and say, 'Damon sent me,' what happens?"

"You'll be interviewed and auditioned. There are no guarantees you'd be accepted, of course, but I am intrigued. Intrigued enough that I would also consider training you personally to prep you for the audition..." A hint of that cocksure tone crept back into his voice. "If you were interested."

The sound of two pairs of high heels clicking reached my ears. His companions were returning.

"I'm really not interested in you personally, Damon," I said, "but I am intrigued by the club."

"Good. Did you want to talk to them?" He gestured to the women.

"That seems like a good idea."

"If you're free now, I think you should go for coffee."

"Right now? I thought you were about to, um..."

He laughed. "I know what you thought. You thought if I couldn't fuck them right here in the gallery, I was going to do it the second we got into the limo. It's tempting, of course. But part of being a handler is not giving in to temptation. Or, at least, knowing when to. I see a much greater opportunity in front of me here, to bring you into our midst."

"Oh?"

"And then maybe in the future I'll get to fuck all three of you here in the gallery *and* in the back of the car. Who knows?" The mischievous grin was back. "I am willing to raise the stakes on my bet."

Part of me was saying "no way, buddy," but the offer was intriguing as a way to search for James... And maybe it was time to find out if what I was craving in James's absence was really James, or just the sexual domination he'd addicted me to. "All right, fine. The girls and I will have coffee, and you should go have a cold shower or whatever it is you do."

He laughed a delighted laugh. "Excellent. Call the guard to lock up and we'll get out of here."

The two women were named Nadia and Juniper, who told me to call her Juney. I would have bet money on them being Scandinavian fashion models or something, but once they started talking, they magically transformed into hardworking women from Manchester. Damon ensconced us in a booth at the very back of a dimly lit café and then left us alone.

"He's trying to recruit you. Exciting!" Juney enthused.

"Is it? I mean, tell me about this training program. How long have you been doing it?"

"About six months for me. Nadia, you?"

"Around eight," the brunette said. "That doesn't count the first three months with Damon, though."

"So you took him up on the—how did he put it—*personal* training offer first?" I asked.

"Well, more like we had a wild fling for three months, at the end of which he foisted me onto the club," she said with a chuckle. "Being with him for three months was fun. Training for the club is more exciting, though."

"Is it? What sorts of things do you have to do?"

"Well, it starts with basic stuff like waitressing at the club itself," Nadia said.

"I should be able to breeze through that..."

"Some trainees provide specialty services, like massage or barbering."

Juney slapped her lightly on the shoulder. "She doesn't want to hear about the boring stuff. She wants to hear about the S-E-X." She leaned forward and cradled her coffee mug. "The sex is amayyyyyy-zing."

"Okay, that's what I'm trying to figure out though." I leaned forward myself. "Are you getting paid for this? Is it...prostitution?"

They both laughed like I was being ridiculous. "The whole point is that we aren't paid," Juney said, "because if we were, it would be. We're doing it because it's exciting and fun and a fantastic way to meet ridiculously rich men."

"And women," Nadia added. "Maybe once upon a time the club members were gentlemen, but these days, it's equal opportunity for tops *and* trainees. We're the eye candy at the club and the practice dummies for tops in training, too. Kinky rich people need play partners who aren't always other kinky rich people, or it gets complicated."

"But then sometimes you want it to get complicated," Juney said. "I know I'm kinky as fuck, but I've had it with the dumbass doms at the nightclubs. They don't know how to treat a submissive right. And the online dating thing? Ugh. They look real kinky online, but then you meet them and it's the same old thing. They want to spank you a couple of times and then: 'Hey dearie, make me a sandwich so I can watch Manchester United on the telly.'"

"Wait, so, you won't make your boyfriend a sandwich, but you don't mind waitressing for rich people?"

Juney rolled her eyes. "It's not the *same*. Nadi, you explain it."

Nadia cleared her throat and took a sip of her tea. "Training has some specific steps. You have to learn general service, a specialty skill, and show progress in sexual uses. But there are rules."

"I assume everyone's sworn to secrecy?"

"Naturally. What I mean is there are rules regarding what they can and can't do to trainees." Nadia glanced around before continuing. "Some are obvious. I mean, they can't hurt you or make any permanent marks, for example."

"The big one, though, is you get to pick something you won't do," Juney said, eyes alight. "So, you know, if you're afraid of fire you could say no fire play."

"Fire play?"

Nadia clucked her tongue. "It's not as bad as it sounds. But you know, the whole thing is about limits and rules. And honor, personal honor. That's the real basis of this lifestyle. It's all about who can be trusted. If you can't be trusted, you're out."

I wondered if that was part of James's hang-up about honesty. "Okay, and Damon's in charge of your training?"

"No, we're actually mostly working under a woman named Vanette. Mr. George is testing us tonight, though." Juney giggled. "I can't wait!"

"I'm keeping you from him, then," I said, taking a gulp of my coffee.

"Oh, he would have come up with some other diabolical delay, I'm sure," Juney answered. "I'm hoping the wait has made him randy as a horse. He's the best lay I've ever had by far."

Nadia smirked. "He is good. And pretty, too."

I couldn't help but smirk back. Sounded like "handler" Damon George was going to have his hands full keeping a rein on these two frisky fillies. "Thank you for talking with me."

"You're welcome!" Juney jumped up and gave me a kiss on the cheek before stepping back to put her blazer back on. "I hope we'll see you there. You'll see. It's a blast. If you've got any masochistic or submissive tendencies at all, it's the best."

Nadia stood and patted me on the arm. "And of course, you'll keep this all private. Strictly."

"Of course."

"Let's exchange phone numbers, in case you want to call us with any other questions," Juney said, jotting hers down on a piece of paper. Nadia added her number as well.

I hesitated for a moment. I'd never given the "James phone" number to anyone before. But it was the phone I had to rely on here. I wrote the number down, tore it off, and gave it to them.

They hurried to the front of the café, where I saw Damon standing. He paid the cashier, and all three of them waved to me as they went out the door.

I thought, well, that was quite a different evening than I'd expected. I walked around a little, looking at the sights while I went in the direction I thought the Underground was. I ended up browsing in a bookshop, then meandering along the edge of a park where a band was playing.

I had just come to the Underground when my phone rang from an unknown number.

My immediate thought was: James?

"Hello?"

Surprisingly, it was Damon George. One of the girls must have given him my number. "Where are you, Karina? Do you need a ride?"

"I can find my own way home, thanks," I said. "Are you done with Nadia and Juney already?"

"Ha. It's been well over an hour, more than enough to finish their night's lesson. Let me come get you in the car."

"Damon, my mother always told me not to get in cars with strange men."

"Even if I promise I won't touch you?"

He couldn't have known that saying so would send goose bumps all over my arms and across my neck, as I thought about the things James could do to me without ever touching me. "I said 'no,' Damon."

"Ahem. Actually, Karina, you didn't say no. You said your mother told you not to get into cars."

"You're maddening! All right. I *meant* no, then. And I'm saying it now." I looked around the street, wondering if he knew where I was, if he was nearby. But he wasn't James, and that sort of thing happened only with him.

"Okay. I understand. I do want to talk to you about my offer, though."

"Your girls convinced me. I'll call the number on the card you gave me."

"All right. I think I can help you, Karina."

"Help me pass the audition, you mean?"

"No. I mean help you understand your interest in dominance and submission."

"Well, if I pass the audition, you'll have plenty of chances for that."

"True. All right, Karina, if you're *really* not interested in talking, hang up on me now."

"I will! Ahhh!" He was so infuriating! If I didn't hang up, that meant I kept talking to him, and if I did hang up, it was like I was following his orders. I hung up and resisted the urge to throw the phone at the ground.

The truth was I did want to talk about it with someone who understood it all. *But not him,* I told myself. *Not like that!*

I went back to the ArtiWorks, alternately fuming about Damon and trying to imagine what the audition for the secret society would be like. Michel was nowhere to be seen, and Paulina was in her studio. I could hear her singing along to some music while she worked. I went to my room rather than disturb her.

I meant to spend some time working on the books, but the moment I got in I set up my laptop on my bed and took the envelope of photos out of my purse.

I was searching for information on the Internet about UK postal codes when Becky popped up in the video chat window.

"Hey, Becks!"

"Hey, Rina! How's it going so far? I got your e-mail! Are you at Misha and Paul's right now?"

"I am. And I think I have some leads, too."

"Oooh, like what? The postmark thing?"

"That's one. Here's the envelope he sent." I held it up so she could see it. "I don't know yet what—"

She leaned close to the screen, and it looked like she was writing something down. "I'll look right now."

"Okay, Watson," I joked. "But there's more."

"I'm all ears, Sherlock."

"Ha. So, remember when you were telling me Renault was drunk and ranting about something called the Crimson Glove Society? I met a man tonight who had a red glove in his pocket."

"Is that unusual?"

"A single glove, satin, and oh, by the way, he had two female sex slaves following him around the museum? Yeah, I'd say it was unusual."

"At the museum!"

"He was the big-money donor who got a private tour. Anyway, he sort of flashed the glove and then handed me a business card. Next thing I know, I'm invited to a sex slave job interview."

"What!" Her image jiggled as she grabbed her laptop like she was trying to grab on to me. "You're not serious."

"I don't mean slaves like illegal trafficking, Becks. I mean, you know, doms and subs. There's a club here in London and they train the subs to do stuff. The point is it must be the same secret society that James is in. And if he's here in the UK, how much you want to bet he gets in touch with them?"

"Oh. Well, I can tell you one thing," Becky said, typing some more as she talked to me. "Whoever mailed that envelope mailed it from York, England."

"You can tell from the code?"

"Yep. Here. I'll send you the link to the info site about it."

I didn't really need to see the page about the postal service, though. I was already doing a search on York. A tourist info site came up, and I clicked on one of the links there touting "Art in York."

Jackpot. "York has glassmakers!"

Becky was apparently looking at a different website from me. "And a ton of chocolate shops. What is up with that?"

"I don't know, but I think I'm more likely to find him through the glass artists, don't you?"

"Of course! Looks like York is only two hours from you by train. I'll send you a link to that, too." She tapped on her keyboard. "So. You've got two solid leads now. The glass people in York and your kinky rich people's club."

"And Paulina and Michel," I added. "They seem to think there's a chance they'll hear about his whereabouts at some point."

"You'll find him, Karina. I know you will."

"I'm sure you're right, Becks." It was nice to hear her say it. But I wondered if he wanted to be found.

Four

This Girl Is Made of Loneliness

The next day I called the number Damon had given me. I was a bit surprised that a woman answered. I'd been expecting someone like Damon, I guess. She told me the earliest they could audition me would be the following week. When I asked what the audition would include, she told me that not knowing was all a part of the test. She did tell me the date and time, but said that the exact address wouldn't come to me until an hour before so I would have time to get there. When I asked what I should wear, she laughed, called me a "dear thing," and hung up.

Fine. In the meantime, Michel had just finished stripping the back hallway of the ArtiWorks and we started retiling the front entrance. I planned a trip to York for two weeks later, by which time I'd have collected enough of my pay from Martindale to have a little to spend on getting there and back.

I also started leading an afternoon group tour of the exhibition every day, filling in for one of the regular docents when she took her summer vacation. Many of the visitors seemed to think it was charming that they got an American art student to lead them around the museum. Tristan followed my tour a couple of times, but claimed he could never speak so knowledgeably and authoritatively about the subject. I knew from chatting with him over lunch that he knew plenty about the pre-Raphs, but he shrugged it off.

By the day of the "audition," I had a blister on one hand and some scrapes and bruises on my arms from renovating, and I still hadn't figured out what to wear. I took a hot shower and then sat on my bed, contemplating the clothes I had to choose from.

What would James have wanted? I thought suddenly. Thinking about him brought everything into focus. It was a job interview, right? I put on the outfit I wore to meet Martindale that first day, matching blazer and slacks, but with one difference. I left my underwear off. Just in case.

My phone rang as I was slipping my shoes on. "Hello?"

"Go to the address you're about to receive by text," said a female voice that I thought was probably the same woman I had spoken to before, but I couldn't be sure.

An address appeared on my phone a few moments later, and I set about figuring out where I was going, in other words, which of the London Underground trains to take. The Underground wasn't that much trickier than the New York subway, but sometimes it took some figuring out.

I took the train to Green Park, and as I came out of the station, my phone pinged with another text. It read: *Ring #3.*

I walked a few blocks to the address I was given and was surprised that the building seemed to be a modern block of apartments. A mother escorting two young children was making her way down the front steps as I approached. I pressed the buzzer for number three. A moment later the door un-latched and I went inside. Number three was on the first floor, at the back. A large envelope with my first name on it was taped to the door. I opened it and pulled out a letter.

If you are to join us, the bond will be built on trust.

If you believe you can trust us, you will follow these instructions. Place your phone inside the envelope along with this letter and tape the envelope to the door again. Then take the Tube to Holborn. The address you seek is printed on the card.

Card? I looked in the envelope again and saw a business card at the bottom I had missed before. It had only a street ad-dress, no name or even the city. I put the card in my pocket, put my phone in the envelope, then stood there thinking.

This was fairly heavy cloak-and-dagger stuff, although it seemed very unlikely they were trying to steal my phone. I supposed they didn't want me taking a camera where I was going, and they had to be careful I hadn't brought the police or a TV news crew with me. They were probably watching me right now. I taped the envelope to the door and went on my way.

It felt distinctly odd to be without a phone. I'd gotten so used to having it, using it to check the weather, the map, read the news, and so on, all the time. Not having it was like wear-ing a blindfold. Which was probably the other purpose for them taking it away.

Fortunately, it wasn't hard to get to Holborn Station, and there was a map on the wall of the train station that let me get my bearings and find the address I needed. I walked a few blocks from the station on a quiet residential street that opened onto a square running around a small park. The buildings here were what I thought of as brownstones, only larger than I was used to. Each was four stories tall and quite wide. The sidewalk was paved in large, flat stones, and each building had a front patio surrounded by a wrought-iron fence.

This looked much more like what I was expecting, but I braced myself in case this doorway, too, had another hoop to jump through. I went up the stone steps and saw the entryway had only one doorbell. There were no envelopes in sight. I pressed the button.

A moment later the door opened. A slender woman in a pillbox hat and stylish suit, her skirt tapering to her knee, looked me up and down. Her eyes were shadowed by the netting from the hat, and she looked like the starlet of a noir film. "Your name?" she said coolly.

"Karina. Karina Casper."

"Come in." She stepped aside so I could enter and then shut the door firmly behind me. I was in the plush-carpeted front hallway. A large staircase led upward and parlors were off to either side. She cleared her throat. "If you'll go forward and to your right."

I went down the hall and then into a sort of library or sitting room. One wall was built with cabinets up to waist height and then bookshelves going up nearly to the high ceiling. A rolling ladder was attached to one side. In the middle of the room was a large table with a sculpted edge. Three chairs sat on one side of it, a single chair on the other, with a folded napkin in front of it.

She gestured to the single chair and I sat in it, my knees

suddenly feeling a bit shaky. What was about to happen? Were they going to ask me to do anything? Or were we just going to talk?

She stepped up beside me then and picked up the napkin. "Call me Vanette. This is a blindfold." She snapped it in the air and it unfolded.

"Oh."

"You don't have to wear it if you don't want to, but I think it actually makes things easier."

"All right."

She went around behind me and smoothed my hair with her hands, then lowered the cloth in front of my eyes. She tied it snugly, but not too tight. I wondered how she knew how snug to make it. Maybe she had a lot of practice. She was right, though. I felt more secure with it on. Maybe it was like calming a horse by putting something over its eyes. I felt my breathing deepen in the peaceful dark. It was time to let whatever was going to happen, happen.

I heard voices then, two men talking. They must have been coming down the stairs.

As they came into the room I recognized one of the voices as Damon's. "That's something for the finance committee to work on," he was saying.

"No doubt you're right," said the other man. He sounded older, and his accent was different from Damon's, with more *r* sounds. "Ah, and here she is. Good to see you, Vanette, my darling."

"Good to see you, Director."

I heard the sound of the chairs being pulled back on the carpet and them settling themselves. Vanette cleared her throat again. "State your name and that you are here of your own free will, that no one coerced you into appearing here, and that you are not being paid or compensated for your attendance."

"Karina Casper, and yes, I'm here of my own free will and no one is paying me."

She then addressed the other two. "American, as you can hear. Turned twenty-seven recently. No known family in the UK."

"What's she doing in London?" the director asked.

"Working at Tate Britain," Damon said. "That's where I met her. Karina, why don't you tell us why you're interested in serving us in the society?"

Well, it was your *idea,* I wanted to say, except now that I had decided on checking the place out to try to find James, I couldn't very well say that. "You made it sound very intriguing," I said. "And so did Nadia and Juney."

"How would you describe your experience?" Vanette asked, her voice sharp and serious, like her clothes.

"You mean, my sexual experience?"

"With service or other S-type roles."

"Oh." How should I describe my relationship with James? "I don't know if I'm really what you could call submissive, but I do follow instructions well. I've done some rope bondage." Let's see, what were the other things I'd seen described on the Internet? "Medical play and shaving. Orgasm denial. I've been . . . played with in public a fair bit—"

"In front of the general public?" Vanette asked. "Or at play parties?"

"Mostly the general public," I admitted. "Secretly, like going to a restaurant with my . . . partner, when he had me wear a sex toy, and also at things like performance art."

"Performance art?" The director sounded a bit amused.

"At an art gallery in New York. Well, it was invite only, so I don't know if you count that as public or private, but I was sort of a spectacle. People in the audience could pick up a riding crop and try to hit me on the ass."

"Did you enjoy it?" Vanette asked.

"Yes. It was very intense. And arousing." How much of my arousal was caused by the sensation of being struck, how much was the thrill of being naked and exposed, and how much was the fact that James was in control? I wondered.

"And your partner, did he also perform more, *ahem*"—the director cleared his throat, and I was amused that a man who was the head of a secret sex club seemed to stumble over these words—"overtly sexual acts in public?"

I paused before answering, trying to figure out which things would be considered overt or not. I decided the best thing to do would be to give a frank description. "If making me come in public, like in restrooms or public libraries, counts as overtly sexual, then yes."

"Did he fuck you?" Vanette asked, and I heard a bit of a smirk in her voice.

"Yes. Once." I pressed my hands together. I hadn't realized that cataloging everything I'd ever done with James was going to make me miss him even more. I didn't think it was possible to miss him more than I already did, but now I felt his absence like an ache all over my body. *Oh, James, does it have to be this way? And is it you I need so much, or the things you used to do to me?*

I drew a deep breath. Was I ready to find out the answer to that question? One more reason why I had to find him. I had to know. Did he miss me as much as I missed him? If he didn't, then maybe it really was over. Maybe it was time to move on. But I had to believe, deep down, that he felt the loss. He was running scared from how much he loved me and how vulnerable that love made him. Right? He was a man of masks, but love stripped them away—or at least I had stripped them away. I had to believe he wouldn't have let me go that far if he didn't love me too.

And I had to believe that if I could find him, I could break through the wall he'd built around himself. I could make him see he didn't have to run.

The questioning turned away from directly sexual topics after that, and it became almost like a job interview. We talked about art and my previous job as a waitress. I even told them Jill's tips for reading customers. But things came back to the topic of submission when Vanette asked, "Have you thought about what your training goal is? What you hope to get out of serving the society?"

"Well, I would like to understand what's going on in the minds of dominant men," I said. "Nadia said you become a sort of mind reader if you're good. I would definitely like to develop that knack."

I think it was Damon who stifled a snigger. Vanette went on. "Society trainees have two other things to determine. One is what your slave name will be, and the other is your personal dictum."

"Dictum?" I repeated. Nadia and Juney hadn't used that word.

"You may choose one thing that you do not allow," Vanette said.

"Ah, right. I didn't know that was what it was called."

"Have you given any thought to what your prohibition will be?"

I had given it a lot of thought, actually, but until that moment I hadn't known what to ask for. It became suddenly clear to me, though, as I sat there. "Intercourse."

"Oh, now that's interesting," the director said, his voice light and animated. "You mean to say you won't allow anyone to, *ahem,* fuck you?"

"Yes," I said.

The director slapped his hand on the table. "In other words, you're not interested in the job as a way to get laid. Excellent! You see, Vanette? That's the spirit we've been missing in the society. Not that I object to all the luscious creatures we have about the house, but these days, they're all so . . . so loose. Even when their discipline is tight as a drum."

Vanette's voice dropped in pitch. "I don't think that's it at all, Director. I think she's saving herself for someone. Is that what it is, Karina?"

I bowed my head. "Yes."

"A real someone? Or your fantasy master whom you hope to meet among our ranks?"

"A real someone."

She huffed. "If we're going to spend the time to train her, then I don't want her flitting off the second Mr. Right comes to his senses and realizes what a plum he has before him."

Damon hadn't spoken for a long time, but now he answered. "I find it more likely she'll forget all about Mr. Right once she's exposed to our ways. And then if one of our members wants to make a permanent partner of her? Well, isn't that part of our job?"

Vanette snorted. "Karina. I take your suggestion to mean that you won't allow *penile* penetration."

"Yes, that's what I mean."

"That means, however, that you'd be available for every other form of sexual play or torment."

"I figured that . . . um . . . ma'am." Was ma'am even the right thing to call her? Mistress? I didn't know.

"Well, I am all for accepting her into the training program," the director said. "I find her a very intriguing and bright candidate. Something different."

"I am not convinced," Vanette replied. "She lacks experience, and I worry that she will be unable to perform adequately when it comes to sex. Service talents are all well and good, but, gentlemen, none of us here is deluded into thinking that is enough."

Damon spoke up then. "And if I took her for a weekend and put her through her paces? If I find her adequate sexually, shall we reconsider?"

They went quiet for a moment, and I had the urge to lift the edge of the blindfold to see what they were up to. If I had to guess, they were all glaring at each other, or at least Damon and Vanette were.

Vanette gave in. "Fine. I'll be interested to see what you can do with her with that dictum in place."

Damon made a surprised noise.

"Because of course that's the condition that needs to be tested," she went on.

Damon sighed. "Very well."

"That sounds like we're in agreement then," the director said, "that is, if Ms. Casper agrees. Karina Casper, if you agree, you'll belong to Damon George for a weekend and operate under all the usual rules of our trainees. Your society dictum against sexual intercourse will be honored."

So, Damon had come up with a reason to get me in his limo after all. But it seemed the only way forward, and I realized that as long as he wasn't trying to fuck me, I felt fine about being alone with him. "Yes, I agree," I said.

"Good." Damon clapped his hands once. "If you really agree, you'll crawl over here and kiss my shoe."

I chuckled inwardly, thinking, *Let the games begin.* "All right."

I slipped to the floor and crawled across the thick carpet under the table in the direction his voice had come from. I felt for his feet with my hands. There. I had my palm on the instep of one of his well-shined leather shoes. I pressed my lips to it.

I felt him stand up. "From this point forward, I'm Mr. George to you."

"Yes, Mr. George." I swallowed. My clit began to throb the moment I answered him.

He hummed in appreciation. "Follow my voice."

He was backing away. I crawled slowly after him, and I felt my lower lips moving slickly against each other.

"Stop there," he said. "Turn around."

I did as he asked, crawling in a circle. Then I felt his hand give a firm caress to one of my ass cheeks. His cupped hand slid between my thighs, and I squeaked, wondering if he could feel the wetness.

"She's very turned on," he said to the others.

"Then I suppose you have a good weekend ahead of you," Vanette said.

"Just remember, old boy, no wetting the dipstick!" I heard

the director slap him on the shoulder. "Now, we should discuss that balloon payment."

"Yes, of course, Director." To me he said, "You will stay still, with your head down, until your dominant has left the room."

"Yes, Mr. George."

"Excellent. I will message you about the weekend."

I stayed where I was, listening to the sound of feet crossing the carpet and then the parlor door sliding shut. I wondered if that meant it was okay for me to get up.

I startled as Vanette's voice came from my left. "Is he telling the truth? Are you wet?"

I squeezed my legs together. "Gushing, ma'am."

"All right. I wanted to be sure spending the weekend with George wasn't going to be a total chore for you. Is he very much like your previous partner?"

"No, ma'am, not really."

"And I told you to call me Vanette."

"Oh! Sorry, ma—Vanette." I felt her approach me and then gentle tugs on the knot of the blindfold.

"Watch your head when you stand," she warned.

I opened my eyes and saw I had ended up with my head partway under the table. I climbed to my feet and straightened my jacket. "Can I ask a question? About the whole names and titles thing?"

"Of course," she said.

"Some people use aliases, some people don't, some people have titles, some don't . . . How is someone supposed to know what to use?"

She smiled. "Well, that's one of the things you start to learn, but generally speaking, it's considered polite and proper to ask how people should be addressed. Now that you know it, you'll be listening for when people say things like 'Call me Vanette.' And if they don't, you'll know to ask, with proper deference of course, 'Excuse me, but how would you prefer to be addressed?' Some of them will tell you sir or ma'am is acceptable. Others will insist on a title or a name. It will be your job to remember what they tell you, of course."

"I understand." I wondered if I should have asked James what to call him sooner than I did. Then again, I realized I had asked very early on. And he had actually told me his real name. I just hadn't known or believed it at the time. "What about the society itself? What do I call that?"

"Well," she said, an amused smile twisting her lips, "you're forbidden to speak of it to anyone, so why would you need a name for it?"

"I meant among us."

"We have no name. Just referring to the group as *the society* is enough, since among our company everyone would know what you were talking about."

"Ah, I see."

"You should make your way back to the Underground now," she said. "Nadia is here to escort you and return your phone." She clapped her hands twice, and the parlor door slid open, revealing Nadia.

I made a quick trip to the restroom before we got going. Neither of us said anything until we were a few blocks away, and then she handed me back my phone. "Here you are."

"Thank you. Wow, talk about giving the third degree."

"They do grill you pretty good. I don't know how many they turn down. It's not as easy to get an interview as it might seem from how taken with you Mr. George is."

"I'm supposed to spend the weekend with him for evaluation."

"Oh, truly? That sounds like him. He makes sure everyone else gets sloppy seconds." She blushed as she said it and put her hand to her cheek, holding in a laugh.

Her comment made me giggle. "What's funny is . . . well . . . I picked sex as my dictum. I mean, sex-sex."

"Oh, you wicked girl!" She squeezed my upper arm as the train station came into sight. "He will hate that. He absolutely loves to rule with his 'love rod.'"

That made me snort, and we both laughed. "I think he thought he was going to have his way with me," I said. "Vanette put a stop to that."

"Oh, she is such a wonderful ball-busting bitch when she needs to be," Nadia said with a sigh. "She's fantastic. She's supposedly only a handler, but none of the tops or masters dare get out of line when she's around. Well, not that they get out of line much anyway, and risk expulsion or censure. They're very, very big on rules."

"I noticed." We passed through the turnstiles. "Which way are you going?"

"I'm following you to make sure you get all the way home safely," she said.

"They're really paranoid, aren't they?"

"We have to be," she said.

I supposed she was right.

Five

Boys Always Work it Out

I arrived back at the ArtiWorks and headed straight for my room. I hadn't been this aroused in all the time James and I had been separated.

I dug to the bottom of my suitcase, where a separate case was nestled among my dirty clothes. I opened it and took out the largest of the glass dildoes he had made for me. I took off my clothes and lay down on the bed with the dildo on my chest. While I waited for it to warm up, my mind went into fantasies. Not of Damon or the club, but of James.

James as Lord Lightning. I could remember the scent of his limo, the sound of the traffic outside the tinted windows. Normally, he would be conservatively dressed in an expensive and fine button-down shirt and jacket, if not in a full suit and tie. But I imagined him as he appeared in some of the fan photos, in a skintight shirt cut off above the waist exposing his toned abs and pants so form-fitting that the shape of his cock was visible through them. I slicked the dildo between my legs until it was well coated, and then began easing it inside.

It had been a while. I remembered how patient James was with me, though, coaxing me and taking his time putting it in. I imagined it was his hand keeping my lips spread. The bulk stretched my insides deliciously.

With a groan, I felt it slide the last inch into place.

It felt wrong to come too quickly because I wanted to make the feeling last. But I knew if I stroked my clit now, it wouldn't take long at all.

I sat up, a sudden idea burning in my head: LL limousine stories were a thing, eh? I crossed my legs, careful to keep the glass in place, and opened my laptop. I still had a browser window open to the LL fan site I had been reading.

Creating an account was free. I picked the username GlassTiara and clicked on *Post a Story,* then started to type:

We hurried into the limousine, but once we were safe behind the tinted glass, once we were on our way, we could relax for a time.

"Come here, my pet," he said, and I nestled close to him, thinking I might nap on our way.

But he had other ideas. His hand slid down the small of my back and under the waistband of my underwear. He teased, slipping it further and further until my clothes impeded him. I predicted that I wouldn't be wearing them for long.

I was right. He whispered into my ear to strip from the waist down, and I did. He pulled me against him again, his other hand finding the space between my legs and then his finger finding the slick entry into my body. I gasped as he slid it inside of me.

He fucked me with his finger, his eyes roving from the place where it disappeared into my body up to my face, checking me for any signs of distress. The only sign I gave was to whisper, "More."

He worked a second finger in next to the first, fucking me slowly and murmuring into my ear. "Do you like that, my darling? Does that feel good?"

"Yes, oh yes, but I want more. I want you."

"I know you do, my pet." He pushed his fingers extra deep and wiggled them, his thumb flicking my clit.

He said nothing more, only continued to stimulate and tease me that way, sometimes speeding up his hand to fuck me hard for a few strokes, then slowing down to a torturous, gradual pace again.

After a while, I reached the edge of orgasm, my breath catching in my throat and my hands clutching at the jacket of his suit. He kept me on that cruel edge for a long time, while I wailed and tugged on his lapels and shook, to no avail.

And then I started to cry. "Please, please, why can't I have you?"

His laugh was deep and low. "You know why, my pet."

"I don't!"

He pushed his fingers deeper, but it wasn't enough.

"I need you! Please!" I cried out.

"No. You know what happened the last time I gave in to your demands."

"That won't happen again! I won't hurt you! I promise!"

But he clucked his tongue and shook his head.

"Please, James!" I whispered, pushing the laptop aside and crushing my clit against my fist as the first wave of orgasm swept through me. "Oh God! Please!" Tears of release came at the same time as the shudders and spasms of pleasure, shaking me and leaving me damp and limp all over.

I was still lying there, half-asleep, when my phone chimed with a text.

My heart jumped for a moment. I was still used to James being the only one with this number. I picked it up and looked at the message.

It was from Damon George: *I have booked us a hotel suite in London for the weekend. I will forward you the exact address. Plan to arrive Friday after dinner, 9pm, and not leave until Sunday at least noon, possibly late afternoon or evening if warranted. If you agree, text me back: Yes, Mr. George.*

I texted him back as he instructed, thinking that would be it for the night.

But another message came a second later. *And now text me a photo of your cunny.*

I knew what he meant, but my mind raced. I still had the dildo in, my pubic hair sopping wet. Everything was swollen. I sent: *What?*

Ha-ha. Your private parts, my dear.

I froze, a bunch of lies coming to the front of my mind. My camera doesn't work. I'm in a public place and I can't right now.

No. We're not doing that anymore. I realized I had a better thing to say. *I don't have to do what you say until I set foot in the door of your hotel suite. Isn't that right?*

For long moments, nothing happened. Then another text. *That is right. Merely testing you. Good to see you can maintain appropriate boundaries. Very important skill.*

I wasn't sure if he was serious or if he was saying that to make it look good. Whatever. *See you at 9pm*, I sent, and he didn't answer. Phew.

I put the phone aside and slid the dildo free carefully. I was exhausted. And it was going to be a long week.

I settled into something of a routine for the next few days. I'd spend the late morning answering questions from people at the exhibition, have lunch with Tristan, give the two-thirty group tour, and then after the museum closed, head back to the ArtiWorks to help Paul and Misha with the renovation work. There was a partition wall in back that had to come down. Misha handed me a heavy metal bar with a bend in one end and a hook on the other.

"What's this?" I asked.

"It's a wrecking bar," he said.

"What do I do with it?"

"Wreck!" He pointed at the wall with a gleeful gleam in his eye.

I hefted the bar in my hand before swinging it at the wall. The hooked end sank satisfyingly into the wall plaster. As I pulled it out, it ripped a hunk of the wall free.

"You get the idea," he said. "Have fun."

Swinging the wrecking bar turned out to be a lot of fun and must have been a good workout because my arm and shoulders were sore as hell the next day. I spent three days reducing that wall to rubble but I managed it. I wouldn't have wanted to do that for a living, but it was very satisfying to see the pile at the end and the nice big room that was created when the wall was gone.

I told them while we sat around one night in the wreckage, covered in plaster dust, eating Indian takeout (they called it "takeaway"), that I would be leaving for the week-end.

"Oh, are you going to take that trip to York you wanted?" Paulina asked. I'd told her I wanted to see York but not why. Not yet, anyway.

"No, that'll be next week. This weekend, I've actually got sort of a date right here in London," I said.

Michel brightened up. He had started growing a beard, and with his apple cheeks it gave him something of the look of a beaver or woodchuck. "*Sort of* date? That sounds more inter-esting than a regular date."

"Weekend-long date?" Paulina asked. "I take it you met someone."

You could say that. Even if I hadn't been sworn to silence about the society itself, I wouldn't have been prepared to tell them what was going on. "I gave a private tour of the exhibit to someone who took an interest in me."

"Hmm, but you don't sound that interested in him." She scooped curry from a container onto her plate. She had brought china plates with a painted pattern of bright blue and yellow flowers on their rims from upstairs for us to eat on. "Am I right?"

"I don't expect it to turn into a relationship," I said. "But I think I might learn something from him. And a weekend at an expensive hotel seems like it ought to be fun."

"Ah, chérie, I wish more young women had your attitude," Michel said. "Your eyes are wide open. You see him for what he is. Go. Have fun. Be open to the experience."

Paulina, though, was looking out for me. "If you need us to come get you, you know, just in case you don't like him or you feel like you can't stay, text or call us, eh? We'll pretend to be your parents."

"I'd like to think that if I need to leave there I could honestly say to him: 'This isn't fun. I want to leave.'" I tore off a piece of Indian bread and took a bite.

"But you're not so naive as to think that's always the case," Paulina said. "Sometimes, you have to do what you have to do to keep yourself safe. We'll come get you. Promise."

"You're so sweet! I'm pretty sure I can handle myself, but thank you."

It was very nice knowing someone had my back if it turned out Damon George was not what he seemed.

The hotel Damon had picked was near yet another famous place I had read about in books: Charing Cross. When I had first arrived in New York to start grad school, the same sort of thing had happened to me in the city. Broadway, Wall Street, Times Square, Madison Square Garden, these were like mythic place-names I'd heard all my life. Once I got used to being a New Yorker, they turned into mere addresses again. Here in London that feeling was even stronger, though, everything more historic, more ancient.

The summer sun was setting as I made my way across Trafalgar Square. Tons of people were milling about, including lots of tourists taking photos of a big statue of a guy on a horse. I didn't attempt to get close to the statue, concentrating on figuring out which of the streets leading away from the park I should take.

The hotel entrance faced the plaza in front of the Charing Cross train station and had various flags flying. I breezed past the main reception desk, and in the hallway beyond it was

greeted by the flickering of tiny candles in glass jars all along
the marble floor and on every stair of a grand staircase spiral-
ing upward. Damon, I mean, Mr. George, had texted me the
room number. I climbed the stairs, the candles making everything seem surreal and magical. On the second floor I found
the elevators and up I went.

At the door to the suite I saw a small envelope taped
next to the door handle. *Please don't make this another wild-
goose chase*, I thought, as I peeled it free and opened it.
Inside was the room key. Okay, at least it wasn't instructions
to go to some other hotel. I checked inside the envelope to
make sure. Wait, there was a note.

Printed in small, neat letters:

*If you are willing, unlock the door, come into the room,
close it behind you, and strip. Leave your clothes in a pile
by the door, along with your overnight bag. Crawl to where
you find me. When you demonstrate your willingness, you
also demonstrate your trust and your understanding that I
will not harm you. If you do not trust me to keep you safe,
leave now.*

I paused to think about it. Did I trust him not to hurt me?
Yes. Did I trust him to keep to the society's rules? Definitely.
But did I trust him beyond that? Not a chance. Damon George
had his own agenda, somewhere underneath it all, but that
wasn't really all that relevant to me. I had my own agenda,
too, after all.

I'm doing this for you, James.

I slipped the key card into the lock and the door opened. I
closed it behind me. Looking around the room, I saw it was a

spacious parlor done in rich eggplant purple and cream colors, with a sitting area to one side, a small dining table, and then through a wide entrance, the sumptuous bedroom with windows overlooking the plaza.

I could see the back of his head. He was seated in an armchair, looking out the window. His suit jacket and tie were draped over the back of the chair.

I took off my clothes and folded them into a neat pile as instructed. When I had nothing on, I dropped to the velvet-soft purple carpet and crawled over to him. I debated as I went whether I should stop next to the chair or go all the way around to the front.

Hmm. Was I allowed to ask? Or was the instruction sheet a kind of "silent treatment"? Or was it all a test to see how I would interpret its meaning? That seemed like the sort of thing he would do.

I settled on crawling around in front of him and putting my head down on the carpet like it had been at the end of the "interview."

Seconds ticked by. I figured that was part of the test, too. We'd see which one of us got impatient first.

He did. "Please me," he said.

I looked up. "Excuse me?"

His expression was stern. "Did you not hear me? I said *please me.*"

I blinked at him for a few more seconds, trying to think of what to do. "I don't know you well enough to know what pleases you."

"Then it is your job to guess and find out," he said.

His shirt was unbuttoned partway. That gave me an idea.

"May I touch you?" I asked.

"Yes."

I reared up on my knees and shuffled forward to finish un-buttoning his shirt and untucking it from his trousers. Once it was free, I could see he was so erect that the red tip of his cock had pushed past his waistband. That gave me a very *definite* idea of something that might please him.

I put my hands behind my back and worked his belt open using my teeth. At first it was a little tricky, but once I got the end free, it took one smooth pull to undo the buckle. His fly was a single button and not overly tight, which made it sim-ple to open.

All the movement made him even harder, and a good inch or two was protruding by the time I was ready to tug his waistband down farther with my teeth. I didn't pull it far, only enough to expose another inch, and then I licked what was showing. He smelled spicy and clean, like he'd showered when he got here. I maneuvered the head into my mouth and sucked gently. I couldn't tell how long he was, but the head fit easily in my mouth, making me think he was smaller than James.

"Well, well, Karina, if I worried you were going to be frigid, I guess those worries are gone now." He chuckled. "Without taking your mouth from where it is, what I'd like you to do next is reach between your legs and make yourself come. Keep sucking me. Do I need to tell you to be careful of your teeth? No? Good. Now go on."

My cheeks flared with heat as I did as he asked. Somehow sucking him wasn't as personal as this. But I slid two fingers down my seam and wasn't surprised to find how wet I was. My clit throbbed. I ran my fingers on either side of it and sucked a little harder to keep him firmly in my mouth.

It became tricky as I got closer, as my breathing grew choppy and little sounds of desire burbled up my throat. Concentrating on not biting him, keeping my tongue and head moving, while also trying to get myself off, was difficult. I think it was supposed to be.

He made it easier when he got impatient, I think, or overwhelmed with desire, and sank his fingers into my hair, taking charge of my head and moving me up and down on him. Now all I had to do was keep breathing and rubbing myself furiously.

I expected him to stop me before I could come. That was what always happened in these situations, isn't it? Doms seemed to deny you at the last second.

Not this time.

When I started to come, I made seal noises, muffled by the cock in my mouth. *Ngh ngh ngh.*

"Keep going!" he hissed, his voice rough. "Make yourself come again!"

Ngh ngh ngh!

I didn't really have a second orgasm so much as that first one didn't end and instead went to the next level. He came with a shout, his cock jerking in my mouth as he shoved himself deep. It was too sudden for me to even try to pull away, and he held me firmly. As it turned out, it was probably better that I didn't pull away. Everything I'd ever heard about it tasting bad or being difficult to swallow was negated by the fact his come went right down my throat. After he backed away from me, I coughed a little with a kind of tickling burn in my throat, but that was all.

I thought for a moment he was going to tug me up into a kiss. Maybe he almost did. Then we both came to our senses a little.

"Is your clit sore?" he asked.

"Not particularly," I answered.

His smile was evil as he shed his clothes. "It will be. On the bed. On your back. Legs spread."

Oof. My legs were weak from coming, and I stumbled a little as I climbed up onto the silky duvet. The bed had a long decorative strip like a pashmina scarf laid across the foot of it. He wrapped one end around my ankle, ran it behind my neck, and then wrapped my other ankle. As bondage went, it wasn't very challenging, even when he pulled and bunched it behind my head, making my legs spread a few more inches.

The next thing I knew, he dove face-first into my pussy, licking and sucking and snarling like a lion at a piece of tasty meat. If that sounds comical, that's because it was. I didn't laugh though, figuring that would probably not go over well. And he was good with his mouth. I was coming again within minutes, bucking against his tongue and crying out. James excepted, I wasn't used to men who actually knew how to please a woman.

He pulled my hips to the edge of the bed then and kept licking, this time sucking hard on my clit until it was trapped between his teeth and torturing the most sensitive bit with jabs of his tongue. I couldn't really struggle with my flesh in his grasp like that, and I cried out instead and drummed my fists against the bed. He didn't relent until I'd come again, even though I hadn't thought I could, the pitch of my screams going up as I did.

When he let go, he stood with a triumphant grin. "And to think that frigid bitch Vanette thought you were too repressed to perform sexually. Come here."

By "here" he meant his arms; he threw himself onto the bed, and I dragged myself up to put my head next to his on the pillow. He spooned me, but if I thought we were going to rest, I was wrong. His hand immediately worked its way between my legs and over my clit until he had a finger inside me.

I groaned as he stroked me deeply.

"Okay, Karina, truth time," he murmured in my ear. "Why no sex?"

"Ngh. This isn't sex?"

"You know perfectly well what I mean."

Even though I had just come four times, the sensation of him touching me inside was so delicious. "Vanette was right. I'm saving myself for someone."

"Some dom."

"You could say that."

"But you're not a virgin. This isn't your marriage bed we're talking about."

"No. I've had sex with him."

"And is this prohibition his idea? Does he know you're being trained by the society?"

"No. We're . . . we're separated right now."

"Ahhh, so it's your idea to try to be loyal to him while you're apart."

"Yes."

"A very noble, if inconvenient, idea."

"What's inconvenient about it?"

"That I want to fuck you so very much." He rutted against me, and I could feel him regaining his erection. I stiffened in his arms, but he murmured to me, "Don't worry. I keep my promises. Although now that I think about it, you didn't say I couldn't fuck you in the rear."

"I...you're right...I didn't." Argh. Had I created a loophole?

"You're very tense, Karina."

"Um." What was I supposed to say? I'm sorry? Wait, can I get a do-over? I'm not sure I want you to fuck me up the ass? "It's just that I suck at this submissive stuff."

He nuzzled the back of my neck, which was rigid as a board. "Karina, Karina. I'll be the judge of whether you, ha-ha, *suck*. You did not suck at sucking, by the way."

"I didn't?"

"No, I was quite pleased."

"Really? Then I did it. I pleased you. Literally." He wiggled his finger inside me and a wave of lust ran through my body. "Ah, stop it! You're trying to weaken my resolve."

"I'm not. I promised I wouldn't fuck you and that means even if you begged me to now, I'd know better than to do so. We've moved on to discussing whether you forgot to count anal sex, too, though?"

"It's hard to keep track of what we're talking about when you've got your hand up my snatch!"

He laughed and said, "I know. That's the whole point. But you're right. I'm undermining my actual goal, which is to hopefully figure out the puzzle that is you." He slid his hand free and dragged his damp fingers across my belly. "Up. Into the shower with you. We'll discuss this more when we're clean."

He slapped me on the bare ass then and I yelped. "Oh, you infuriating, confusing man!"

He rolled off the bed and sauntered toward the bathroom. "Ha. More infuriating and confusing than the master you're saving yourself for?"

"Yes!" I threw a pillow at him and he danced out of the way, laughing.

Washing up was a brisk, genial affair. Despite the room's luxurious size and the fact that there was a Jacuzzi tub for two, the shower stall was not large enough for both of us. We took turns; he went first. Damon made small talk while he scrubbed himself.

"So have you had a chance to see the sights? Parliament, all that?"

"Not yet. I've been working days at the museum—plus some nights, as you know—and I'm helping my landlords renovate in exchange for rent in the evenings."

"Oh, painting, that sort of thing?"

"Demolition, mostly. This week, anyway. I'm going to try to get to York next week, though."

"For sightseeing?" He stepped out and toweled his hair, leaving it a mass of glossy black, not unlike Perseus's in those Burne-Jones paintings.

"I hear it's really nifty. The old medieval city and all that. Plus lots of chocolate shops." I got into the shower and shut the door. The glass was clear, not frosted, so he could see me perfectly well, and the stall was open at the top, so I could hear him as long as my head wasn't under the spray.

"Really? I was only there once, for a big to-do at the Minister. That's the big church there. Always figured I'd go back, but, you know, it's a big country."

"I'm planning to take the train." The water was still hot from him using it.

"Train is definitely the best way to get around. Ah, here's a tip. Don't be confused by the so-called National Rail. Unlike

in America, there are lots of train companies. They're like air-
lines."

"That would explain why there are so many train stations
here."

He laughed. "I suppose. Never really thought about it."

I ducked my head under the water and when I came out
he was in the bedroom, dressing. He had put on a casual shirt
and what looked like soft pajama bottoms or sweatpants. He
was pulling on a pair of socks.

My bag and the pile of my clothes that had been by the
door were nowhere in sight. I had a towel wrapped around
my head but didn't see anything else for me to put on. "Do
you have something you want me to wear?"

He looked up. "Your skin. I want you to be completely
comfortable in your skin. Although, you're actually far more
at ease about it than I thought you'd be, Karina. I was expecting you to be all shivery and blushing when you crawled
over to me."

"I wasn't?"

"Not like you were ashamed of being naked, or de-
graded by it. Which you shouldn't be. You're gorgeous.
It's no crime to be beautiful and it's no shame to show it
off. Something the Greeks understand much better than the
English."

"It's also a lot warmer in Greece," I pointed out.

"True. The warmer climates certainly encourage one to
show one's skin. Look at Brazil. Hmm, but then again, Fin-
land, Sweden, they love their nude saunas..." He stood and
went back into the bathroom, emerging with a hand towel.
He gestured for me to follow him into the parlor, where he
put the small towel down on one of the two padded dining

chairs. "Here's something you might not know about sauna etiquette. When you go inside the sauna stark naked, you always bring a towel, so that you don't leave a stain on the seat. Whether sweat or other."

I sat on the towel while he picked up the phone and ordered tea and dessert.

He took the other chair then, and ran his fingers through his still-damp hair. "Now, where were we? Ah yes, your demeanor. I was expecting you to be less comfortable with nudity because most Americans are."

"You've seen a lot of nude Americans?"

He gave me a wolfish grin.

"Okay, fine. But did you miss the part about me doing performance art? I think that kind of got me over any nudity issues I might have had."

"Ah. You hadn't actually said you were bare-arsed, so I didn't make the assumption. Hmm. I would have liked to have seen that performance. Were you entirely naked?"

"I was. Although my face and upper body were hidden from the audience. I was..." How to describe it? "Sort of inside a sculpture, with my ass and legs hanging out."

"All in the name of art?" he teased.

"Ha. I guess. And because my partner wanted me to."

He nodded. "Let's talk about this partner."

Yes, let's, I thought. *You try to figure out the puzzle of me, and I'll try to figure out the puzzle of James.*

"I take it he's a dominant man, but is he a sadist?"

"I'm not sure."

"Well, did he like to hurt you?"

"At least sometimes. Like the riding crop, or paddling me, or spanking me. But it wasn't the main focus."

"And it doesn't sound like he was into humiliation, or your shame about nudity would be intensified, not lessened," he said. "What kind of dominant was he, then?"

"Um, is *control freak* one of the types?"

He snorted, holding in a laugh. "Yes, dear, I suppose you could say it is. Describe to me what you mean by that."

"Aside from the whole public exhibition side of things, he seemed to get off on—and I mean that figuratively and literally—controlling me. And himself, actually. Having rules and plans. Asking me to do things and having me obey." That first night we'd met, if I'd laughed and said no way when he'd asked me to go looking for the marble in his pocket, what would have happened? He would have laughed, too, and moved on. He would have gone home alone, like he said he had planned to.

It struck me then how much I had derailed James's plans by saying yes. And what had spurred him to invite me into the game? He had once told me, in a romantic moment, it was because there was something special about me. Did I still believe that?

Did he?

"Your mind is somewhere far away," Damon said softly.

"Sorry. I got caught up in thinking about him."

Damon pursed his lips, examining me. Then the door chimed. "Aha. Stay where you are." He hopped up.

The room service deliveryman was Asian, and he averted his eyes from my nudeness, concentrating on lowering himself so that the tray on his shoulder settled neatly on the table. He then transferred the various items onto the table with brisk movements. Damon signed the check and closed the door behind the fellow, who scurried out.

"I think he was more embarrassed than I was," I said, as Damon sat back down.

He plopped a sugar cube into his teacup. "Perhaps. Or at least he felt he should act like it. I'm sure hotel employees see honeymooners looking much more compromised than you."

"What if he comes from a country where they're more repressed? That was kind of cruel to him, then, wasn't it?"

"First of all, how do you know he's not English?"

"Well . . . Oh." It hadn't occurred to me until then that there were the equivalent of Asian-Americans in other countries. "You mean, Asian-English? Asian-British?"

He chuckled at me. "I know. Not the English stereotype at all. London is nearly twenty percent Asian. In fact, less than half of London's residents are white British."

"How do you know that?"

"Demographics are part of my business," he said smoothly. "I believe we're about forty-four percent white British in the city. When you add in white Irish—"

"Irish is different?"

"Yes, dear," he said with a snort, "and all the others who count as white, the total is close to sixty percent. But that still leaves four out of ten London residents something else."

"How many Greeks?" I asked, only half-joking.

He had the answer right on the tip of his tongue. "Probably about thirty thousand total. London has the most Cypriots outside of Cyprus itself. But how did you get me off the subject? We're supposed to be talking about you."

"We are?"

"We are." He poured a cup of tea for me and waved at the platter of cookies and pastries they had sent up.

I could not eat a miniature éclair without thinking of James and the treats he had fed me from the catering table after the private show in the gallery. I took an éclair and savored it.

"So, the man you pine for is a control type with a taste for public display and art. But you're separated. Whose idea was it to separate?"

"His," I admitted, my throat closing suddenly. I took a sip of tea and blinked away tears.

He gave me a moment to gather myself. When he went on, his voice was softer. "And what is it you hope to gain out of training with the society?"

I couldn't tell him I was there to hunt for James. I simply couldn't. I had to wonder what James would think of me sitting there naked with another dominant man. Would he be jealous? Hurt? If so, would that mean he still cared? I tried to focus on Damon and his question, though. "We had a terrible misunderstanding. I misjudged the boundaries, I guess. I want...I need to know more about how these kinds of relationships work. So if I can get him to give me a second chance, I won't fuck it up again."

"And if he doesn't give you a second chance?"

"I can't even think about that."

"You should, Karina. You're young and beautiful and desirable, not to mention kinky. There are plenty of men who would love to collar you."

"I'm not a stray cat who was put on the street, you know." Though I felt kind of like one. *Hiss.*

"Ah, but the society could be thought of as a pet adoption center. For some, anyway." He sipped his own tea and then steepled his fingers, his eyes dark and smoldering as he considered what to say next. "Please be open to the possibility that your man is in your past, not your future. Having had a taste of what he offered—what *we* offer—could you go back to a vanilla relationship, now?"

I sighed. "Not like my old ones, anyway."

"How so?"

"It's taken a while to sink in, and I don't always get it right, but I think the thing that really gets me is the honesty." I forced myself to look at him while I said it. "Having to be honest about what you want, what you need. I don't think any of my previous partners could be honest with me about that."

"Or with themselves, perhaps," he murmured against the rim of his teacup.

"And I don't think they necessarily cared what my desires were. They wanted me to want to be their girlfriend. Like everything would have worked out fine if only we were on the same page, and then they couldn't understand why I didn't automatically want exactly what they did. I don't mean only sexually. I mean who they wanted me to be."

He nodded.

"I mean, I wasn't exactly the clearest about communicating my needs either, but I feel like when I tried, I got shut down. Like, 'Why are you making waves? Aren't we getting along just fine? Isn't this good enough for you?'"

Damon set down his cup. "Don't settle for 'good enough,' Karina. Never settle for that. Any man who lands you has caught himself a prize."

"So I should make sure he's a prize, too?"

"Make sure he's right for you, anyway." Damon wiped his lip with a napkin. "I'll be honest. I know you think this fellow was *all that*, but I hope if you widen your experience, you'll see perhaps he wasn't. You'll always love him for being the one who opened the door to the BDSM world, but if you realize there are more fish in the sea, it might make it easier to forget him and move on. Especially if he doesn't want you back. Have you been in contact with him?"

"Sort of."

"Explain."

I toyed with another pastry on my plate. "I leave messages for him. I don't know if he gets them. I know he had more than one phone. He doesn't answer, anyway. He hasn't communicated with me at all since the night of...the big blowup."

"And you aren't taking that as a sign he doesn't want to speak to you?"

"Well, maybe I'm deluded. But I think if he really wanted me to stop, he'd tell me to stop. Or change his number."

"Then why is he ignoring you?"

"Because he's a chicken-shit bastard who's afraid of love, that's why."

Damon nearly snorted his tea. He coughed a little. "Aha. All right. I won't be solving this puzzle tonight, but you've given me some food for thought." He looked at me, though, as if he were hungry for something other than food. "How old were you when you figured out you were kinky?"

"What do you mean?"

"You know. Did you tie up your friends playing pirate captain or what have you?"

I shook my head. "I didn't know until J—" Shit, that was close. "Until my partner pulled me into it. In fact, I'm not sure I would call myself kinky."

He gave me one of those skeptical looks. "So you think the only reason you get turned on when a lover takes control is because you imprinted like a baby duck on this one guy's style?"

"Is that possible?" I asked. That was exactly one of the things I wondered about. "I mean, you are a little bit similar to him, the way you order me around. Bringing Nadia and Juney to the museum, leaving me the written instructions, all that...I could picture him doing the same things."

"And was it his cock you imagined when you took me in your mouth?" he snapped.

I sucked in a breath. Damn. I hadn't meant to insult him, but don't they always say no guy likes to be compared to the one who came before? And I *had* thought about James when I'd pleasured him. "I'm sorry. I didn't mean it that way."

"Didn't mean it *what* way?" He looked sullen.

"You're hurt. I'm sorry. I didn't bring him up to be hurtful or push you. I'm just trying to figure it out. I thought you were trying to figure it out, too. I mean, am I actually into this stuff or is it only because of *him*, you know?"

Damon closed his eyes, clasped his fingers together, and was silent for a long moment. When he opened his eyes he sounded calmer. "He wasn't there when you kissed my shoe," he said. "He wasn't there in the bedroom tonight. I'm not saying that I"—he pressed his hand against his chest—"am *all that*, but that you, Karina, do respond to dominance and submission."

"Okay, but what does that mean?"

He sighed. "It doesn't have to mean anything. It just is. The play with power and control turns people on sexually. It doesn't have to be more than that."

"But people make it out to be something terrible, something we should hide. That's why the society is secret, isn't it?"

I poured a fresh cup of tea for myself. The room was comfortably warm even though I was wearing nothing.

"Well, first of all, the society has been a secret since the days when there were thousands of secret societies. It was totally a thing in the mid-1800s. Some men were in several societies, dozens maybe. Some were more secret than others. The Freemasons aren't secret at all these days. Our particular society was built for those who were sexually excited by power but who didn't want to have to abuse their power. At least, that's how I imagine it came to be. One moment." He got up from his chair, went to the other room to retrieve his jacket, and then showed me the red satin glove in his pocket. "Did Vanette explain this?"

"Not exactly. She told me the society has no name, but it's pretty obvious to me you use the crimson glove as some kind of signal or calling card."

He nodded and sat back down. "Now, imagine you lived in a society where to get your kinky needs met, consensually that is, you couldn't reasonably speak to anyone about it without fear of being exposed. If you met a woman you wanted to tie up, spank, and fuck until she cried, how were you to ask her if she was willing to do such a thing? After all, she doesn't dare admit aloud to her desires either."

"Well, couldn't you meet at the club?"

"I believe we're speaking of a time before the club building was established," Damon said. "Say you met at a polite function of some sort. Perhaps you even flirted a little. The story goes that the man would say to the lady something like, 'Oh, I happened across this. Is it yours?' And if she was in the know, and willing, she would reply, 'Yes.' If she was in the know and not willing or not able to take up his offer, she would say,

'Oh, I don't believe that will fit me.' Or many other variations. The woman could initiate it, asking if the man had perchance seen a glove she had lost. And so on. Once the actual calling card came into fashion, of course, it became as simple as what we do today, merely flashing the token as the card is handed over."

"I see."

"Of course, today one can also go down to a fetish night-club that advertises in the newspaper, pay the cover charge, and go in and mingle like any other singles bar, except everyone's in black."

"If that's so, then why is the society still secret?"

"Ah. Well. As you say, there are some people who still have a problem with it. Many of our members are politicians and the like."

"And rich people."

"Why, yes, and rich people," he said with a chuckle. "That's always been so. That's how we came to have five town houses connected together for the club. And society members live in the adjacent buildings and most of the other buildings on that cul-de-sac. It was quite the expensive neighborhood at the turn of the last century, and still is today."

"Makes sense. Back then, though, couldn't a man with, er, perverted tastes go and beat up a whore if he wanted? That's what all those terrible books make it sound like."

"I'm sure many did," Damon said. "And those are not the type we admit. I thought you knew that."

"Yes, but—"

"But what? Is it so hard to believe that decent but kinky men—and women—might have banded together to do it in a way that their morals of human decency could accept, yet kept them safe in the eyes of polite society? And what about the man who doesn't want that companion for a night, but for a lifetime? It has worked marvelously in that regard for generations. And for a rich kinky fucker like myself?" He grinned. "All the willing, prime-grade ass I can spank."

I laughed. "All right. It makes sense to me."

"I pity the poor sods who can only get off if they're actually forcing someone," he said as he stood and yawned. "They're the truly perverse. Trapped in a world of lies and coercion and sickness. You see it all the time. That CEO in Georgia who was fucking his secretary all those years, made her do all kinds of nasty things, but she turned around and sued him the second she had saved enough to put her mother in a home? Otherwise we'd never know about him. That one here who had been doing it with his Irish Catholic housekeeper and forcing her to abort the babies he got on her? Sick. *That's* sick. And people classify us in the same way because they don't realize there's a difference. A huge, huge difference."

"You can get off your soapbox, you know. Preaching to the converted and all," I said. "Maybe they just don't realize there's a difference because it's so secretive."

He shook his head and beckoned me to follow him into the bedroom. "It's because there's so fucking much of the sick stuff." He went into the bathroom but kept talking. "You want demographics? How about this: A third of British teenage girls eighteen and under report they've experienced sexual violence. A bloody third! But the rate of conviction here is staggeringly low. Maybe one out of a hundred. Maybe the U.S. is different. I don't know."

I followed him as he brushed his teeth. "It's not that different. They say one in six American women will be the victim of rape, or at least attempted rape, and at any given time, five percent of the women on a college campus experienced it at their university."

He rinsed and spat. "That sounds like a pretty specific statistic."

"Yeah, well, I got real familiar with that topic."

He stood straight, his eyes serious. "You were a victim?"

"Of an attempt. By my own thesis advisor. I told him to fuck off, though. It took me a while to get around to accusing him publicly." I blew some hair out of my eyes. "That's why I'm in England. Waiting for it to blow over."

"Ah, so much becomes clear," he said. "I looked into your academic record before your interview and wondered why your coursework was complete but not your thesis. I thought maybe you were here for the exhibit to finish your research."

"If only. I think it will all come out fine, but it's good I'm not there for the summer."

"Okay. Thank you for telling me that. Your bag is in the closet. Get ready for bed and join me there."

"Wearing nothing?"

"Ideally." He smirked. "I didn't say we were necessarily going right to sleep."

Six

The Stars Look Very Different Today

The next morning I woke to the feeling of the bed jiggling under me. I looked up to find Damon masturbating with his eyes shut, his arm moving quickly as he worked his fist up and down his shaft. He had kicked his pajama bottoms off and was outside the covers, so I had a very clear view of what he was doing.

He held his breath when he came, coating his fingers with ropy come, then opened his eyes when he started breathing again.

"Karina," he said.

"What?"

"Nothing, just seeing if I remembered your name right." He grinned.

"You bastard."

"Ah ah, calling your dom, even a temporary one, names? That's a spanking offense." He sat up and wiped his hand on the sheets. Then he used his pajama bottoms to wipe off his penis before he tossed them on the floor. "Come on. Across my lap."

"You're kidding!"

"I'm not. Besides, a good spanking will wake you up better than coffee. Come on. Around the side of the bed and lie across my lap. And say 'Yes, Mr. George.'"

Right. "Yes, Mr. George."

I climbed out of the bed and lay across him, my feet hanging off the bed. I still wasn't wearing anything, so he had a nice eyeful as I did.

He rubbed my ass cheeks with his hand. "You mentioned you've been spanked before?"

"Yes, Mr. George."

"Did you like it?"

"Yes."

"Were you a naughty girl or did he merely like hitting you?"

I had to think for a moment. "Once it was because I did something I wasn't supposed to, and once was when he had me all tied up and I guess it was just the thing to do."

He switched to scratching me lightly with the backs of his fingernails. "That's it?"

"That's it."

"All right. Then let this be a lesson. Why am I spanking you?"

"Because I called you a bastard."

He laughed. "No, no, I didn't mean the fake reason, the scene reason. What's the real reason I'm spanking you?"

"Um—" This had to be some kind of trick question.

"I'm spanking you, really, because you have a gorgeous arse and I want to. I like spanking women. I like feeling how you react. I'm a dom and I like to inflict pleasure and pain. It's that simple."

"I see. Do I have to count them?"

"No. I'll stop when I feel like it."

And with that he began to swat me on the ass. At first the swats were light, and they hurt less than I expected them to, but as he went on and on with a steady rhythm my skin heated up and got more sensitive. That was when he started hitting harder. Soon I was squealing and kicking my legs on each smack. All he did was keep his other hand between my shoulder blades, keeping me in place.

And then he stopped. His hand went back to caressing my cheeks in a circle. I shuddered under the gentleness of that touch.

Then his hand slipped between my legs. "Wet. As I predicted."

He slid one finger into me and I gasped at the sparks of pleasure shooting through my body.

He finger-fucked me a few times, then pulled his hand free. "It is absolutely maddening that I can't fuck you. I'm sure Vanette knew it would be. Up. Go clean up a little and we'll go to breakfast."

In the hotel restaurant, Damon seemed moody and distracted as we sat near the wide windows overlooking the plaza in front of the train station. After a cup of strong coffee, though, he seemed to revive.

"So a spanking wasn't actually better than coffee," I teased.

"I meant for you, not me," he said, but smiled. "I am not truly awake, or human, until I've had my first cup. Now. I have to rethink my plan for what to do with you today."

"You do?"

"Yes. My plan revolved entirely around gradually wearing down your aversion to sexual pleasure. You pretty much threw that out the window within the first minute yesterday." His hair was glossy black in the morning sun. We were sitting across the small table from each other. "So I need something else to challenge you with."

"Like what?"

"You're reasonably obedient when I insist on it, so I don't think there's much challenge there. I suppose I could put you through some tests of physical endurance, but they get boring for me, and I dislike being bored." He yawned. "What's your least favorite thing?"

Getting dumped in the middle of a party after the best sex of your life, I thought, but didn't say. *That's my least favorite thing ever.* "You mean like what toy did I like least?"

"Or activity."

I had to think about that. I hadn't really liked the Wartenberg wheel but I didn't hate it. The paddle had been kind of fun. The riding crop hurt, but the way he used it was thrilling. Activity? Going out in public, wearing Ben Wa balls, those things were fine.

Oh, I knew what I was going to say. I glanced back to make sure a waiter wasn't about to appear over my shoulder. "Once he made me go a whole week without an orgasm."

Damon cocked his head. "Was that a very long time for you?"

"Well, he insisted on seeing me every day, and, you know, playing with me and bringing me to the edge, but not letting me come."

"An entire week? Every day?"

"Sometimes more than once a day."

"That is dedication to training," he said with a nod. "So what was it you didn't like?"

"The delayed gratification, I guess."

"You don't sound sure."

"Well, I was still getting plenty of attention, and seeing a lot of him, and it was...It was very hot, in its way. It was just a long time. You asked what my least favorite thing was. That's what it was."

"Huh. Then it sounds like you liked what he did to you, no matter what he did."

"I guess. Every time we tried something new, I liked it." I wasn't about to tell him about how I'd discovered the hard way that James was larger than my body was ready for. Besides, we'd gotten past that and that wasn't the sort of thing Damon was after, anyway.

"Then either he was very good at reading you and predicting your tastes, or you were exceptionally compatible," Damon said with a small frown. "No wonder you're so stuck on this fellow."

Or maybe it's because I'm so in love with him, anything he did felt wonderful. I shrugged.

"Let's start over," Damon said suddenly, tossing his napkin onto the table.

"What?"

"I'm going to go back upstairs. Follow me in half an hour." He stood. "Let's start again."

"If you say so."

"Indeed, my dear, it is my job to say so." He grinned like a Cheshire cat, then disappeared.

The waitress brought fresh tea and asked if I wanted a copy of the newspaper. I thanked her and told her no. I'd rather read it on my phone.

I looked up more details about York and checked my

e-mail to see if Martindale had e-mailed me back about the days off I would need. The dear man had answered not only saying that I could take the days, but he'd booked me a guest-house, too. Apparently he wanted me to find James badly enough to lend some assistance.

A half hour was done quickly, and I signed the check to the room and went back upstairs.

This time I wasn't surprised to find a small envelope on the door. The note inside read:

Come into the room and remove your clothes. You will find a notepad on the desk. You are to write three things you deserve to be punished for. Then go stand in the corner.

Well, that's different, I thought. I went in and saw the bathroom door was closed. He must have been in there. I considered writing three fake things, as if it were a schoolgirl thing, like "didn't do my homework, lied about my dog eating it, talking in class." But that wasn't what he was after, I figured. Like with this morning's question about it, he didn't want the "scene" answer. He wanted the real answer.

I picked up the pen and sat down at the desk, the contoured leather of the chair feeling cool to my bare bottom. How to start? What to write? To get myself going, I wrote at the top of the page:

Three Things Karina Deserves to Be Punished For

I wrote a number one and circled it. If I were writing this list for James, what would it say on it? Well, I had already been reporting via text all the little white lies I'd told. There hadn't been many, but there were a few.

For the little lies I told the customs agent and other people, trying to make my way easier, when I had promised not to lie anymore.

Okay, that was one. What was number two? Was there something else I actually felt sorry for?

For not reporting my advisor for sexual harassment and attempted assault earlier. I might've saved other women some trouble.

I closed my eyes then. Think, Karina. What else would you want James's forgiveness for? Well, of course I wanted him to forgive me for forcing him to tell me his name, but I sure as hell didn't feel I deserved to be punished for that. What did I feel sorry over, though? Or what did I want to feel sorry about?

An idea struck me suddenly. Oh. Did that make sense? Maybe it didn't have to make sense. I wrote:

For letting Mr. George touch me and give me pleasure and make me come.

My hand was shaking when I put down the pen. I hurried to the obvious corner that had been cleared of furniture and hunched with my face in my hands. What the hell was I doing here?

I heard the bathroom door creak and I sucked in a breath as I heard him moving closer. The paper on the desk rustled.

When he was standing directly behind me, he spoke. "You're a very confused woman."

I could only nod.

"And I would like to smack the man who confused you this much. Since he's not here, though, I'll have to settle for punishing you instead. You know what to say."

"Yes, Mr. George." It came out a whisper because my throat was so tight.

"Good. Now let's see. I can see why you might feel guilty over not reporting the creep. Now, the lying thing. That was something your former master told you?"

I wanted to argue that I hadn't called him master, that we didn't use titles, but this wasn't the place for that. "Yes, Mr. George."

"And you're trying to comply with it, even though it's difficult. And even though he's no longer around."

"Yes."

"Very well. Let's clear your slate then. Come and put your hands on this chair."

I turned and saw he was dressed in a full three-piece suit, his tie smartly knotted, and I swallowed hard. He had no way to know that was how James dressed. It had to be a coincidence. But it made me feel even weaker in the knees than I did.

I leaned over to put my hands where he showed me, gripping the seat of one of the dining chairs. Then he displayed a long, slender piece of plastic, flexing it slightly between his hands. If it hadn't been bright red it would have looked like a shade pull.

"Canes were traditionally made from rattan," he said. "But the synthetic ones last longer. Head down and tell me how many lies you think you've told."

"Total?" I asked.

"No. How many you think you need to be punished for."

"Oh. Ten or twelve for sure. Maybe as many as twenty over the past couple of months."

"Let's do twenty to be sure your slate is wiped clean. Have you been caned before, Karina?"

"Is it like the riding crop?"

"Not exactly. The way this works is I deliver the punishment, and you keep the count and thank me after each one. If you mess up the count, you go back to the beginning."

"That is devious."

"These things usually are." He chuckled and rubbed the tip of the cane against my ass. "Now, if you are ready, you know what to say."

"Yes, Mr. George."

He cleared his throat, and then a second later, a burning stripe of pain cut across my ass. I clamped down on the noise I wanted to make, waiting for the pain to dissipate. When it did, I was panting and immediately thinking, wait, nineteen more of these?

"What do you say?"

Right. "Thank you, Mr. George. Th-that was one. Nineteen to go."

He smoothed his hand over where he had struck and it felt wonderful. He sounded amused. "The traditional way to do it is, 'One. Thank you, sir. May I have another.'"

That sounded sort of familiar. There had been a man saying it at that party James had taken me to. "Should I call you 'sir,' Mr. George?" I asked, remembering what Vanette had said. "And do you prefer the traditional way?"

"You know what, Karina? I don't prefer the traditional way. I'm interested to see how you do. And I love it when you call me 'sir.' It's like every time you say the word, you lick my cock."

He stepped back again and I knew the next one was coming. There was a second of silence and then *bam,* a new line of fire on my ass. He didn't seem to mind that I wiggled as if that would make the pain lessen faster.

"Two, sir, and eighteen to go," I said. "Thank you, Mr. George."

"Good," he said, and did not wait to hit me a third time.

"Three! Thank you, Mr. George." I squeezed my legs together. Oh, it hurt. "Seventeen to go."

He hit me again and I gasped a little as I said, "Four, M-Mr. George! Sixteen to go! Ahhhh.... ah, thank you!"

He stepped close and rubbed my inflamed skin again. "You know, if you're not ready for the next one yet, you can take longer to answer."

"But isn't that cheating?"

"I don't think it is, dear. I think the point of having you count is to give you a chance to set the pace. If I think you're going too slowly, I'll harangue you about it."

"Oh. How was I supposed to know that?" I asked.

"Well, since it wasn't obvious to you, that's why I'm telling you. If you're worried that you're taking too much control of your own punishment, don't worry. I can always gag you if I want to. Remember that."

"Yes, sir." It was an odd sort of back-and-forth, but I guess it made a kind of sense. "I'm ready for number five, sir."

He said nothing before delivering it, and this time I heard the cane cut through the air. I think that meant he hit me harder. This time I screamed. And it took me several breaths before I was ready to say, "Five, thank you, sir. Fifteen to go. I'm ready for another."

The next one wasn't as hard, but that didn't mean it didn't hurt. The next few, in fact, felt like he backed off a little, and I didn't have to scream on each one. I counted them off dutifully until I got to "Ten, sir, and ten to go."

Instead of caressing me with his hand now, he ran the tip

of the cane up and down the backs of my legs and across my shoulders. "You're doing very well. Ten is often as many as a punishment might be for."

"But we said twenty?" I squeaked.

"Yes, we said twenty, so we should see it through. I'm going to put a few of these down your thighs, which I imagine will mean no miniskirts or short-shorts for you for a few days, unless you want to have to explain the welts."

"Yes, Mr. George."

The next five he did like a ladder climbing up the backs of my thighs until he had reached my ass again, with me dutifully counting each one. It hurt differently on my legs from my butt. I preferred it on my ass.

"Five to go, sir." I gasped.

"These five will be the most difficult to take," he said. "Your skin is already sore now, and I won't be holding back."

So I was right, I thought. He *was* holding back. "Yes, Mr. George. I'm ready."

The next one made me scream loud enough my throat felt raw. "Sixteen! Sixteen." That meant how many? The strike had driven all the thoughts out of my head. Think, Karina! "Four left. Thank you, sir." Was I actually ready for another one like that? We'd find out. "May I have ah . . . another?"

He said nothing, merely delivered the blow. This one making my knees buckle. It took me a moment to realize that what I was feeling then, as the pain slowly ebbed away, was him tapping me gently on the thigh with the tip of the cane. Aha, trying to get me to straighten up again. I did with some effort. "Seventeen. Oh God. Three to go. Thank you, Mr. George. I—" I took a few deep breaths. "I'm not sure I'm ready for the next one."

"You're doing very well, Karina. I'm so proud of you. You're doing terrific."

Hearing the words made me feel good, but I couldn't help but feel they were kind of empty. They didn't mean what they would have if James had said them. The same way the sex play we'd had yesterday didn't mean anything. Though I still felt guilty about it.

"Thank you, sir. I'm . . . I'm ready for another."

Oh, the bastard. What he did next was hit me hard, not once, but twice in quick succession, which made me crumple all the way down to my knees, screaming and hanging on to the chair. He didn't touch me this time, leaning back and waiting until I made myself straighten up again.

"That . . ." I was shaking like I was angry. "Did that count as one or two?"

"Two, dear," he said.

"Wasn't that cheating, then? Hitting me before I was ready?"

"Would you prefer I count it as only one?" he asked. "Then there would still be two to go, instead of only one more."

"Oh." I tried to clear my head enough to understand that.

"You give me feedback by asking. It helps me gauge how much you can take," he explained. "But you are not the one in control here."

"I see. Thank you, Mr. George. Does that mean there is only one left, then?"

"It does. Are you ready for it?"

I had to take a couple more breaths. I'd come this far. I could do it. One more. I could do it. "Yes, sir. I'm ready for another."

"Good," he whispered. "Here you go."

He tapped me ever so lightly with the cane and then

rubbed his hand over my ass, kneeling beside me and pulling me against him.

Don't ask me why that was what made me burst into tears. Somehow getting all worked up to one more shot of pain, expecting the worst, and then having him turn gentle, melted my resistance away and I started to cry.

"There, there," he said, stroking my hair. "You did very well. And now you're forgiven."

But I'm not, I thought. *You're not the one I need to forgive me.* The thought only made me cry harder.

He held me and let me weep until I was cried out. I got tears all over his lapels, and he gave me the silk handkerchief from his pocket for my nose.

And then, because I wasn't in any shape to stand up, I guess, he brought me a glass of water and a bathrobe.

After I drank the water, he helped me into a chair, and I belted the robe. He opened the curtains again, and the afternoon glow brightened the room.

He took off his jacket and laid it over the back of the chair, then sat down. "Do you feel better now?"

I looked at the glass in my hands and he refilled it for me. After another sip I said, "I do and I don't. I feel lighter now. My mind feels clear. But I still feel guilty about why I'm here."

"Explain." His expression, rather than stern, looked concerned.

I realized I had to tell him the truth. The big lie was that I hadn't told him why I wanted to join the society. Duh. And that was tied up with the reason I'd let him do what he did to me in the first place. I wondered how I would start.

"Maybe you should say a bit more about why you wrote

you felt guilt over having sex with me. Wait, not-sex. You wrote 'pleasure.' Do you not believe you deserve pleasure and release, Karina?"

"It's not that." I turned the glass in my hands. "I do. Everyone deserves that. It's just . . . I don't actually want it from you. Not that you're not great at it. But . . . but it's true. I'm thinking about him the whole time. Part of me says if I were really going to be loyal to him, I wouldn't even do that much. And part of me says I'm being bad to you, too, by thinking about him instead of being here with you."

He said nothing, digesting my response.

"And then there's the fact that I haven't told you everything."

He kept silent, the peaking of his eyebrows the only indication that his interest sharpened.

"The man I'm trying to find? I think he's a member of the society. I . . ." I tried to cover my nerves with a sip of water, but my hands shook. "I'm hoping I'll find him. I'm hoping if he sees me there . . ." I couldn't say any more. I had to hold my breath to keep back the tears.

Damon took the glass out of my hand and set it aside before I could drop it. He then held my hands in his. He still didn't say anything though.

"I'm so stupid!" I said. "I don't know what I was thinking. I saw . . . I saw a chance and I thought I would grab it, and here I am in trouble again because I didn't tell the truth."

"No," he said softly. "First of all, you're not in trouble. Secondly, your situation is as much his fault as yours."

I looked into his eyes. "Surely, I'm in trouble with the society for trying to join them on false pretenses."

"I didn't hear any false pretenses in anything you said." He rubbed his thumb across the back of my hand. "I think you meant every word."

"You're bending the truth."

"Am I? The truth is relative, perhaps. Karina, seriously, you're clearly very deeply in love with this individual. Enough to make your judgment questionable, perhaps. But don't beat yourself up about having not-sex with me. If he abandoned you, I'm sure he doesn't expect you to go live in a nunnery or something now."

"I guess."

"If a man abandons his cat, is he going to be angry at the cat for getting fed by a neighbor?"

"Well, he shouldn't be, but that doesn't mean he won't feel betrayed anyway."

"True. Is your former master that irrational? If so, I'd say he's not worth your loyalty."

"It's not that simple. I'm the one who feels guilty anyway." I squeezed his hands in mine, hard. "What should I do?"

He pulled his hands away then, shaking one of them like I'd overdone it. "I think you should get dressed and have lunch. We'll talk about it after."

"We're not allowed to talk during lunch?"

"No, dear. You're going to go have lunch. I'm going to fuck Ms. Juniper's brains out while you do." He stood as a knock came at the door. "That's probably her now."

"Really?"

"Really. You turn me on tremendously. Since I can't have you, why should I suffer?" He opened the door and Juney came in, grinning from ear to ear. She gave me a little nod and a wave.

"Hey, Juney." I smiled. "Okay, I'll leave you two alone for a bit."

I wandered down to the gym, which was deserted. I wasn't planning to work out—I'd already had my workout, thank you very much—but I wasn't hungry for lunch yet and I wanted to stretch my legs a little. Everything in the gym was black and red, with the most stylish-looking barbells I had ever seen. They looked like they belonged in a science fiction movie.

As I walked around the hotel, I thought about James. And myself. I didn't come to any big conclusions, but when Damon met me for lunch I was a lot calmer.

Instead of lunch, in fact, we had tea, and although it wasn't quite as fancy as the Buckingham Palace Hotel tea, it came pretty close.

When we were settled with a pot of tea each and a tower of tiny sandwiches and pastries between us, he shook his hair out of his eyes and said, "Now, where were we?"

The next closest table to us was across the room, four women who were chatting animatedly and paying us no mind.

"I think we were talking about whether I was going to join the society or not."

"Ah, yes. I think you still should."

"Even though I'm doing it to find this guy?"

"Look at it from my perspective, Karina, or from the club's perspective. We see a bright young woman who is delight-fully responsive to sadism and dominance. She's old enough to have her wits about her, educated enough to be good con-versation, but young enough to maybe turn into a lifetime companion for someone. What's that? She's had her heart broken by some lout? Well, that doesn't make her different from half the girls we take in. And what's the other thing? Oh, if she met the right fellow while at the club, she might marry him? Well, that certainly happens often enough, too."

"I guess so. So I wouldn't be breaking any rules by it."

"No. Though of course if the director and Vanette thought the only reason you joined was to search for him, well, they wouldn't take too well to that. However, I think you have plenty of good reasons to join outside of this one motive. After all, what if you find this fellow and then he rejects you? You will need a support system."

"I guess you're right..." I let out another long breath. "There's also the fact that I'm supposed to go back to the States at the end of the summer. What about that?"

"Tell me truthfully. If this man turned up at the club, reconciled with you, and asked you to stay with him here in London, would you?"

"Yes," I said, without hesitation.

"Then I think you have as much chance of staying after your training is done as any other S-type we take on these days. No need to mention to the others what may happen." Damon set down his teacup then and leaned forward, staring into my eyes until I felt all I could do was stare back. "I will make you a promise if you make me one."

"What promise is that?"

"I will promise to do everything I can to help you find this man, if you promise me that if he rejects you, you come to my bed for one night. One night of anything I want, no restrictions."

His eyes were intense in the afternoon light, wide but lit with a hunger in them.

"Not being able to fuck me really has you bothered," I said quietly.

"It does. Do we have a deal, Karina?"

"Okay. I promise. One night with you, I'll do anything you want if J-Jules rejects me, and you'll do everything you can to help me find him. The first thing you can do is buy me a train ticket to York on Thursday."

He smiled brightly and sat back, clearly pleased with himself. I could see him already plotting what he wanted to do with me. "Easily done. One moment." He pulled out his phone and sent either a text or an e-mail. "There. It's as good as done."

"You really think I'm a masochist?" I asked.

"I do. Are you worried about that? All that means is you get sexually excited by intense sensations like spanking or being caned."

"Pain, you mean."

"Pain, and other challenges. On the psychological side, you find control arousing, too. Honestly, I think most people do, they just tell themselves they don't because it's not socially acceptable. You're supposed to be turned on by, what, bouquets of roses and bubble baths? That's nice if what you want is to fall asleep side by side. Physically, we're a lot more complicated than that."

"You get turned on by seeing a woman in pain."

"Physical pain, yes. I'm not so big on emotional distress." He sipped his tea. "Making women cry has never been my thing."

"Oh. Then I'm sorry about before."

"Sorry? For what? It was fantastic to make you cry."

"But you just said . . ."

"I said I didn't get sexually turned on by it. But I was very pleased to get that result out of you, Karina. You opened up. It helped you tell the truth. And now that you told the truth, I can help you."

"You're right. It did." I nibbled at the cucumber sandwich. "Well, what should I tell you about him?"

"How about starting with his name?"

"He told me in the U.S. society a lot of people don't use their real names, so they never even know sometimes."

"Someone in the group must know because they run background checks." He frowned over his teacup.

"Yes, but the members don't necessarily know one another's names, I meant. He went by the name Jules, or Jewels, I guess, depending on your accent? He said he got the nickname because he wore a lot of diamonds and gems when he first started going to their parties."

"Diamonds?"

"That was what he said. They have elaborate balls and people get quite dressed up."

"So I've heard. Trying to imitate us, though we hardly do that sort of thing anymore. I mean, we do, but not for the society. You have the regular ones for nonerotic purposes, and then you have private ones on various estates by invitation. But anyway, that's fascinating. Sounds like he was quite ostentatious, then?"

"I have no idea. He made it sound like a long time ago. Anyway, he told me about the group here, too, so when you pulled out that card, I jumped on it."

"How did you know it was the same group, though?"

"Oh, I wouldn't have, except you know the professor I turned in? He was trying to gain membership, and I scuttled it by reporting him. He showed up at my building drunk and ranting. My roommate tried to tell him I wasn't there. He went on and on to her through the intercom, and she told me he used the phrase Crimson Glove Society."

"Ah, so that's where you got the designation *crimson*. I wondered why you used that word instead of *red*."

"He might have been saying *crimson-gloved society*, but she heard it as a name, anyway. And so when I saw yours, it clicked."

"All right, and this Jules, describe him?"

"About six foot, built like a dancer, all muscle but no bulk, blond. His mother was British and I guess he did some school here. Sound familiar?"

He shook his head slowly. "Can't say that he does. But don't be discouraged by that. But you still haven't told me why you think you'll find him here, rather than back in the States. Is he in York?"

"He might be. Another mutual friend, my boss at the museum, got a letter from him with a York postmark on it."

"And you're going to walk up and down the streets calling his name like a lost puppy?"

"Jerk. I figure I'll start with the post office, ask around, and there are a few art-world-related connections I may be able to follow."

"Aha. All right. You pursue him that way, and I'll start inquiries within the society. It's a shame we can't start your society training this weekend if you're out of town, but there will be ample opportunities to get worked over at the club."

"You think I'll be approved?"

"Vanette will go along if I give you the thumbs-up. Which I will. The director is already quite taken with you. You'll be fine, Karina."

Seven

Camouflaged Face

My weekend with Damon wrapped up with much more "not-sex." He definitely kept his word when he said my clit would be sore, but we didn't have any more deep talks. On Monday I went back to work, and if I sat somewhat gingerly because of the welts on my butt, no one noticed.

If I thought the previous week had gone by slowly, this week dragged even more. I gave two more after-hours tours, both to couples, none of them remotely like Damon. One was a man in his sixties and his slightly younger wife, both quite knowledgeable about the art, and one was a late-forties-ish couple who didn't know much but were enthusiastic listeners. I was a bit hoarse after the evening with them. The daytime tours I was giving had become monotonous, though. I started to wonder if people were even listening to what I was saying. Then again, *I* was barely listening to what I was saying. Damon messaged me to say Vanette and the director had accepted my application for training, which would begin after I got back from York. The demolition finished at the gallery and we moved on to plastering. I chatted online with Becky a few times, but now that I was on a schedule I was usually asleep by the time she came online.

The night before I was to leave for York, I checked my e-mail and was surprised to see a ton of notification messages from the LL fan site. I had nearly forgotten about the story post I had made.

There were more than a hundred comments. I started to read them in the e-mails, then logged in to the site, where I could see them all at once.

I was amazed at how many messages I'd received, most of them surprisingly sympathetic. "I miss him, too!" one wrote. "Oh, GlassTiara, you have perfectly captured the longing we all feel in this superb piece of writing!" said another. "I feel your heartbreak," said a third.

I had thought it was nothing more than a silly porno piece. But somehow what I felt had come through. It hadn't oc- curred to me before that there was any emotional connection between me and Lord Lightning fans. And yet they all felt like I did: abandoned. Why? Because they loved him too much? It made me wonder: why had he decided to retire from per- forming? It was yet another thing I wanted to ask when I saw him again.

I would see him again. I had to believe that.

I caught the train on Thursday morning from King's Cross. There were several trains leaving, every five minutes or so, for all different parts of the country, but exactly like they did at Penn Station, everyone would stand around until the track number for their train was announced. It was nowhere near as confusing as I feared it would be.

The seats were assigned on the train I was on, exactly like

an airplane. Unlike on a plane, however, I had a window seat
at a table. The trip would take about two hours, so I brought
a book, but I ended up spending most of the time staring
out the window. Very quickly we seemed to move past the
city and into countryside. There were places we passed, with
green rolling hills divided by hedgerows, that looked so idyl-
lic I expected to see the doors to hobbit holes. Quite at odds
with that were the gigantic nuclear power plants, towering
over the landscape, sending up massive clouds of steam. I
saw at least two like that.

The York train station was very historic looking to me, but
it was new when compared to the rest of the town, much of
which was built in medieval times. The guesthouse Martindale had booked for me was a few blocks from the train and
just outside a massive stone gate that looked like something
from a Dungeons & Dragons book. Except that cars were
driving through it. The guesthouse had a pub on the ground
floor and the rooms above. I dropped off my bag in the room,
pocketed the metal key, and went out to look around.

I passed through the stone gate and walked on a narrow
cobblestoned street, which opened up at the intersection to
the plaza in front of the church Damon had told me about. It
looked huge compared to the buildings around it, and likely
full of fascinating art and architecture.

But I wasn't here to look for art. I was here to find James.
As I walked, it became quickly clear to me that wandering
the warren of streets was only going to result in confusion for
me. I found my way to the tourism center I'd passed when
walking from the train station and picked up some maps and
brochures.

My first stop was the post office, which turned out to be a

counter inside a shop, which was confusing to me at first until I found it. There were about twenty people in line and two clerks working. When I saw how slowly the line was moving, though, I decided to go back later. I looked in the brochures I had picked up, trying to decide where to go next.

There was a shop called York Glass. That was as good a place to start as any. I took their brochure and went looking for it. It took some time, as the streets were narrow, winding. A few times I took the wrong side street, but ultimately the walled city wasn't that large and I found the even narrower street called the Shambles, where the shop was located. In New York it would have been called an alley, not a street.

"This is like something out of Harry Potter, isn't it?" said a woman standing on the corner looking at her map just like I was. Her accent was American. She got out her camera and took a picture of the alley. "It's like right out of the movie."

"Did they film it here?" I asked.

"Oh, I don't think so. They built a wider version anyway, so there would be room for the cameras and everything."

"Ah, I see."

She wandered down the street. She hadn't even looked at me through the whole conversation, and it was a good thing there were no cars, because she wouldn't have seen them, either.

York Glass was a tiny shop, with barely room for a handful of customers. A shopgirl sat behind a register in one corner, and the walls were lined with brightly lit cases and shelves of glass knickknacks and baubles, everything from glass Christmas ornaments to cat figurines.

I lingered while a few other people came in, and the shop-girl came out to help them. She had reddish brown hair and freckles across her nose. The people, a woman and her two daughters, made a fuss over what color glass cats they were going to buy, then left without buying anything, leaving the shopgirl standing there with several cats in the palm of her hand. She carefully put them back onto the rotating shelf in a case where they were displayed, waiting until an empty space for each one came around so she could replace them.

She turned to me as she closed the case door. "Can I help you with anything?"

"Oh, um, I'm trying to find out more about the glass artists in the area."

"Are you, now? A collector?"

"I work at a museum," I said. That was true, after all. "I've got a special interest in glass. I'm fascinated by how it's made. Are there studios nearby?"

"Oh, I suppose. Most of this"—she waved her hand toward the shelf—"is made by our own people, 'specially for the shop. I don't know much about the artists around here. I'm just helping out the owner of the shop. You might come by later when my boss is here?"

"That's a great idea. I'll do that, thanks." I stepped out into the alley again, deflated. That wasn't much of a start. I would go back as promised and ask again. Meanwhile, I needed to eat something. Right across the alley was a small place—I mentioned they were all small, right?—called the Earl Grey Tea Shop. Perfect.

Inside was a series of low-ceilinged rooms. A very nice lady sat me down and explained the menu. I picked a rose-flavored tea and she bustled away to get my order started. I felt like I was having tea at someone's grandmother's house, which was perfectly charming.

The sandwiches were large compared to what I had been getting, made on full-sized bread, and the pastries included a whole slice of cake, so I was quickly stuffed. The rose-flavored tea made me think of what Damon had said. If all I wanted was roses and chocolates and bubble baths, I might as well be asleep.

I could see the appeal of that, but I wanted to feel I'd earned it. The cuddles and the bubble bath should come *after* the mind-blowing sex or whatever intense thing I'd experienced. Right?

I was toying with the remaining half slice of Victoria cake that I couldn't eat when the hostess came back to bring my bill. "And what brings you to York?" she asked. "Seeing the sights?"

"Oh, pretty much. I'm in England for a summer job in London and I wanted to get out and see a little of the country." *Now's your chance, Sherlock,* I told myself. Ask. "I'm also interested in glassmaking and glass art. I hear there's some of that here?"

"Oh, goodness, yes, a little bit," she said.

"Do you know where? I'd like to meet some of the artists."

"My daughter's an artist. She might know. Let me ring her. I won't be but a moment." She went out to the front counter, which was in the next room over, where they sold tea and accessories, and I heard her pick up the phone.

I still had some tea in my pot and a pile of brochures to look through, so I contented myself with waiting around a little to see if the lead turned up anything.

A short while later, a woman about my age, in jogging

shorts and a tank top, her hair in a bandanna, stuck her head into the tearoom. "You the American who wants to see the glassworks?"

"Me? Yes!" I closed the brochure I was reading.

"Mum says you're keen to go down there. If you give me a minute, I'll take you."

"Great! I'm Karina."

"Helen." We shook hands. Hers was sweaty. "Back in a mo'."

I continued with my reading, and a short while later Helen returned to collect me. I paid my check and followed her through the narrow streets, an actual alley that was barely wide enough for a bicycle, and we emerged on a wider thoroughfare. Another two blocks down and we went into a parking garage.

"Is it far?" I asked.

"About ten minutes' drive," she said. "That all right? It's a few miles." She unlocked the doors and we got into a small car. "I mean, kilometers. No, wait, you Americans use miles, don't you?"

"We do. Isn't it metric here, though?"

"Some things are. We British invented the mile, though, so I guess we feel we've still got a right to use it, eh? Anyway, we're headed to an old factory-type building up the river. A bunch of art going on there."

That sounded promising. "Really?"

"Mostly sculpture. There's a fellow who welds industrial scrap into things. All manner of crazy good stuff and some glass. York's always had glassmakers, though not always the arty type, if you see what I mean."

"I'm not sure I do."

"I grew up here, so here's the schoolbook version, all right?" We pulled out of the garage onto a busy street. I had to suck in a breath as my instincts said we were on the wrong side of the road. She didn't seem to notice my anxiety and barreled us cheerfully onto the road out of town. "All business in York was controlled for hundreds of years by the guilds, the guild of Merchant Adventurers—"

"Adventurers?"

"I know. Sounds like something made up, don't it? Anyway, they allowed kind of monopolies to various companies. This one for shoes, that one for combs. You had to apprentice in a shop to get anywhere, and the license to run a shop was passed from generation to generation. The early glass companies weren't making art. They were making medicine bottles for the apothecaries and such. When industry came along, it was industrialized of course, but you didn't have the kind of horrible mills and factories here that you had in a lot of West Yorkshire. The guilds didn't allow it. So it stayed small scale. There were three glassworks with a dozen or so employees each. One by one they moved out or outgrew the area. Redfearns left in the sixties and their building got turned into a hotel. So all that was left was little guys again, some hobbyists and artists."

"I see."

"What I'm saying is there's a tradition of glassworks, but what we're doing now isn't really part of that." Helen gestured around with one hand, then put it back on the wheel. "It's a new thing."

"Art."

"Yeah."

"So what kind of art do you do?"

"I was in painting for a long time, but that world is so hard. So competitive, and you're being compared not only to every painter working today, but everyone who ever put paint on a canvas. You look at Rembrandt and Titian and van Gogh and you think, why do I even bother? Dalí. Rossetti. It's all been done. And it's so restrictive. So I moved into sculpture, where...I can't say there are no rules, but there are a lot fewer of them." She hunched over the wheel as we zipped along on a two-lane highway, with a river on one side and fields on the other.

"What medium do you work in?"

"That's the fun of it. Sculpture can be anything. Metal, wood, glass—your own poo if you're into that sort of thing." She cackled. "Don't worry, I'm not. Lately I've been using animal bones, though. And doing things like casting them in metals. Thousands of years from now they'll dig up the site of where some piece of mine was and wonder why the hell they have a pig skeleton that is partly copper, partly bronze, partly steel. I hope in the future we're smart enough to say it was art and not some weird pig-worshipping cult."

That made me smile. "I hadn't thought of that before."

"Glass, too, glass lasts forever. There's a glass artist from America. He makes these globes that look like planets. Think paperweights, only he makes them all sizes, up to huge like this." She took her hands off the wheel for a second to make a space bigger than a bowling ball, then quickly grabbed control of the car again. "And he marks them with the infinity symbol and hides them all over the world. He wonders what people will think in three thousand years when they've found hundreds of these things all over. If his name is forgotten, will they think space aliens put them there, or what?"

"What is his name?" I asked.

"Josh something," she said. "Super-nice guy, too. Came to visit the glassworks here, gave a talk. Singleton? Simpson? Can't remember. I'm not good with names. He was really nice and his work was gorgeous and amazing." She pointed up ahead. "There's our destination."

We pulled into a cleared parking area lined with gravel, next to a stone building that made me think of an old firehouse. In each of what would have been a garage for a fire truck, there was a workshop. The bay doors were open, and she showed me one was for melting, smelting, and forging, one was for glass blowing, and the third was for woodworking. There were very solid stone walls between each section. Other parts of the building had some offices and smaller studios.

Some glassblowers were working together making something, and we watched them for a while. A man and a woman seemed to be the two leads, with a few assistants. When they took a break, Helen introduced me to them as Linae and Peter.

We made a little small talk about art and such while Helen went over to check on some of her materials by the forge. I felt I didn't want to waste a lot of time, so I tried to get right to my main question. "I'm looking for an artist, a glass artist, who has been working around here recently."

"Oh, what's his name?" Peter wiped a bit of sweat from his forehead.

"Well, I think he might be under an assumed name, you know?"

"What, is he wanted by the law?" Linae joked. She was blond, her hair tied back in a ponytail, with a smudge of soot on her temple.

"Worse," I said. "By the *Tate*."

That set them laughing, which was good.

"But seriously, my boss at the Tate has been trying to track him down for a while. He's about six feet tall and blond."

"Like this?" Peter stood up straight. He had a dark beard, shaved close to his face.

"About that," I said. "Anyway, blond, or he was last time I saw him."

"He hasn't been working here," Peter said. "Sorry. Can I get you a drink? I'm afraid water's all we've got, though. No beer until we're done with the dangerous stuff."

"Oh, that's all right. I drank a gallon of tea earlier."

Linae grinned. "You'll be wanting the ladies', then. Come on with me."

I followed her around back to the toilet facilities. Once we were alone she said, "I think I know who you mean."

"You do?"

She nodded. "He came around more than a month ago, looking to borrow some things. Peter was in London at the time. I was under the impression the fellow was setting up a workshop but didn't have everything he needed yet. We helped him out, of course."

"Oh my goodness, that's great. Do you know the address of the workshop?"

"I don't exactly. But I helped him to move some things, so I've been there. I could probably figure it out again."

"That would be fantastic."

"Here's the thing. Peter gets ragingly jealous. We can't let him know I went to this bloke's workshop by myself while he was gone, and I can't leave here now. We could go tonight."

"Tonight would be fine. I'm free." I gave her my number

and the name of the guesthouse, and then we took turns using the facilities.

We hung around a bit more, and then Helen offered to run me back into town. At the guesthouse I got online but Becky wasn't around. I ended up taking a nap.

My dreams weren't exactly hard to interpret. I was Snow White, and my prince was put in a charmed sleep under glass. The only thing I had to smash the glass, though, was an apple. I brought it down as hard as I could, cutting my hand on the glass as it shattered, and thumping him hard on the chest with my fist. I woke suddenly, clutching my hand. No glass here.

When Linae came to get me later, after dinner, she pulled up in front of an old university building where there was a driveway, around the corner from the guesthouse. I was surprised to see Helen in the car, too. "Well, hello."

"I thought I'd come along for the ride," she said. She was wearing a dress, and so was Linae, who looked much more refined when she wasn't wearing a heavy leather apron and covered in soot.

"Peter gets much less suspicious of me if I bring a girlfriend along," Linae added. "He thinks we're going out drinking."

I got into the backseat and buckled myself in, glad that I was wearing something relatively nice, too. In case we did find James I didn't want to look like a slob. As we were headed out of town, the houses dropping away and the countryside taking up both sides of the road, Linae asked, "So, tell us more about this fellow."

"He's a recluse," I said. "Used to work in upstate New York mostly. I'm not sure why he's in England now."

"A mystery man! And what's his art like?"

"Abstract mostly, but with some odd representational pieces. One of them looked a lot like a house, but made of glass. I guess it was a whole 'glass houses' concept."

"Where did you see that?"

"A gallery in New York City. They had a bunch of his smaller works, too. And they installed a piece in the art history department building at my university last semester."

"Oh, are you at university? I thought you older," Linae said.

"Graduate school."

"Ah, that explains it. And now you're at the Tate."

"Yes."

"So what name was he working under when you knew him in the States?"

"J. B. Lester," I said. I didn't see how I could get around telling them that.

"Oho, the infamous. Now I know who you mean. But this fellow looks nothing like the photographs of Lester I've seen."

"He uses an actor to play him so that he can hang back and observe the audience at his installations," I said.

"Ahh, clever, clever lad. So sneaky!"

"Oh, we don't know any sneaky artists," Helen said with a snort.

"No, none," Linae agreed, giggling a little.

They didn't let me in on the joke, but I took it to mean they had some shared secret.

We drove for a while. The sun was setting, and I didn't have a sense of how far we had gone. We turned off the road onto another small highway, then another. Linae and Helen debated where we should try if this didn't turn out to be the right road.

"No, wait, there it is," Linae said. As we cleared the trees coming down the side of a hill, we could see a lone house on the next hillside. Maybe house wasn't the right word. It wasn't big enough to be a mansion, really, but it was pretty grand looking, with another building off to the side that looked to be a barn or carriage house or something. We could see several parked cars in the circular driveway.

"Is it his?" I asked.

"I don't think so. I was under the impression he was merely staying there," Linae said. "He set up the workshop in the carriage house and mentioned some wealthy couple from Romania or somewhere. I think they own the place, but they weren't there at the time."

"Looks like they're having a party," Helen mentioned.

"So it does. Think we should come back later, Karina?"

"No. Let's go in and see." Maybe if it was a party we could have a look around. "Let's act like we belong, eh? If anyone asks, we're neighbors, right?"

"Sounds good," Linae said. "After all, we did help that fellow out."

We parked at the end of the line of cars and then walked up the rest of the drive.

Where the driveway met the walkway to the front door, a butler stood in full livery, despite the summer warmth. He had a red silk cravat tied around his throat, black tails, and very shiny shoes. The only thing that looked modern about him was the piercing in his ear. As we approached, he looked at us somewhat curiously. "Good evening, ladies?" he asked cautiously, as if not wanting to offend us by challenging our presence there, but not sure if we were invited.

I was about to go into the "neighbor" explanation when I

realized his earring wasn't just a hoop. It was a flattened silver loop with a smaller loop hanging from it, like a miniature slave collar. If I hadn't seen people wearing collars of that type before, I wouldn't have made the connection. Was this one of *those* kinds of parties? "Good evening. We seem to have . . . lost our gloves," I said.

"Oh, indeed?" His smile grew wide. "I might have seen them."

"If they matched your tie, then I'm sure you did," I said coyly. I had the urge to wink but thought that might be overdoing it.

"They indeed did," he said, and bowed. "Please proceed inside and have a lovely evening."

The other two hurried after me as I went up the walkway between towering hedge trees. When we were out of sight of the butler I whispered to them, "Okay, gals, you want to know what that was all about?"

"You bet I do," Helen said.

"This party, it's not like a regular hoity-toity garden party," I said, trying to think of how to explain it. "It's kind of like an orgy."

"Oh my goodness!" Linae's eyes lit up. She looked far from distressed by this news. "Karina, you are full of surprises."

"Well, keep your cool, okay? I'm still trying to find this guy."

They nodded in agreement.

"And don't do anything. You know. These people are very big on rules. So if you say don't touch, they won't touch you."

"All right," Helen said.

"That doesn't sound like any fun." Linae wrinkled her nose. "But all right. We'll try not to get in trouble."

Another butler opened the front door for us but didn't challenge us in the slightest. My heart began to hammer as we went into the parlor, where a buffet was laid out, as if I might run into James at any moment. But no one was in there except a pair of servants, one of whom offered us crystalline glasses of fruity punch. We took the glasses and then followed the sound of voices through the back of the house and into the garden.

There was a sudden cheer as we appeared, and it took me a moment to be sure it had nothing to do with us, but as I looked around it became apparent what the commotion was. They were running races, human pony races. The riders were all done up in these sort of fox-hunty outfits, and the ponies were people—mostly naked, with leather tack on them like for horses, except clearly made for humans. They raced by pulling their rider in a kind of buggy or rickshaw. Racing lanes had been mowed into the grass between the patio and the ornamental hedges.

With everyone watching the racing, no one paid us much attention, and I got a good look at everyone there.

None of them were James. I wondered if he could be in the house, or down at the workshop building. I told Linae and Helen that I was going to sneak down there. They stayed put.

There was a stone walkway from the house down to the other building. The sun was down now, and the staff was lighting lanterns and torches for the pony racing, but I made my way in the dim twilight.

The door was not locked. It opened easily. The entryway was dark. I felt for a light and managed to hit one. British light switches tended to be large and easily hit with the hand.

I was in a sort of mudroom, with hooks for coats and shelves for shoes. I passed through from there into a large central room. The scent of turpentine and burned wax filled the air.

It took a bit longer to find the switch for the lights in there, but when I did, I found myself looking at a studio full of art. The worktable was covered with sketches, some of them technical, some of them figure studies. My breath caught as I realized one had to be me, in rope bondage, a pose he had tied me into at the party. Once I had seen that, I saw another, this one the way I had been tied that time at the hotel, the time with the string of pearls. The pearls were even in the picture, the suggestion of them anyway, a series of shaded curves off to one side. I still had that necklace. I'd nearly sold it to get the plane fare for this trip, but I was glad I hadn't.

Under a drop cloth stood a canvas with a painting in progress. It was reminiscent to me of Degas's ballerinas, except this was a woman in a blue ball gown and a glass tiara. Bits of glass had been affixed to the canvas, yet it remained unfinished.

In the center of the room I saw what James had photographed and sent. The glass slippers. They were mounted on a platform over which loomed a much larger glass sculpture. It looked like Hokusai's breaking wave, except instead of blue and white, this was white and deep red, and the spiky forms of glass towering overhead resembled a giant mouth of teeth about to eat the shoes. Parts of the sculpture were suspended by near-invisible wires to look as if splashes were ricocheting away from the negative space. One "splash" rose up from the center of the breaking wave like a tongue.

Or a phallus.

Deep red, it was the only part of the wave's underside that

was rounded and liquid-shaped rather than spiky and harsh. It had a pattern on it. I looked more closely and saw it wasn't a pattern but words etched into the glass. The etchings were on an interior layer so when I ran my fingers over it, I felt only smoothness.

PAIN OF DESIRE OF PAIN OF DESIRE OF PAIN...

The words repeated around and around the protrusion. I ran my fingers up and down it lightly; my heart caught in my throat.

Oh, James.

If I had wondered if the photographs of the glass slippers meant he was thinking of me, now I was completely sure. But the angry red and the dangerous-looking spikes made me think he wasn't thinking of me fondly.

I turned the lights back off and slipped out the door, hurrying back up to the patio. Linae and Helen were standing very close together, punch cups still in their hands. I sneaked in behind them. "I'm back."

"Jaysus, give us some warning next time," Linae said. "Well, did you find him?"

"I don't see him anywhere, but that's definitely his workshop down the hill," I said. "Let's try to come back when there isn't a party going on."

"Oh, Karina, you're no fun!" Linae said.

Helen saw the sense in us making a quick getaway before we were found out. "If you think Peter's going to be angry about us going out, what if he gets wind of this? We better get out of here, Linae."

"Oh, all right. That door guard is going to know something's up if we just waltz right back out again, though." She turned to me. "Can you sick up on command?"

"You mean vomit?"

"Yeah."

"Not that I know of."

"All right, I'll have to do it." Linae sighed and set down her punch cup on a cocktail table. "You two act like you're helping me because I can't walk straight."

She was much taller than either Helen or me, which made for a comical stagger down the walkway toward the butler.

"Everything all right, ladies?" he asked, one of his eyebrows arched in concern.

"Oh, I think I'm going to be—!" Linae threw her head into the bushes and made puking noises. When she pulled free, she had twigs and leaves in her hair. "I think I better go home."

"Um, we'll take her home," Helen said and steered her toward the car again.

When we got to the car, Helen took the keys and got into the driver's seat. Linae lay down in the back and I took the passenger seat. Helen waved to the butler as we drove past him and then turned us onto the lane toward the highway.

Once we reached it, Linae sat up, cackling. "Was that brilliant? Tell me I'm a brilliant actress!"

"You're a nutter, you are!" Helen said. "I can't believe you! And *you*!" She glanced at me a moment before turning her attention to the road again. "Taking us into some kind of secret sadomasochistic soiree! We need the story on this, sister. This isn't merely some artist who owes you a piece, is it?"

I sagged against the seat of the car. "No."

"He's your ex-lover!" Linae guessed.

"I hope not," I said. "I hope we're still...I mean, he dumped me, but I think it's all a mistake. I think if we could sit down and talk, he'd stop overreacting about everything! He's afraid. I get that, but come on, tons of guys are afraid of commitment!"

"That's true," Helen said. "But flying across the Atlantic is more than your usual bloke will do to avoid a talking-to, don't you think?"

"I'm not stalking him, if that's what you're thinking," I said. "If anything...he's as obsessed with me as I am with him." I told them about the sketches and the painting. "You girls have to help me. I want to talk to him. That's all. There's got to be a way to get us in a room together. You have to understand, the way he dumped me. There's been no chance to talk it over. He just disappeared."

"And came all the way to England, aye? All right," Helen said. "Say we kidnap him or trap you in a room together or what have you. What happens if he says no again?"

"If he really, truly, rationally says no, he doesn't want me, doesn't love me, then I'll cry a lot but I'll believe it's over. I'll stop chasing him."

"And then we'll go out for a right night of drinking for sure," Linae said. "We'll try at the house again tomorrow, a'right? I'll go myself, say I'm bringing him news about that new art market day we're starting. If he's there, we'll come back the three of us and block the exits while you talk to him."

"Yes!" Helen shouted. "I've got a Viking sword I can carry and everything. He won't be getting past this Valkyrie."

"Viking sword?" I asked.

"Have you not seen all the Viking stuff in town? Not yet?

They pay folks to dress up as Vikings and answer questions
from the tourists. Quite fun." That got her off on a tangent
talking about the history of the Vikings in York and burial
sites and various bloody battles that had been fought. My
mind drifted a little as she spoke.

James, I thought. *I'll see you tomorrow. Maybe.*

But when I reached my room and was settling down to
check my e-mail, a text came from Damon.

Jules is here, it read. *In London. Club party Saturday night.
Get on the next train you can.*

Eight

Strange Doors That We
Never Close Again

I told Helen and Linae the news. The earliest train I could get was early afternoon, so I wandered the streets of York for a few hours before it came. The narrow, cobblestoned streets full of charming little shops still seemed more like something from a fantasy book than a real place to me, but I couldn't really concentrate. All I could think about was James.

Damon texted me throughout the day, winding me up even more. Especially when my train was late. *I'll pick you up at King's Cross,* he messaged. *We'll need to go directly to the club. I don't suppose you have anything suitable to wear with you.*

While on the train I ended up texting him a complete list of everything I had with me, to which he replied: *Perhaps you'll have to go naked...*

And then a bit later: *With no time to prepare you, V. has an ingenious idea for your debut.*

He said nothing about what the ingenious idea was,

though, which I'm sure was intended to key me up. Knowing that didn't keep me from getting keyed up, either.

He teased me with a few other texts, too, like: *The director makes his own floggers and flails. When he approved you he told me he was making one especially to use on you himself.*

In other words, I was a nervous wreck by the time I arrived in London. I tried to imagine how the reunion with James would go. Maybe they would put me to serving drinks, which was something I was certainly qualified to do. I would be carrying a tray with a glass of whiskey to a man seated in the parlor, talking politics. He would look up to accept the glass, see me and...?

Or maybe I would be lined up with the other trainees. I remembered the pony players from the party in York and imagined us lined up like horses waiting for riders, each one tethered to a post, as club members would come by and look us over. And then along would come one tall, well-dressed man, whose eyes would light up in delight and relief when he saw me...

The party was probably going to be nothing like that, but I couldn't stop myself from hoping and dreaming.

At King's Cross, Damon was waiting on the other side of the turnstiles, as if taking no chances on us missing each other. He swept me into a kiss that bent me back before I even realized what he was doing.

"What—?"

"Sh. Making it look good for the constables," he said into my ear, as he righted me and began walking quickly, one arm around my shoulders, toward the exit.

"Are you kidding me? Damon—"

"Ah ah, it's Mr. George, remember?"

Shit. "Yes, Mr. George."

"*Tsk-tsk*, and I'll have to punish you for that."

"Of course you will," I said, somewhat sarcastically, "Mr. George."

He opened the back door of a limousine at the curb and then followed me in. I didn't get a look at the driver, but the car began to move and then my attention was on other things.

"I enjoy your wit and playfulness," he said, "but some club members will find it too irreverent. Others will think it is an invitation to punish you. Is it, Karina? Are you doing it to provoke me?"

"I'm not. You didn't say I shouldn't be sarcastic."

"I shouldn't have to, if you have any instincts about how to act around authority. But as I said, there's no time to train you more properly before tonight. Next week you can start lessons with Vanette. For tonight, maybe we'll just gag you." He drummed his fingers against the ledge of the window. "I assume you're as eager to get this resolved as I am."

"If you are thinking about putting it off, with all due respect, *no way.*" I wasn't going to miss this chance after coming so close.

He nodded. "I figured you'd feel that way. I want it resolved quickly. Now get your trousers off. You have a punishment coming."

"Right now, Mr. George?"

"Yes, right now, and expressing reluctance by asking bogus questions is another no-no." He shrugged out of his jacket and rolled up his sleeves.

Meanwhile, I shimmied out of my jeans, thinking how familiar this was, stripping in the back of a moving limousine, and yet so totally different because I didn't have the feelings for Damon I had for James.

He gestured to his lap and I hesitated, not sure what he wanted. "At the risk of asking a bogus question, sir, I'm not sure how you want me or what that gesture means."

"Across my lap, your bare arse up, please," he said with a wicked smile. "And now, you see, that was an appropriate question, respectfully asked."

I crawled across him so that my ass was in the air at the edge of his lap. His hand was warm and dry as he rubbed circles against my cheeks.

"What's the proper way to display reluctance?" I asked.

"I'll show you later. Asking questions in the middle of your punishment is also not correct, Karina."

"I'm sorry, Mr. George."

"No, you're not. But you will be when I'm done."

I nearly opened my mouth to ask if this was going to be like the caning and if I should keep the count, then thought, *Duh, Karina. He said no questions right now.* James never told me not to ask questions. In fact, he'd told me I should. I pressed my lips together, waiting to find out how this was going to go. If there was a pause after the first swat, I thought, then I could give the count of *one* like in a caning.

There was no pause. He started to spank me with brisk slaps of his hand on my backside, several on one cheek before moving to the other. The rhythm was quick and steady, but where his hand was going to fall I couldn't predict. As he moved around my ass and down my thighs, the slaps were getting heavier and harder the longer it went on. It wasn't long before I was yelping, kicking my legs involuntarily on each heavy blow, as if I could launch myself off his lap to freedom. His other hand slid warm and solid against the back of my neck, holding me in place.

And still the spanking continued. The driver was probably used to hearing all kinds of noises from the backseat, but I wondered what it sounded like to him anyway.

When Damon stopped, we were both out of breath, and I coughed a few times, trying to catch mine.

The next thing I knew, Damon's hand was in my face. I looked at it, his palm as swollen and red as my buttocks felt.

"Kiss it and say you're sorry," he said.

Oh. I kissed his palm and it was scalding hot. He ran it through my hair, like he was petting a cat, and I remembered to say, "I'm sorry, Mr. George, for getting your name wrong."

"That's better." He hauled me off his lap and onto the leather seat, which felt cold against my scalding-hot ass cheeks. "Take off the rest of your clothes."

"Yes, Mr. George." My voice was breathy, not in a sultry way, but more like I'd run up a flight of stairs. He smiled at me like he found it sexy, though. I slipped out of my shirt, wondering what he was going to make me wear.

But now that I was completely naked, he ignored me, looking through the heavily tinted window with a brooding expression on his face.

I looked out my own window, but couldn't really make out where we were or what we were passing. The air-conditioning in the car was chilly, and the sweat I'd broken into during the spanking cooled down fast. I crossed my arms.

Without looking at me, he said, "Don't do that."

"Cross my arms? Sir?"

"A sex slave should never make herself less available to her master," he snapped. "She should always be making herself more available to him."

I slowly straightened my arms as I cleared my throat. "Forgive me if I'm incorrect, Mr. George, but I wasn't under the impression that you were my master."

He shook his head as if to clear it, then looked at me. "Of course not. Not yet, anyway." He moistened his lips with his tongue. "And you're not a sex slave. You're a club trainee. But if I have my way, Karina, you'll not only be my sex slave, you'll beg to be."

I didn't know what to say to that, so I said nothing.

"Spread your legs. Show me," he said.

Remembering how James had liked me to do so, I brought my feet up onto the seat, then let my knees fall apart.

Damon ran a finger lightly down the inside of my thigh, then upward between my folds, spreading my own natural wetness over my clit. He massaged it with two fingers, moving in a circle. "The fact that you can get this wet from a spanking, *ngh*." He grunted. "It's truly difficult not to fuck the living daylights out of you. But I shan't. Not until you've given up on this loser."

He spanked me on the clit then, with much lighter slaps than on my ass; these made me yelp but also thrust my hips up into each swat.

"Greedy girl," he said as he pulled his hand back. "Could you come from that?"

"I don't know, Mr. George." I was so aroused the entire area between my legs felt inflamed.

"Perhaps later we'll find out if you can. Your masochistic streak is very intriguing." He looked out the window again. "All right. Time for a blindfold."

"But I already know where the club is..." I said, confused.

"Who says this is to hide anything from you?" he said with a grin. "Maybe I merely like you helpless."

"Whatever you wish, Mr. George."

He grinned and slipped the tie from his neck, then wrapped it around my eyes.

A short time later I felt the car come to a stop and heard him hop out before the driver could open his door. My door opened and I heard Damon's voice. "Reach out for my hand and I'll guide you."

I stood carefully. The floor felt like concrete and it sounded like we were indoors. Some kind of garage. They wouldn't risk anyone seeing a naked woman walking up to the front door, I guessed.

The air in the garage was cool against my bare skin, and Damon pulled me gently by my hand. "Forward, forward. Now step up."

I stepped up onto carpet. We were in a hallway now. He led me into a room and closed the door.

I jumped at Vanette's voice. "Is that really necessary?"

"Don't be such a spoilsport, Vanette," Damon said as he lifted the tie off my eyes.

I saw I was in what looked like a small bedroom. The early-evening sun filtered through diaphanous white curtains onto a twin bed. Several implements sat on the coverlet, leather, metal, and rubber.

Damon looked them over. "She's not voice trained at all," he said. "Have we got a gag that matches this?"

Vanette frowned. Today she was in a black cocktail dress with gray piping, her hair in a bun and her feet in strappy black and gray shoes. "If we're making her other orifices unavailable, don't you think we might need to leave her mouth free for use?" She turned to me. "If you can't abide by a gag order for one night, then we certainly can't have you here."

"I can only try my best, Vanette."

To my surprise, she smiled at me. "Your best is what I want. All right then. Once you leave this room, you will not speak. If you are in distress or need help, the one word you may use is *Mayday.* That will bring a member of the staff straightaway." She glanced at the slim watch on her wrist. "Your role tonight will be that of new girl. You won't have to do anything specific like serving tea. Everyone will want to admire you and try you out. I regret I won't be able to supervise you myself tonight as my attention is required on another matter. In fact, I must go." To Damon she said, gesturing to the stuff on the bed, "I trust you can manage this?"

"I am certain I can."

"Once it locks, only I can open it," she reminded him. "So be sure you have it on right."

"I will."

They nodded to each other and Vanette left briskly.

I looked at the items on the bed. "I take it this was the brilliant idea of hers you texted me about?"

"Indeed. Have you ever worn a chastity belt before?"

"No, Mr. George."

His smile was gleeful. "A first. I do love firsts. Bend over, darling, and rest your upper body on the bed."

I did as he asked, and the next thing I felt was his fingers spreading my wetness around even more. Up to my anus and all around my lips. Then I felt something more rigid pushing against me.

"This is rubber," he said. "It's a two-pronged toy, with a

small plug for your arse and a small dildo connected together. They'll obviously prevent any unauthorized entry."

He teased me with them, though. Instead of putting them into place immediately, he fucked me with one prong first, then the other, before using both at once, making me whine and moan. I was still aroused from all we'd done in the car, and this was a deeply pleasurable sensation. Being penetrated in both places at the same time sent ripples of pleasure all through my abdomen.

"You're enjoying that far too much," he said. "Stand up straight now, and spread your legs."

His hand kept the double-prong in place, and with the other he pulled the straps off the bed and wrapped them around me. This was the belt part of the chastity belt, with one strap that went around my waist and another shaped leather piece that fit between my legs. There was a small split here as well, although it held the prongs in place, exposing my clit and upper lips. The lock was on the side, at one hip, and he clicked it into place.

He pressed against me from behind, his hand snaking down my front until his fingertip could tickle my clit with light flickers. "You'll be allowed to come as many times as you want tonight," he said. "Unless the club member playing with you at any given time orders you not to. Do you understand? Different people will demand different things. You'll have to do your best to obey them."

"Yes, Mr. George."

"Vanette, that minx, she knows how tempting you are. The belt makes good sense. Any member who forgets your dictum won't be able to get too carried away. Myself included." He growled in frustration. "I want you more and more, Ka-

rina. It's going to drive me mad to see the others having their
turns with you tonight."

I pressed back against him, aroused and needy, but glad of
the belt myself. Would it drive James mad with desire to see
me in the hands of someone else? Would many men make
me come tonight?

Damon's finger slid over my clit and I bucked. "You . . . you
said you like firsts, don't you? Mr. George?"

"Yes, I do."

"I've never come while wearing a chastity belt," I said.
"That would be a first."

He chuckled into my ear, rubbing my clit harder for a few
seconds, but then pulling his hand away as I writhed back
against him, whimpering. "You've also never been tortured to
the edge of orgasm again and again while wearing one either," he said. "I think I like that one better."

"Ahhh, sadist!" I cried as he did it again.

"Yes, dear, that's the point," he said with another chuckle
and then stepped away. I put my hands on the bed to steady
myself.

He rummaged in a drawer of the chest behind me. Next
I felt his hand stroking my hair. "Vanette convinced me, no
gag, but let's put one more thing on you."

He slid a black nylon hood over my head, turned me to
face him, then tugged at it until the holes for the eyes and
mouth were in place. He looked quite serious now. "This way
you'll have a chance to observe your Jules before he realizes
it's you."

Ah. "Good thinking, Mr. George."

"I knew being sneaky would come in handy someday."
He raised his eyebrow conspiratorially. "And here's something

else." He held up what was like a very short robe made of sheer black silk, almost see-through. It had no belt. I slipped my arms through it, and he had me turn so he could inspect how it looked. It hung just above my ass in back. "That'll do. Now, I have a few other rules to go over with you."

They were commonsense things, mostly. There was a dining room where they didn't allow sexual acts to go on for sanitary reasons, and he explained some of the etiquette around the slaves or servants people brought with them. Since I wasn't supposed to speak, I didn't have any need to worry about forms of address or other spoken formalities.

"And be sure to alert me if you need to use the water closet," he added.

"You really think of everything."

"You're far from the first submissive I've put in chastity. Last thing. We haven't discussed your name."

"Oh." I blushed under the mask. How could I forget? This was always a big thing.

"It's customary for most to use a pseudonym," he said, as if I didn't know that already.

"I know. I have one."

"*Tsk.* And here I was hoping you'd let me name you."

"Like a stray cat you adopted?"

"Exactly."

"I'm not yours yet, Damon."

His grin grew toothy, predatory. "Ahem."

"Ack! I mean, Mr. George!" Dammit, why did I slip?

"Now I have to punish you again, Karina."

"Ashley, my name's Ashley," I snapped.

"Very well, Ashley it is! Come with me. I'll punish you out there for everyone's entertainment." He hooked a finger under the belt and pulled me toward him, then turned and strode out of the room. I hurried to follow.

He went up a flight of stairs to a large parlor. Two men were sitting in one corner, chatting.

"What have we here?" one of them asked.

"A new trainee," Damon answered. "The night's barely begun and I've already got to teach her a lesson. Ashley, over here."

He gestured to a nook in the wall lined with bookshelves, but in the archway of the nook I saw restraints hanging from bolts embedded in it. They were fur-lined cuffs for the wrists, with chains to adjust their height. He turned me so I was facing him and the room, and strapped my wrists into place above my head.

Then he reached down and rubbed my exposed lips and clit until I was flushed and panting. While he was doing that, other people came drifting into the room, most of them men, some women, and a few S-types. I heard myself described as "new trainee" several times in the snippets of conversation I could make out.

"Lift your leg," Damon said. "I don't care which one."

Back when I had been dancing, one of my teachers had told me my right leg was stronger, so I stayed on my right foot and lifted my left, bending at the knee.

"Wider," he said. "Show me your pussy."

I didn't have to worry a lot about balance since my wrists were affixed to the arch, and I held my leg off to one side.

"Perfect. Stay like that."

Stay like this? It was a pose I could hold for a little while, but I wasn't sure how long. Was he going somewhere? His facial expression was pure mischief, of course, as he pulled down the flaps that covered the eye holes on the hood. He really liked blindfolding me, I guess. I took a deep breath and tried to relax as much as possible in the darkness behind my eyelids.

Then I felt something soft against my inner thigh. Something tickled and I bounced a little. Then came a soft swat on my thigh and I yelped in surprise, not pain.

"These tails are a lovely, soft suede," he said. "They'll only sting if I want them to."

The next swat of the flogger fell against my leather-framed cunt. It didn't sting at all; rather, it was a pleasant sensation, a gentle impact against my sensitive parts. He hit me like that again, then a third time, before setting up a rhythm. He must have been twirling the suede tails such that they caught me on the way around each time.

I had already been aroused when he started, and now the sensation of being struck again and again softly right where I was most sensitive was making my hips buck. He had asked earlier if I could come from something like this. I had a feeling I was about to find out.

I drew closer and closer, but oh so gradually. The leg I was holding in place began to tire, but when it drooped, the tails didn't catch me in the right spot! He didn't even have to order me to fix my posture. Every time I slipped, I straightened up again because I wanted that touch, needed it, needed more of it, wanted it to be harder, faster. I couldn't ask for it with words, but I bucked my hips and hoped he was in a generous mood.

As I grew closer and closer, my breathing went ragged and I let out little cries and whimpers.

"Can she come like that?" a male voice asked.

"I don't know," Damon said. "Do you think I should let Nadia down there lick her to completion?"

I whimpered hopefully.

"I'm of half a mind to lick her myself," the man said.

"This is supposed to be a punishment," Damon pointed out. "I think she'd enjoy that too much."

"Ah, understood. Well, carry on then."

The strokes never stopped during that conversation. My cries grew louder again as he ramped up the intensity, hitting harder now, but I was too aroused for it to feel like pain. The only pain was in my leg muscles, which were cramping a little from holding up my leg.

And then they were cramping a lot as he continued relentlessly whipping my crotch. Finally I couldn't keep my leg up anymore and it collapsed against the other one. I moaned in dismay, so close, so close! But now with my legs closed, my clit wasn't getting anything.

The blows stopped, though, and a moment later something touched me there. I assumed it was his fingers again and bucked against it.

No, it was his cock. He slid the long bulk of it between my legs, along the flesh the belt exposed. I clamped around it instinctively, knowing he couldn't get inside with the plugs in place and needing that friction against my clit so desperately. My hips jerked as I sought to stimulate myself against whatever I could get.

"That's a pretty picture," said another voice nearby. The director. "Ingenious. You have her in chastity and yet utterly wanton. You do have a way about you, George."

"Thank you, Director. Would you care to take my place?"

"Does the belt not chafe you? I think I'll pass."

"Oh, only a little. Anyone else?" Damon called out.

I was nearly there, and he wasn't stopping me, so I rubbed as hard and fast against his shaft as I could.

"How about you?" he asked teasingly to someone else nearby. "Help a girl in need?"

"Thank you, but no."

James! I'd know that rich, honeyed voice anywhere. But at that moment Damon gripped my buttocks and thrust against me, triggering my orgasm at last. I screamed, helpless to do anything else, as the powerful spasms tore through me.

Nine

Breathe For a Long Time

My body went slack in the restraints, my legs completely giving out and Damon supporting me with his arms tight around my body. I could barely move, but inside I was frantic. James was here. I knew it was him. What was I going to do now? This wasn't anything like what I had imagined our first meeting would be like. I was grateful now for the hood over my face and the fact that he couldn't tell it was me.

Damon undid the restraints and carried me to a couch nearby. The voices were farther away, and when he opened the eye flaps I saw we were in a side room to ourselves. The doorway to the hall was wide open, but we were alone. He had also put his dick back in his pants and looked as put together as ever.

"He's out there," I whispered.

"Yes, I believe he is," Damon answered in a low voice. "I definitely heard his name."

It occurred to me then that Damon might not know what

James looked like. He might know him only by nickname and reputation. "How are we going to—"

I didn't get my question out before the director appeared in the doorway. "How is she? Revived enough for another round?"

"I daresay she is," Damon said, straightening his shirt cuffs. "Quite a masochistic streak in this one."

"Bring her to the Rose Room then, would you?"

"We'll be there shortly," Damon said. After the director had gone, he continued. "No rest for the wicked. Come on. Up one more floor. And remember, no talking."

I nodded in answer. He gave me a glass of water and then we went up another flight of stairs.

The front parlor on this floor would have overlooked the park, except instead of a regular window, the large oval niche inset in the wall contained a huge stained-glass window in the design of a rosebush. I could see it had been soundproofed with an additional layer of clear glass, as well. The chairs were arranged in a semicircle facing the rose window, and there was a thick curtain rod across the oval niche.

The director smiled as he saw us come in. "Ashley, so glad you could join us. If you would grasp hold of that bar and do not let go unless either I tell you to or you physically cannot any longer?"

I bowed my head in acknowledgment. So it wasn't a curtain rod after all. What else was I supposed to think a bar across a window was? The wood was warm and smooth, well polished.

"She's not allowed to speak, but she can make sound, is that right?" the director asked Damon.

"You're welcome to forbid her from making sounds," Damon said.

"Oh, no, no, it's no fun if the songbird doesn't sing," the director said. "I'll refrain from asking her questions, however. If you'll gather the others?"

"Of course."

Damon left the room. The director tucked some stray wisps of my hair into the hood and then took hold of the short robe. "Let go of the bar, now," he said, as he slid the robe from my shoulders. "Now grasp it again." He ran his hand across my bare shoulders and I shivered. He was a nice enough man, older and distinguished looking, but I wasn't particularly attracted to him and I didn't know what he was going to do to me.

"I made something especially for you," he said. As some people came filtering into the room, he showed me a cat-o'-nine-tails made of purple leather, intricately braided at the handle end, a long leather tassel at the other. "Have you been flogged before?"

I nodded, then shook my head, then nodded again, trying to figure out if what Damon had done to my pussy earlier counted as what he was talking about.

"Ah, here I go, trying to ask you questions. Clearly the answer is more complicated than a mere yes or no." He chuckled. "I'll ask George."

To that I nodded emphatically.

I heard them speaking about it behind me a few minutes later, and other conversations were taking place as the audience settled into their seats. I had goose bumps all across my bare back and shoulders.

And then I heard James's voice again. "I'm more interested

in the window than the girl hanging in it," he said. My heart did a little flip, and I reminded myself he had no idea it was me.

"Have you not been here before?" another voice said.

"Not in many years," James answered.

"The window has an interesting history," his companion told him. "It was originally in the private home of a member, but his wife didn't like it, and it was moved here. Designed by Burne-Jones, they say, and manufactured in William Morris's workshop."

Really? Apparently I couldn't escape the pre-Raphaelites, even when naked and about to be turned into some kind of erotic performance art. Well, maybe that made sense.

The voice went on. "Yes, the rosebush is clearly meant to represent female sexuality in all its lush fullness."

"And don't forget that the lovely, silky petals are matched by the wicked thorns," said the director. "With pleasure, comes pain. With desire, comes agony. Or so our little trainee is about to learn. Aren't you, dear?"

I nodded.

"Take a deep breath, dearie," he said.

I did, and as I let it out again, he brought the flail across my shoulders. I jumped at the impact and the sound, but it didn't actually hurt. The sensation was stimulating and sensual as the tails slid off my skin after the initial smack. Not that different from what Damon had done to me earlier.

I tried to relax into the strokes, which got gradually harder but at the moment felt only good. Over the sound of the flogger I could still hear James's voice out of all those in the room.

"Yes, I've been working on a major piece, but it's not quite done. My benefactors have been quite patient with me, thank goodness."

So these people knew him as an artist. Interesting.

"And then there is one, the one that is actually taking up all my time and energy. It's essentially done, but it isn't what they are looking for. I don't know whether that one will ever see the light of day. Few institutions are daring enough to exhibit that sort of material. With glass, all they want is beauty. Dale Chihuly's work is astounding and wonderful, but overall it is beautiful. But where is the angry glass? Where is the glass art about war and heartbreak and tragedy?"

I heard Damon joke, "Well, no one likes *broken* glass," and several polite laughs.

All through this, the tails of the flogger were slapping against my skin, so rhythmic I almost felt I was being hypnotized by it. My body was there, my skin heating up under the touch of the leather, but my mind was in the corner of the room where James sat. What was he wearing? Was he there with someone? Could I toss my head and catch a glimpse of him? It sounded like he was behind me and to one side.

Suddenly the flogger tails swung sharply across my ass, making me yelp.

"Making sure you're still with me," the director said. "Now that you're warmed up, we can begin."

Oh. He started a new rhythm then, faster and harder, and all my thoughts flocked to the surface of my skin. The leather battered me like relentless wind or rain, feeling less like violence and more like an irresistible force, wearing away my tension, my fear, everything I held so tightly inside.

I lost myself in that sensation, in the waves of impact, my resistance washing away. Eventually I began to cry, not because of any physical pain, but because of all the pain I held inside that I couldn't keep in any longer. The director made crooning sounds at me, encouraging me to let it all out, his flogger never stopping in its rhythmic path tearing me apart.

The last time I'd felt like all my boundaries were worn away by sensation had been when James had made love to me at that party. To have it happen again now, with him sitting in the room, was too much. I cried and sobbed and shuddered. This wasn't like some romantic, sexy misting of my eyes. I was flat-out bawling. The director didn't seem the least dismayed by that. In fact, he seemed quite proud of himself for having brought me to such a state.

When he was done, he praised me for being so obedient, for never letting go of the bar, for letting him take me "so far." He wrapped a blanket around me and lowered me to the floor right on the spot, not even trying to get me to a chair. He petted my hair and asked someone to bring a glass of water.

Various people drifted out of the room, now that the show was over, but I could hear James and Damon had stayed put.

Their conversation was smattered with art-world talk. "Yes, I take two or three trips a year to Greece, dealing in antiquities, so my relationship with the museums is quite good," Damon was saying.

I realized Damon must have figured out he was the one, though, when he began to ask James leading questions.

"I hope you've been enjoying the hospitality on this side

of the pond. I haven't had the chance to go to America yet. I've heard the society is quite different?"

James cleared his throat. "Yes, quite. The socializing is much more centered on private parties."

"That must make it more difficult to find suitable partners. How do they bring in fresh blood?"

"Oh, well, there is recruiting of various kinds. People meet partners outside the society and bring them in, or through the nightclubs and the Internet."

"Daring," Damon said. "You never know who you'll meet through the Internet. Here, with the trainee program, you know the submissives are extensively screened."

James chuckled. "All the screening in the world won't guarantee love, though."

Damon chuckled in return. "Well, of course not. Some members, of course, are satisfied to have a juicy fanny at their disposal."

"Trophy submissives instead of trophy wives?" James asked, his voice deep with skepticism.

"Sometimes," Damon allowed. "But we do pride ourselves on being able to play matchmaker. What sort of woman would you be looking for, my friend?"

James made a noncommittal noise, deflecting the question with a question. "You have submissive members of the society, too, don't you? Do you train doms as well?"

"We do. Vanette is very skilled at teaching women to bring out their dominant side, and both she and the director have a skills-training curriculum. And of course we have an endless supply of practice bottoms with the trainees. Ah, here come two of our recent trainees now. Miss Juniper, Miss Nadia, come say hello."

While they made their introductions, the director pulled my hood free and I gasped in fear. But I was still turned away from the room with the director curled behind me, dabbing at my tear-stained face with a handkerchief. I held it over my eyes. No one but the director seemed to be paying any attention to me, though.

From the chatter and rustling, I could hear it sounded like the two women were settling in with Damon and James. I heard the sound of kissing.

Then Juney's voice. "Oh, what have we here? Oh, sir, I'm trained to take care of problems like tha—Ahh!" She yelped and I heard a thud as if she had fallen to the carpet.

"I say!" said the director.

James's voice was tight, and I could hear he was livid. "Is this how you train them on this side of the ocean now, to be wanton, undisciplined creatures?"

"I was only going to suck it a little," Juney said, sounding confused. "No one's ever complained before."

"My apologies, Miss Juniper, if your training did not include such niceties as asking first. It takes a very special woman to get into my trousers. Now, if you'll excuse me, I think I've had enough for one night."

He left amid a burst of protest from Damon and the women.

"Well, la-di-da," Juney said. "I guess I'm not special enough for Master Fancypants."

The second she said it, I knew it was a mistake. I finally lowered the handkerchief to look in Damon's direction.

His jaw was set. "Miss Juniper," he said in a very low voice. "Strip and take your place at the bar."

"Here you go, darling. Let's get out of the way," the director said to me. He helped me up and we moved to a nearby chair while Juney pouted and started to shimmy out of the black minidress she was wearing.

Damon stopped her with a hand on her waist, pulling the dress down just enough to free her ample bosom. He discarded her bra, then hiked the bottom of the dress up to show she was wearing thigh-high stockings but no undies. Her pubic hair was as blond as her head.

"Nadia, my dear, fetch my canes."

"Yes, Mr. George." She hurried out of the room. When she returned, Vanette stood in the doorway, her cool eyes taking in the scene.

She gestured to me. "If I might borrow Ashley a moment, Director?"

"Why, certainly," he said, helping me to my feet, taking the blanket from my shoulders and replacing my short robe.

I followed Vanette down the hallway to another door. She opened it and led me into a small but elegantly appointed bathroom.

"I thought you might need this," she said. When I nodded, she pulled up one of her sleeves to show a gold charm bracelet. One of the charms was the key that opened the locks on the chastity belt. "It's much neater if you take everything off. When you're done, you can replace the items and close the locks again yourself. I'll wait outside the door. Knock if you need help."

I nodded and she smiled, seeming pleased that I remembered not to speak.

I did as she suggested and then sat down tiredly, taking the opportunity to collect myself. I was aroused from the flogging, from the environment, and from hearing James's voice.

I felt a surge of hope, and even a little pride, thinking about what he had said to Juney. He was back to the way he was when we'd first met. Damon George would let any woman suck his cock who offered. Not so James.

Only a special woman could get into those pants. What could I do to show him I was still that special woman, the woman he fell in love with? What could I do to find out if he was still in love with me?

Ten

Driven by the Night

Damon gave me a ride home that night. All my things were still in the car, after all. The spacious back of the limo was much larger than the town car Stefan drove. This one had seating for six or seven, more than enough room for Damon to drag Juney along. I sat on one side, while he held her by the hair on the seat across from me. Her hands were bound together, a gag was in her mouth, and although she was still wearing the black minidress, it remained bunched up around her midsection, leaving her as good as nude.

Once we were in the car, Damon thrust his fingers into her and made her moan around the gag, but he wasn't looking at her. He was looking at me. "So that was him," he said.

"That was him," I affirmed. "He...he has a habit of running off when he's upset."

"So I gathered, and why this one"—he thrust his fingers into her harder—"is being punished for scaring him off."

Juney made a whining noise like she was trying to say

something in her own defense, except she couldn't speak. Damon responded by thumbing her clit until she grunted.

"What are we going to do now?" I asked.

"Well, I'll do my best to entice him back to the premises," Damon said. "In the meantime, you'll start training with Vanette. I'll apologize and explain we'd like to make it up to him. If he's polite, he'll realize he can't refuse entirely without making enemies of us. By then you'll be trained in voice and service of some kind and it will be easier to isolate you two for your crucial conversation."

I sighed. How long was this going to take? I'd already waited long enough. But if that was what it was going to take, I could suck it up and hang on.

"You're hopeful, aren't you?" Damon said.

"I am."

"Because he rejected Juniper, here?"

"Well, yeah."

"I wouldn't get your hopes up too high. He's probably one of those repressed types."

Well, sort of, I thought. That was the James I knew, anyway.

"I'm going to have you, Karina."

I looked and saw Damon had his cock free of his fly and was stroking it. I looked away.

"After tonight, I want you even more than before. In the same car with you like this, I can barely hold back. Good thing Juney's here, eh?" With that he mounted her, pushing her down on the seat so that she was flat on her back with her knees in the air.

He was still fucking her when I got out of the car at the curb outside the ArtiWorks. I could see the lights were burning on the second floor. Even in the wee hours, either Paulina or Michel was awake. I exited the car quickly and slammed the door, though there was no one on the street at that hour to see what was going on inside.

Upstairs I found Paulina in the midst of baking half a dozen fruit pies. She served us some while it was still steaming hot, with vanilla ice cream on it.

"Your stomach is happy but the rest of you is not," she said, as she put the kettle on. We had eaten the pie sitting on stools in the corner at the one bit of countertop space that wasn't covered in kitchen gadgets, cookbooks, jars of pasta and flour, or cans of tea. "Something wrong?"

I was still brooding about having to spend however long as a trainee at the club, hoping that James would come back. What if he didn't? Did Damon hope I'd forget him eventually? That all the chastity devices and flogging would wear me down? It occurred to me then that Damon could lie to me, too. He could say he was trying to get James to come back, when really he was just training me to be his own personal sex slave.

Okay, maybe that was a bit extreme. I felt like I could trust Damon because he clearly stuck to the rules, but I didn't think I should rely solely on him. Sitting there with Paulina, I realized I had another avenue to try. "So when do you think the gallery will be ready to open?"

"Oh, we're drawing very close now. Not more than a month. In fact, we'll probably be finished before then, but it takes at least thirty days to promote the opening show, you know. To get in all the listings calendars and book everyone."

"I really would like to see the place in operation before I have to go back to New York," I said. That reminded me I needed to book my ticket home soon, but I couldn't really think about that yet. A month. This might work. "I have an idea for an artist who might be suited for the opening."

"Do you? We need someone edgy and underground but famous enough to give us some oomph, you know?" She flipped the kettle off and let the water cool a few moments before she poured it over a basket of tea leaves sitting in the pot. "Which is a difficult combination to find. Michel has a friend who knows Damien Hirst, but he's gone so mainstream now, ugh."

I didn't know contemporary art that well, but I had a vague memory of Hirst as the guy who did a lot of paintings of spots. Or was he the guy with the dead animals in formalde-hyde? That might have been the same guy. Either way, yuck. "You don't want something that is just stuck on the wall, either," I said. "You want someone who can bring a perfor-mance art aspect to things."

"Most definitely!" she said excitedly. "That might be our slogan. You know, 'Art is in the air, not on the wall!' Or some-thing like that. I want to have musicians, too, and maybe some dancers for opening night. The ArtiWorks should be multimedia, a space where all art thrives. The performing arts *are* visual arts, don't you think?"

"I totally agree," I said. "You still haven't heard my sugges-tion."

"So I haven't! What is it? Or rather, who?"

"J. B. Lester," I said.

"Oh, the glassblower?" She pulled the basket from the pot and then poured two cups, setting one in front of me.

"Glass*worker* is probably a more accurate description," I said. "It's not all blown glass." Some of it, I knew, was cast, some fused, some etched. Not to mention broken, glued, and constructed. "I know where he's working in York."

"Oh, you brilliant girl! And you met him there? He's a recluse, yes?"

"I know some people who were working with him and I saw his workshop. He's got a major work, very edgy. It's a whole installation, and he's dying to exhibit it somewhere and has nowhere to do it. The ArtiWorks would be absolutely perfect, wouldn't it?"

"Sounds like it would," she said.

"I'll put you in touch with the people who can talk to him." I sipped my tea cautiously so as not to scald myself. "He'd be an absolute fool to say no." I was already thinking through the logistics. The glass would be heavy. He wouldn't want to ship it overseas. This installation alone must weigh half a ton. Maybe more. It was about the size of a car, and glass was even denser than steel. So he'd want to show it in the UK.

Paulina sipped her tea for a while before musing, "And you say it's a project he has no backer for, no commission, no museum already waiting?"

"Yeah. The Tate is waiting for something else from him and this isn't it. It's like he's got to get this out of the way first."

"The muse works in mysterious ways," Paulina said. "If this is the demon that has been gnawing his soul, then of course it would emerge first."

I didn't know if breaking up with me was on par with a demon gnawing his soul, but I sure hoped it was. I thought of all the drawings of me on his worktable. If he wasn't still in love with me, he was at least still quite obsessed.

A wave of sleepiness came over me then. Between being

flogged to tears, hearing James's voice, and now having schemed a plan to draw him out of hiding that didn't involve Damon's help, I was exhausted and hopeful. I apologized for the fact that I couldn't finish my tea and dragged myself upstairs to bed. The sun would be rising very soon. I collapsed into a very deep sleep.

I called Helen the next day before I left for the Tate. "How'd it go?" she demanded.

"Terrible," I said.

"I thought you raced back to London to go to a party he would be at?"

"I did. He left in a huff, though, before I could talk to him. He might be headed back to York. I'm not sure. But listen, I've got a gallery owner here, opening a new place in about a month. I need you to play matchmaker between him and the gallery."

"Me?"

"Come on, Helen. Say you heard through the grapevine. They want something edgy and challenging and have room for a full installation of the piece I saw in his workshop."

"I'm going to need Linae's help. I'm no good at espionage."

I sighed. "I guess so. I'm a little worried about Linae, though."

I must have sounded jealous. Helen chided me. "Don't you be like that, Karina. I know what you're thinking, that Linae's going to tempt him into some kind of trouble. She's a flirt, but she wouldn't do that to you, trust me."

"All right. If you say so."

I gave her all the details I could about the ArtiWorks and how to get in touch with Paulina to make arrangements.

In the afternoon I led a tour of the exhibit as usual, and then one right at closing time for what I gathered were new and prospective donors of some kind. It was just a forty-five-minute tour, with an additional fifteen minutes for them to look around at the end.

Tristan was endlessly amused by the people. We stood together in the gift shop, smiling as the crowd headed to the exit. But inside I was laughing about the small comments he would make when they couldn't hear him.

"Blue sweater styled her hair for the occasion, but no one told her the modernist sculpture is at a different Tate," he said. Or, "Look at that fellow's lapels! He needs to get a landing permit to go to Heathrow."

Martindale took us to eat after the group was gone, which I thought was very nice of him. He grilled Tristan a bit during the meal on his graduate program in museum studies. Tristan, I realized, rarely talked about himself when we went to lunch, because I hardly knew anything about his internship or his degree program. Apparently he was thinking of trying to transfer to either City College of New York or Seton Hall but hadn't committed to trying it yet. That led to me and Martindale telling him about New York, since Tristan had never been. I promised to show him around the city if he came to visit, though I couldn't put him up, given that Becky had the bedroom and I couldn't imagine sharing the couch with him. There wasn't even really room for a sleeping bag on the floor.

I was amused to find Martindale also took the Underground to get home. He was amused that I was amused. "They say the measure of a great civilization is not how many of the poor have automobiles, but how many of the well off take public transit," he said after we had waved good-bye to Tristan, who went to a different train line.

The platform was lined with poster ads for Broadway shows, except of course there was no Broadway here. While we stood together, awaiting the train, I debated whether to tell him what I had found in York. While I was dithering, he came right out and asked, though.

"I missed him, but I did see his workshop," I told him. "I made contact with some other glass artists in the area, and we went out to where he's staying, but he wasn't home."

"That is disappointing to go all the way there and come so close."

"Well, I have a plan. I know he's working on a piece that he's been complaining he has nowhere to install."

"Indeed? He has not inquired with me about it."

"Which makes me think he thinks it's really not Tate material. But here's the thing. The folks I'm staying with? I've told you about how they're building an art space on their first floor?"

"You mentioned it, yes."

"I'm trying to get a message to him that they want it for their opening show next month. So, fingers crossed, maybe we can lure him out."

"Well, it's enough for me to know he's working and thinking about showing again. I was quite concerned that perhaps depression or the bottle had gotten to him."

I wasn't sure what to say about that without incriminating myself too much. Martindale had an inkling that I'd broken his heart or something, but I'd never gone into detail. "Far as I can tell, he's poured himself into his work instead," I said.

"That's all to the good, then," he said. "So long as he's saner for it."

That I couldn't speak to.

"Oh, Karina, one other thing I've been meaning to mention. We should book your ticket home. If we wait too long, the fares will get out of control. Mention it to my secretary and she'll handle everything, of course."

"I'll talk to her tomorrow," I promised. The summer had flown by, hadn't it? I could hardly imagine going back home.

When I got to the ArtiWorks, Paulina and Michel were waltzing across the newly sanded floor of the gallery to a song Paulina was singing in some other language. When she saw me, she beckoned me over and they pulled me into a three-way hug, still swaying slightly to the music she could hear in her head.

"It's all thanks to you, Karina! We've heard from an agent for J. B. Lester. He hasn't said yes yet, but it's looking very, very good."

"Agent?" I asked.

"A glassworker named Peter Simpson called, said he was speaking on his behalf," Paulina said. "We're negotiating a bit about fees and the date, but if he doesn't back out, it's going to happen!"

"Great. That's great!" I went up on my tiptoes and they swung me in a circle I was so weightless with glee.

I started training with Vanette that week. I met her at the club and on that first day of formal training we mostly talked. She took copious notes.

"Would you say you liked being a waitress? Did you enjoy it?" she asked. We were sitting in a room in what I thought of as the "backstage" area of the club, near the kitchen, where the members never went, only the staff and submissives.

"I didn't enjoy the low pay or customers who were jerks," I said, "but there were times when the work was satisfying. When you get all the orders right on a big table, it's great. When you swoop down, make every last one of them happy, and you see what a good time they're having, you walk away glowing, knowing you made that happen. Especially when an equally crappy server can have the opposite effect."

"Interesting. So making people happy, that was the best part of it? Did you chitchat with the customers?"

"That was the best part. I often didn't talk to them at all, other than to take their orders. Sometimes the way to make them happy was to be invisible, to get out of the way of them enjoying their food or their booze. Other times you would get the feeling they appreciated a little human interaction. That's why they came out to a bar instead of drinking at home, maybe."

Vanette wrote something on the pad in her lap. She was dressed casually, in black knit pants and a white mock turtleneck with short sleeves, the same charm bracelet as the other night on her bare, narrow wrist.

"We used to have a server here, a man, who had memorized each club member's favorite drink and the way he liked it served," she said. "And he could simply ask if someone wanted the usual and bring it to them unerringly. Even if it was a whole table of them, playing cards or what have you. Does that strike you as exceptional?"

"Not if he was seeing the same guys over and over. You always get to know your regular customers. If he could memorize them all after only being told once? That's a little more special. Had he been a bartender before?"

"I believe he was."

"He'd had practice at it, then. Good skill, though."

"It certainly made the members very happy, and they've been somewhat disgruntled since his departure that none of our current trainees seem to be able to handle doing the same." She seemed to be holding in a sigh.

"With all due respect, Vanette, the other trainees I've seen seem a little more focused on . . . How do I say this? They seem more there for sex and sex play than anything practical."

"Just so." A smile curved her perfect lips, which were tinted seashell pink today instead of bombshell red. "The term you're looking for is service oriented. There's a difference between submission and service. I think that's why the director was so intrigued by the fact that you barred intercourse. In recent years it has been easy to find sexually adventurous men and women who enjoy being on the receiving end of lots of kinky attention. It hasn't been so easy to find those who want to *serve*."

"Well, if Damon George is doing most of your recruiting, that's what you're going to get," I said.

She nodded. "He's not our only bird dog, but he is enthusiastic. I do wonder if part of our problem is that the concept of noble service has been lost. The so-called service industries, hospitality, food service, and so on, are now associated with immigrant populations and the disadvantaged. One is expected to move up out of those jobs as soon as possible. No one takes on service as a career unless one is in management, which is the opposite of what we need."

I hadn't expected her to get so philosophical. "That's true in the U.S., too, though I don't think we ever had the concept of noble service. We didn't have the whole *Upstairs, Downstairs* kind of thing going on."

She grinned at my description of the British class system as a TV drama, but knew exactly what I meant. "True. Which may also be why your branch of the society is much more focused on couples and private parties, while here, the gentlemen's club roots show through."

"You mean in how most of the trainees are women?"

"Among other things. Now, to come to the point. The best submissive is the one who seems to be able to read the dominant's mind. Since these fellows often seem to have, as the expression goes, one-track minds, the girls like Juney don't have to work very hard to make them happy. Although that wasn't the case the other night. I believe you were there for the little incident?"

I held my breath and nodded. I didn't think it was a good idea to let her know James was the sole reason I was here. "The member seemed offended that she had touched him without permission."

"I have to say, I wish more members had Jules's attitude," she said. "And when you think about it, if she had been a male submissive and the dom had been female, they would have been scandalized at the sub being so forward. Juney has been getting away with far too much, but I can hardly blame her when the members themselves allow it. This is why self-discipline is equally as important as discipline. Yes, your dom can rein you in easily enough, but he or she shouldn't have to be doing so constantly. If you had a horse you had to continually put back on the path, even if the horse didn't fight the correction, you'd still be thinking it was a difficult horse."

We were silent a moment while I thought that over. Then I asked, "Can you teach me? To not be too headstrong?"

She tapped her pen against her lips. "Perhaps. The smart horse knows where the rider wants to go and so doesn't have to be told. As I was saying, if you can learn to read their minds, you master yourself before they even have to lift a finger."

"My sister, Jill, used to say that about customers, too. 'Learn to read them,' she told me. 'Figure out how much money they want to spend. If they can't make up their mind on the menu, try to convince them there's something they really want.' And so on. But it was basically the same thing. The thing is, though, sometimes what they want is . . . to tell you what to do."

"True. With the ones who get off most on being dominant, it's ordering you to do something and seeing you obey that arouses them. Sometimes the odder or more difficult the request, the more excited they become. Other times it is not whether the submissive can succeed in following the order, but in how much they struggle to try, that turns them on."

That sounded like a description of James to a T. "Those are the doms whose praise means the most," I said, "and who are the most fun to please."

Her smile grew wider. "You and I are going to get along so well. Come with me to meet our bartender."

The bartender was a high-strung blond in his midtwenties named Stuart. The bar itself was at the back of one of the town houses, built into a room very similar to the one where I had been interviewed, only this one had fewer bookshelves, and many of the shelves held games. Some of the tables had inlays for backgammon and chess. Stuart and I got along well and he knew many of the members' preferences already. Perfect.

Two nights later I was put to working like a waitress. This time I wore the locked chastity belt but without inserts and a very cute, short dress and apron that left my buttocks exposed. That became my regular outfit on the nights that followed.

Two or three times members wanted me to bend over to have my ass swatted or the like, but when they realized I wore the chastity belt, they lost interest. I quickly became the queen of the refill. All a member had to do was tap his glass as I moved through the room and I would bring him a refresh. I also learned to make ice water magically appear nearby whenever someone was finishing a flogging or other public scene.

I couldn't work every night. I was still helping with the ArtiWorks renovation, which sometimes went until ten or eleven at night, when we would stop for fear that if neighbors complained of noise we could lose our construction permits. Some days I hurried home right after the afternoon tour and then after putting in a few hours painting or sanding or plastering went straight to the club. Meanwhile, Vanette had me teach a group of half a dozen other trainees how to put a glass down without making either a mess or a noise.

One night at the start of my second week, Damon came up to me as I waited at the bar for Stuart to put up an order. "You're making me look very good," he said.

"Excellent." I smiled at him. "Whoever thought helping out my sister was going to come in so handy for me later?"

He smiled in agreement and then rubbed his palm over the exposed globes of my ass. "By the way, I think our friend will be coming back soon."

I tried to play nonchalant, since Stuart was right there. "Oh? How soon?"

"Possibly tomorrow. I will do my best to arrange it so that you two can talk." He kept smiling while he said this, but his expression was a bit frozen. "I'll let you know when I know for sure."

But he didn't come the next night, or the next, and I was starting to worry. I hadn't heard from Helen or Linae either.

I arrived at the club as usual one night and was locking myself into the chastity belt in the dressing room when Vanette appeared.

"When was the last time a member used you for a sexual purpose?" she asked.

"Damon was the only one to go there," I said, "on that first night I was here."

"Hmm." She looked slightly concerned but she said nothing more about it, and I started my shift as usual. Damon didn't seem to be there that night, at least not that early in the evening.

It was drawing close to midnight, which was when Stuart usually went home, when I learned what she was so concerned about. One member whom I thought of in my head as Lord Sideburns, but who I gathered had the actual name or pseudonym of Burns, marched into the gaming room with Vanette in tow.

"Isn't it the rules, my dear, that aside from a submissive's dictum, they're required to perform a minimum of sexual service for us?"

Vanette was looking very proper that night, with a high-collared jacket that buttoned all the way up to the top of her throat. "The minimum is there to ensure we don't pass off people who should merely be employed for a wage, and that people do not pass themselves off for the sake of—"

"I know why it's there. And I would certainly never force someone to do something they truly objected to. But twenty days have gone by since Stuart's last service of any kind," Burns responded.

Stuart blushed to the roots and bowed his head.

"Isn't that true, Stu?"

"It is, sir."

"The rules say the minimum is once per week. It's been nearly three. What do you have to say for yourself?"

"I ... I've been busy, sir. And no member has demanded it of me."

"Have you offered?"

"No, sir."

Vanette pursed her lips. "If you'd like to have a go at him, sir, it's certainly well within your rights to."

Burns had piqued the interest of everyone in the room, though. "I was thinking, rather, that he needs to be taught a lesson so that he'll not forget to offer himself in the future. I believe it's in the bylaws that withholding sexual favors is punishable by a form of gantlet."

One of the men watching with interest spoke up then. "Gantlet? Of floggers?" he asked.

"That would be right if dear Stuart here had tried to get out of being flogged," Burns said. "It must be a sexual gantlet. All submissives in the house are subject to these rules."

Damn Damon for walking in at that moment. "Indeed, all.

I believe Ashley here has been neglecting her sensual duties in favor of practical ones, as well."

"But she's under chastity," the one who had brought up floggers said.

"She can still come." Damon slid a hand up my throat and tilted my face toward the man. "And her mouth is quite available. I believe the minimum for a gantlet is six, am I correct?"

Vanette let out a long breath. "Five, actually. The original rule was for all present, but that became impractical once the club grew in size."

"Five it is," Damon said. "I know Ashley can handle five orgasms in one night. Can't you, dear?"

Eleven

Run for the Shadows

Aside from how red his face got, Stuart remained stoic throughout the discussion and said nothing as they herded us upstairs. They settled Stuart in a room first, bound lengthwise on what looked like a vaulting horse, his ass hanging off one end and his head on the other. Burns patted Stuart's backside gleefully and I was encouraged to see Stuart wiggle it in response.

After a brief debate, they decided to put me in a separate room. Damon took the lead, bringing me to a room with a metal frame in the center. Wrist cuffs hung from the top crossbar, making it look like a kinky swing set, which was fitting I suppose, if I thought of the club as a sexual playground. Damon stood facing me as he lifted my arms, one at a time, into the cuffs and secured them. The cuffs were leather, but they were padded with fur on the inside.

He then slipped a matching blindfold over my eyes, leather with fur against my face. "Do I have to wear it?" I asked, as he settled it in place.

"If anyone wants to take it off you, they can," he said. "You know I get off on blindfolds."

Sigh. "Yes, Mr. George. So what are the rules here?"

"You have to do something sexual with each of the five members. Usually that would include letting them fuck you, but your dictum prevents that. So I'd say either you or they must come for it to count. Vanette, do you agree?"

"That's my interpretation of the rules, as well," Vanette said. "I'm going to supervise Stuart. I take it you can handle things here."

Damon slid his hand between my legs, his fingers skimming my exposed clit and labia. "Oh yes, I'll handle things." I moaned as his feather-light touch aroused me far more quickly than a rough hand would. "Hmm, but we're only four in the room. Daniel, would you get started while I go recruit one more so we can reach quorum?"

"Certainly," said a voice from behind me.

I felt hands at my wrists, and the next thing I knew, the cuffs came loose from the chains. I was still wearing them, but not attached to the frame any longer. "Follow the sound of my voice, darling," he said.

I turned toward him. He was walking away. I heard the creak as he sat down in a chair. I lowered myself to the carpet and crawled toward him as he said, "That's it. Come on, a little closer. No big surprises here."

That last caused one of the other men in the room to guffaw, and I wondered if that meant I was about to find a huge penis in my face. I found one of his knees with my hand and felt for him with the other.

In fact it was the opposite. His dick was small enough that the entire thing fit in my fist when fully erect. Apparently he was sufficiently self-confident to make jokes about his lack of size. I stroked him for a bit.

"Lick the end, would you?" he said, as if he were asking me to pass the sugar.

I hesitated a moment. Somehow it was no big deal for me to give this guy a hand job, but putting him in my mouth gave me pause.

"That's a good girl," he said. "One little lick won't hurt."

Okay. I swallowed and licked him like an ice cream cone. He tasted clean and a little salty.

"There you go. Get it wet and then use your hand."

I did as he asked, trying to guess how he liked it best, fast or slow, tight or loose, and at what angle. What made him go "Oh!" was when I tugged him away from his body, outward and not upward, with my thumb over the head circling on each stroke. When he got too close to bear it any longer, he closed his hand over mine and guided the last few tugs until he spurted, hot and thick, into my fingers.

"Ahhh. Outstanding instincts," he said, as someone else toweled my hands clean, first with a sanitary wipe and then with a towel. I heard him pulling up his trousers. "I don't know where George finds these lovely prodigies. This one is so innocent, yet sensual. It seems almost a shame to corrupt her."

"Almost," said another man. "Lay her back on the pad there."

"What do you have in mind, Charles?"

"If I can't fuck her twat or her arse, how about her tits?"

"Not sure she's got enough titty for that, but I suppose you could give it a go."

Hands helped me into position, lying back on something

soft. Someone put a pillow under my head, and then a naked man climbed astride my stomach.

I gasped as cold liquid splashed on my chest.

"It's only lube, love," Charles said. "Without it we'd both be sorry. Give me your hand."

I lifted one hand and he poured some lube into my palm.

"Now get me good and hard."

I reached for him, found him easily, and began to stroke. It took a few seconds for his flesh to come to life, but once it did, it felt like a chubby, fat organ in my hand.

"There we are. Now push your jubblies together." He caught me by the wrist cuffs and put my hands on my breasts in case I wasn't sure what he meant.

I'm not one of these ample-chested women, but I had enough to make a tunnel between them, which was good enough for him. His cock slid against my breastbone, into the tunnel I'd made.

It would have been kind of hot if I'd been attracted to him, but I wasn't even sure which man this was merely from his voice. If James, or even Damon, had been doing it, I would have enjoyed it more. As it was, it was mostly a test of endurance, trying to keep my grip on my boobs and waiting for him to get all the way to orgasm.

When he finally did, we were both out of breath. Although he bellowed loudly when he came, his come was a mere trickle on my chest and throat.

Again there were various hands cleaning me up, and then helping me to my feet. Several of the men were chuckling at one of their number who I gathered had been jerking himself off and had accidentally gone too far.

"'Ts all right, 'ts all right," he said. "I can still perform m' duty to the fellowship and the lady. Settle her over here."

They moved me again, this time bending me over another horse, crosswise, this one lower than the one they had put Stuart on. They attached the wrist cuffs to the feet of the horse so my head was bent way over, and secured my thighs to it somehow so that my toes no longer touched the ground.

The next thing I felt was a mouth on my clit. His tongue pushed under the edge of the chastity belt, teasing at my vagina, and then concentrating cat-washing licks across my clit. When he tired of that, he sucked my clit into his mouth and jabbed relentlessly at it with the tip of his tongue. I cried out, aroused but tortured by the sensation at the same time.

"Shhh. Hush, darling. See if you can keep quiet," he said, which gave me a moment of relief since he had to stop in order to say it, but began a whole new form of torture when he went right back to it.

Not screaming or crying out was difficult, but I managed it somehow. The endless sensation right on the button of my clit was pain as much as pleasure, and just when I was convinced the torment was too much and would never go over into orgasm, he slipped one finger under the edge of the belt into me and I began to come instantly.

I couldn't move, bound as I was, and I couldn't scream, so all the energy of the orgasm came out in shuddering. Behind the blindfold I saw colors and heard fireworks. It was only when I calmed down at last that I realized an argument was going on in the room between the last two men left.

James was one of them. "Honestly, George, is this necessary?"

"House rules, old son. Either she comes or you do."

I felt a hand on my thigh and trembled under it. James!

Damon coaxed him further. "It won't take you long. If she comes once, the second one is easy to bring out."

Careful fingers felt along my seam where the chastity belt exposed me, and massaged gently my ravaged clit. Oh, oh James, please! I didn't want him to stop. I needed that touch, that gentleness, so I tried to keep quiet, thinking that the moment he realized it was me, he might stop.

"How long has she been here?"

"A few weeks," Damon said. "As I was explaining, the total lack of sexual use of her is what brought this on."

"The society has some odd rules," James said.

"We never claimed otherwise," Damon agreed. "The British have made an art of creating convoluted excuses to elaborately fuck each other."

"And I appreciate that art," James said, "even if I am perhaps less enthused about this than my fellows. The poor girl at least deserves some consideration." His long, slick finger slid slowly along my clit, then back the other way, like a violin bow making a string vibrate.

And then the whole charade came down, as he asked me a question. "Do you like that?"

I nodded my head, trying desperately not to give myself away yet.

"Tell me how much you like it," he purred.

One sob escaped me before I could begin to speak. "I . . . I like it exactly like that!"

He froze, his finger against my clit but no longer moving. "What—?"

"I told you her name was Ashley," Damon said.

I cried out as his hands went away. "What is the meaning of this?" James sounded so British at that moment, like he often did at times of stress.

I shook my head trying to get the blindfold off. "It's me! It's me!" I shouted.

"You're despicable," James said, though whether it was to me or to Damon I couldn't tell.

Damon answered. "On the contrary, I keep my promises."

"I'll have no part in whatever sick game you're playing." It sounded like James was leaving the room.

"I just want to talk to you!" I shouted, but he was already down the hall. I could hear two sets of footsteps going down the stairs, James fleeing and Damon following.

I pulled at the wrist cuffs, but I was well and truly restrained. I screamed in frustration.

A moment later Vanette was there, letting me loose. "What happened?"

"Damon—" I tried to start. "He—" I blinked as she took the blindfold off me and helped me to a chair.

But Damon was back. "Alas, he's gone."

"You left her unsupervised in bondage?"

"Only for a moment," Damon said. "The door was open and Charles and Daniel are both about."

Vanette looked around the empty room with an accusatory tilt to her head. "She's had enough. And you've more than proved your point."

"The rules state five. If you count that last, aborted one as number four, she still needs one more. I'll do the honors and then she can go."

Vanette crossed her arms, but said, "Fine. You're last. And then she's done. Send her to my room for debriefing."

"Unlock the belt," Damon said with a grin.

"Need I remind you of those rules? So long as she is under this roof—?"

"I am all too aware of her prohibition," Damon said. "I promise I won't penetrate her. Not even with my pinky finger. Not even if she begs me to."

Vanette huffed, but she undid the locks and slid the belt free. She took it with her when she left. Damon closed the door behind her.

"What the hell, Damon?" I said, jumping to my feet the moment we were alone. "Was that your big plan to get him and me together? It sure as hell looks now like a plan to get me alone with you."

"Language," he said, snapping his fingers, "and form of address. Two infractions in one sentence. Turn around."

"I'm not kidding. This isn't a game."

"No, it isn't, which is why you had better do as I say."

"Fine." I turned around and he pressed himself against me from behind. I felt his trousers drop to the floor, his erection hard against my spine.

"Down," he said, and we went down on all fours like a pair of wrestlers, onto the mat on the carpet. He pushed me until I was facedown on the padded surface and his cock was between my legs. "Keep your knees together."

He fucked me then, in the crack between my thighs, his cock rubbing against all my sensitive parts but not, as he'd promised, penetrating me. Yet.

"I'd say your friend's sudden departure today was a fairly unequivocal rejection of you, wouldn't you say?" Damon's cock was long and slender as he drew it back and forth.

"Bullshit. We didn't even get to talk," I countered.

"If he wanted to talk, he would have stayed," Damon countered back. "The moment he knew it was you, he bolted."

"That's because he's ashamed of how he dumped me and he's afraid of dealing with the consequences." I gritted my teeth. *Do I believe that? I have to.*

Damon wanted me to think otherwise. "You're clinging to a pipe dream. He's a loser. He's in your past. Can't you see I'm the man who can give you everything you want?"

"All you've given me is an excuse for even more people to touch me."

"I'll take you away from here, Karina. I'll never let another man touch you again if that's what you want."

"We are not having this conversation!" I tried to struggle out from under him then, but he held me fast. "I'm not yours!"

"Not yet, you're not. But you promised me one night, one night to do whatever I like, no restrictions."

"Only if he rejected me!"

"What else do you call fleeing at the sight of you?"

"Shut up! You don't know him the way I do!" I struggled more, which only seemed to spur him to thrust harder.

"And I thought you were a woman of honor!"

"I am! I'll prove it to you!"

"How?" His breath was coming in short gasps now.

I clenched my legs tighter. "Give me two more weeks! Two more weeks, and if I haven't made up with him by then, you can have your one night with me!"

His answer was to shout in my ear as he came, shooting torrents of come between my legs and then collapsing, panting, on top of me.

He climbed off after a few moments. Something hit the ground near my head. I looked up to see the box of wet wipes. By the time I sat up to start cleaning myself up, he was gone.

I told Vanette everything that night. I used half a box of tissues I cried so much, but she never lost patience with me, never urged me to hurry up and get to the point. Maybe getting it all off my chest was the point. I don't know.

"I take it that the man we know as Jules is the man you told me you were saving yourself for," she said, as she settled me with a cup of tea at the small, round table in her room. She sat at an angle from me instead of directly across. She had her notepad but hadn't written anything on it yet.

"Yes," I said, choking back a sob. "Damon said he would help me talk to him."

"Maybe you better start at the very beginning again with how you met Damon."

"I think I better go back further than that," I said, "because he's not actually my first contact with the society."

"Ahhh. Do tell."

So I gave her the abridged version of both how my advisor, Theo Renault, had inappropriately propositioned me, and how James and I had met, leading up to going to the society party together. "One of the reasons I finally got up the gumption to turn Renault in was that I was told his application for membership in the society would be rejected if I did. When he was, he showed up drunk and ranting at my doorstep about how I'd ruined his chances with what sounded at the time like 'the Crimson Glove Society.'"

She nodded. "Sexual predators try to hide in our midst. It is very much in our best interest to rid ourselves of them. But how did you and Jules come to be separated?"

Now I had to decide how much to tell her. But I realized I could describe the situation, keeping what James told me secret. "Up until then I only knew aliases for him. Meanwhile, though, he knew everything about me, where I live, where I went to school, everything. It was starting to feel to me very lopsided. If he loved me, really loved me, when was he going to tell me?" I had to pause to cry a bit, saying out loud the fears that had gnawed at me then. "I felt we'd already gone far beyond just being a kinky fling. We'd used the word *love*, even if there hadn't been a . . . a big exchange of I love yous, you know?"

"I know," she said, giving me another moment to gather myself.

"Up until then we . . . we hadn't had full-on sex, either."

She was so earnest and calm, I didn't even feel embarrassed telling her.

"We had been working up to it. So here we are at this huge party, which he'd been winding me up for all week, and he ties me up and does all these things, and we finally get in bed, and I t-tell him . . ." God, where had I gotten the chutzpah? If I'd known he was going to react the way he did, of course I never would have done it. At the time, I'd felt it was my only reasonable action. "I told him no, you can't put it in until you tell me your real name."

"Ahhh." She nodded.

"I felt like if I didn't demand it then, he was *never* going to tell me. No one was watching us at that point. It was just us, so it wasn't like I made him say it to the whole room."

"And he refused?"

"No! He went through with it. Told me and then we made love." Okay, maybe it was harder to tell her this than I thought. I tried to calm myself with a deep breath. "Or, I thought we did. I thought it was the most amazing sex I'd ever had in my life. But apparently, all through it he was freaking out. At the end, he ran off and gave orders to Stefan, his limo driver, to take me back to the city."

She let me cry for a few minutes after that, waiting until I had slowed down again before she asked, "Did he speak to you after that?"

"Not a word. Not even to tell me to get lost or to stop calling."

"I can see why that might leave a girl with a burning desire to track a man down." She tapped her pen against the paper but wrote nothing. "Did he change his phone number?"

"Far as I can tell, he hasn't. But he did go into hiding. And came here, to England, I mean. I heard some members talking to him. They seem to know he's an artist of some kind."

"Yes, the society has funded some installations of his in the past," she said.

The private showing of the glass houses piece, the riding crops, it made more sense to me now. "He has a reputation as a recluse. So him going into hiding is something he's done before. I followed a rumor he was in England."

"Very well, but where does Damon come into the picture?"

I sighed. "Jules introduced me at one point to the curator for the Tate I'm working for now. Damon showed up at the gallery for a private tour with Nadia and Juney in tow. When he got an inkling that I wasn't as freaked out by it as your average art history student, he showed me the glove in his pocket and everything clicked."

"Ah, so you knew there was a possible connection between him and your missing paramour."

"Yes. Next thing I know, Damon's offering me a position here and help searching for Jules. I jumped at the chance. At the time, it was my first real lead."

"And, indeed, Damon put the two of you in a room together." She clucked her tongue though, shaking her head. "Tell me more about your relationship with Damon."

"What relationship? He's been trying to get into my pants since that very first day. That's not a relationship."

"True." She gave an emphatic nod. "So would you say it's all one-sided on his part? He's mad for you and you don't particularly care for him at all?"

"I don't think he cares about me," I said. "I think he sees a challenge, and that's why he's so keen on me. It doesn't have anything to do with me at all. I think once he lands me, he'll lose interest and move on to the next conquest."

Vanette stood and stretched at that point before refreshing the tea in her cup, adding a dash more to mine though I hadn't touched it yet. It was lukewarm when I took a sip.

"I can only speculate on Damon's motives," she said. "I've known him a long time. I gather you promised him something if Jules turned you down?"

"I promised him I'd let him have me for one night if Ja—" Oops. "Jules rejected me. He makes out like he'll use that night to make me forget Jules ever existed. That he'll be such a superior lover and master that I'll forget my hopeless crush on the guy who dumped me."

"Do you believe him?"

"That's the thing. If he could really do that, and Jules really did convince me we had nothing, then I'd let Damon give it a try. But I don't believe he really could do that, even if he intends to. Like I said, I think once the challenge is beaten,

I'll be just another trophy like Nadia and Juney to him. In a few months he'll be chasing someone else, and I'll be stuck, again."

Vanette nodded. "So when you said you wanted to learn how the minds of dominant men work, you were thinking of Jules?"

"Yes. Because I clearly miscalculated terribly with him."

"I am not sure you did," she said. "It sounds to me like you knew him so well and that is what scared him the most. He is, as you say, a recluse, a man who lives on secrets."

"That's what I told Stefan! That he was afraid. I think he realized how much power I had over him. I'm sure he didn't hand over his identity to just anyone. But how will I ever know if we have no contact?"

"And now that you have made contact, nothing he said or did tonight contradicts that feeling you have. That he runs from you because he's scared."

"Yeah. Until he can sit down in front of me and look me in the eye and truthfully say 'I don't love you,' I won't believe that he doesn't. I won't believe it's over." My eyes were dry as I said it. That's how strongly I believed he would never be able to tell me that.

Vanette sipped her tea and I did the same, waiting to hear what she would say next. When she did, she brought the subject back to the society. "Well, I cannot claim you were here under false pretenses, since I knew right from that first interview you were stuck on some dom. Damon is in hot water for not telling us everything and for being a general instigator of trouble, but you're not. The question now is whether you continue in training or not. How did you feel during tonight's exercise?"

I couldn't hold in a shiver. "I really have no interest in having sex, even pseudo-sex, with anyone here," I admitted. "I
couldn't wait for it to be over. The...the men have all been
perfectly nice. I enjoyed being flogged. But I'm really not interested in having kinky fun for the sake of kinky fun. I want
Jules back. If training here was the way to do that, I don't regret anything I've done. But I'm really not into it."

"Alas, that was the sense I got from you," she said. "And
you're the only one who actually displayed any aptitude for
service among the trainees. Well, you and Stuart."

"Is he going to be all right?" I asked, before I really thought
about what I was asking.

"Oh, he'll be fine. The membership gangs up on him about
once a month. For the next week or so he'll be walking on
air, completely chipper and well adjusted. Stu's got no capac-
ity to ask for what he needs, though, and is far too obedient
to act out to get it. Burns and his cronies take good care of
him."

I chuckled a little. "And here I thought he was high-strung."

"He'll wind up again gradually over the next month, and
then they'll take him apart again. It works for all concerned."
She smiled dotingly. "But we were talking about you. I'm
sorry to say that unless you have a very strong argument for
staying on, we're going to have to let you go, and it sounds
to me unlikely we'll see your Jules here again, so you've little
motivation to stay."

"You're right," I said. "There's no reason for me to be here."

"I'm sorry we couldn't engineer a resolution for you and
Jules, either," she said. "Keep my number. If he eventually does
reject you, or you decide to give up on him and you want to
come back, I'd be open to speaking with you about it."

"You would?"

"I like you, Karina. You're bright and smart and your heart is in the right place. Not to mention, you're a born masochist with an understanding of service. You'd be very valuable to us, if you wanted to be here. It's good we both recognize that right now, though, you don't."

"Yeah."

"I'll call you a taxi home." She stood. "My last piece of advice is this. Do you know what excites Damon George?"

"Blindfolds?" I guessed.

"Pushing the boundaries," she answered. "The thing that gets him the hardest is pushing against the rules and the strictures. Not breaking them, because that would get him thrown out of too many places, but on seeing how far he can go, how much he can get away with in the gray area before he crosses the line into too far. And this is a man who thinks with his cock."

"Are you saying don't trust him?"

"I'm saying understand what drives him."

"Thank you. That's good advice." It applied equally well to James, too. What drove James to be so secretive, so closed, so careful? I hoped I would have the opportunity to find out.

Twelve

Images of Broken Light

The taxi let me off in front of the ArtiWorks. Despite the late hour, I could see the lights in the gallery were blazing through the paper that covered the front windows. Inside I found Michel with a roll of tape on his wrist like a bracelet, pacing back and forth on the raised section of floor that would serve as a "stage," though it was only a few inches higher than the rest.

"Ah, Karina, you can help me with this." He held out one end of a tape measure, which I took between two fingers. "Hold that down on the piece of tape over there." He pointed to the edge where I could see he had marked an X.

He then measured a distance he had in his head and put down another taped X. He marked out two more spots and then stood back. "Perfect! It will fit. Thank heaven."

"What will fit?" I asked.

"The rather large installation that your friend will be contributing to our opening, of course! This will leave plenty of room along here..." He gestured to the open area that would extend from the edge of the raised step to where the chairs and tables would be. "For the dance performance, which it looks like we will not have anyway, but I am hopeful, nonetheless."

"What happened to the dance performance?"

"Oh. The leader of the troupe has a severely sprained ankle, and her husband, who also dances in the troupe, a broken elbow, I believe. Quite a coincidence, no?"

"Were they in a car accident?"

"Heh. That would be a convenient cover story. But no, I believe it was described as a sex swing accident." He looked up at the ceiling where two large eyebolts had been installed. "They were rehearsing for this very performance and got carried away, I think. And then the attachment to their ceiling gave way. Alas. It will be dull without dance."

I had thought maybe he was going to say it would be dull without sex, but no. I looked up at the bolts. "I guess you'll have to hang a sculpture or a lamp or something."

"Yes." Then he looked at me for the first time since I had come in. "Mon chérie, are you all right? You look as though you have been crying."

"Oh, I'm fine. I'm fine."

"This man who took you on the weekend-long date. Is he a problem?" Michel took my hands in his.

"It's not him, Misha. I . . . I'll be okay. So, this installation. When's he coming to install it?"

Michel cleared his throat. "Well, he is shipping most of it down with two assistants, who will do the initial construction. He won't arrive until the day of, with the final segments. I can see from your face that you are disappointed about this."

I squeezed his fingers in mine. "I should probably tell you and Paulina something."

"Something serious?"

"Very serious. Although first I should tell you...I used to do modern dance. I...I could put together a performance for the opening. In fact, I would really, really like to."

"Truly? All right, chérie, let's finish up down here and then you can tell Paul and me all about your idea and whatever your other secret is."

"Okay."

We turned off the light and went out the front door. Michel locked it with the key and then unlocked the door to the flat. Upstairs, Paulina was emerging from her studio and putting on the kettle as we arrived on the landing.

We settled ourselves in their art-filled sitting room again, with the latest in Paulina's baked creations on the table in the middle, éclairs and cream puffs. "If I can get it right in time for the opening, I'll cater it myself with these," she said, holding up a mini-éclair. They tasted delicious, but some of them were oddly shaped.

"*Tsk*, they are artisanal," Michel scoffed. "I think you should make *none* in the traditional shape! Each one should be unique."

"That's harder than making them uniform," she said, licking chocolate from her fingers.

"No one said art was always easy." Michel looked up at me. "Karina has an idea for the opening, too."

"Um, yes. I heard about the dancers who got injured, and Michel was saying with less than two weeks to go it's too late to find someone to replace them. But I thought I could do something."

"Do something?" Paulina asked.

"Dance something," I said. "It's been a while, but I have an idea. If the piece that is being installed is the same one I saw in York, I even have a way to integrate it into the performance."

"Oh, that's exciting," Paulina said. "Misha, do you have the photos from the e-mail?"

"I'll get them." He set down his teacup and hurried into the other room. I waited until he had come back. The photos were marked with dimensions, height and width, of each piece and the floor layout of the footprint of the sculptures.

"This is exactly what I remember." I looked at the images and passed them to Paulina. "Did he tell you what the art is meant to evoke?"

"Not a word, but I can interpret abstraction with the best of them." Michel cracked his knuckles. "All of the red? You cannot think it is anything but blood. Spilled blood is conflict. And the looming, jagged red maw above? Why, it is the piece of his heart that is left after being broken. No?"

"The entire thing is a carnivorous flower," Paulina said. "The petals turning to teeth, a warning that beauty does not mean passivity. And this protuberance in the center is of course the stamen. Or the pistil. I forget my botany. The sexual bit that protrudes."

"Go with Freud and call it the phallus," Michel joked.

"To me it also evokes the floating world of Japanese art." I pointed to the shape of the overhanging red claw/maw. "This looks like the breaking wave, *the Great Wave* of Hokusai, only in red instead of blue."

"Ah, I see that!" Michel grew very excited then. "This cannot be an accident. It must be intentional. Right down to some of the shards having opaque white parts capping the red. But what do you think the piece means?"

"I've been thinking about it a lot, and I think the association with the wave is saying something about the force of desire, about how once the tide of lust is unleashed, it cannot be stopped. This is a part of nature that mankind thinks can be controlled, but once the wave reaches its crest, it's going to be unstoppable."

"Ah, and your phallic pistil then is truly the phallus," Michel said. "What artist doesn't dream of glorifying his own penis?"

"Female ones, perhaps?" Paulina swatted him on the shoulder. "Listen to Karina."

I went on. "Well, it probably is the phallus in this case. I need to ask you guys, though. Misha said the other dancers were going to do a very…sexual show."

"Well, I think they intended to merely simulate sex, but possibly in such a way as to make the audience wonder whether it was real," Michel said. "Why do you ask?"

"I'd do that, too," I said. "I would interact with the art as if it were a monster of male desire come to life. Some of it might be, um, quite racy."

"Racy is good," Paulina said. "Racy is very good. But what about the artist himself?"

"I would like to keep it a secret from him. And I promise I won't damage any of the art. Here's the other thing I've been meaning to tell you."

They were both silent, hanging on my words.

"I did an art performance with J. B. Lester once before." How could I come out and say this? What if I was wrong and they didn't really know James? "That was before I knew…who he really was."

Paulina nodded. "We've suspected he was J. B. Lester for some time now, but we've never told anyone in the LL community."

I sighed in relief. "Then you understand."

"Yes. I believe one of the reasons he responded positively to the invitation to the ArtiWorks is he knows we'll understand the need to keep his secrets," Paulina said.

Michel cackled a little. "And he's owed us a favor for, oh, only about ten years."

Paulina poured fresh tea into my cup, then her own. "I'm sorry, you were saying?"

"Yes. I was...in a relationship with him. I think I still am. But he's been in hiding from everyone, including me."

Michel's eyes were bright with mischief. "Oh, we must keep you a secret, too, then!"

"Well, I wanted to talk with you about it, because I don't want him to cut you off because you helped me. He can be sort of...irrational at times."

"And a diva, and self-absorbed, and miss the forest for the trees?" Michel said. "That is the nature of being an artist, perhaps. Do not fret, chérie. We can handle his tempers, should they flare. I wholly support your performance art idea. Will you wear a mask and reveal yourself at the end?"

"You read my mind. I'll need to choose music, of course, and rehearse, but I can be ready in two weeks. I might need some help with a costume..."

"My sewing machine stands at the ready!" Michel said, standing up and saluting like a soldier. "Oh, this is going to be great fun. And how wonderful it will be to see James again."

Hearing his name spoken aloud sent a shock through my whole system, an electric thrill that ran from the top of my head to the tips of my toes. It was real. James was real. He would be coming here. I had a plan to confront him and I had real allies this time.

Now I merely had to prepare to perform an art I hadn't done in two years. Somehow being tied up and flogged sounded easier. But I was committed now. I would be dancing for high stakes.

I started practicing. It took us and a crew of about six of Paul and Misha's friends to paint the entire gallery before the floor could be finished. Add two full days for the varnish to dry, but once it did, the gorgeous hardwood was perfect. There were no chairs or tables yet, so I used the entire space as a dance studio, remembering my warm-up exercises bit by bit and stretching. Flexibility came back faster than I expected.

So did Damon George. My phone rang one night while I was practicing in the front and Michel was working on refurbishing a gigantic secondhand espresso machine he had acquired.

"Karina, how are you?" Damon said.

"I'm fine. Do you need something?"

"No need to be snippy, Karina. I know your two weeks aren't up yet. I need your help with a project."

"What kind of a project?"

"An art project."

"Really. I'm very busy, Damon—"

"I need a model and you're the only one who will do."

"I don't have time to sit for a painting."

"Not the painting. The photographs that will be used as a reference. It'll be two or three hours at most, I promise."

"Damon—"

"And I keep my promises. You know that."

"Two hours, no more, and you promise not to try anything."

"Define anything."

"You promise not to stick your cock in me, okay?" I shouted. "Are we clear on that?"

"Yes, yes, of course! God, Karina, did you think I'd forget that?"

"Did you think I'd forget you tried to talk me into it last time?"

"I said two weeks and I meant it. Really. I promise. I won't penetrate you with anything, cock or no. Okay? How about tomorrow?"

"Fine. What time?"

"I'll pick you up at the museum after your last tour. How's that? And I'll have you back home before sunset."

"Sunset isn't until like nine o'clock," I said. "It's summer."

"Nonetheless."

"All right. Will I need to bring any clothes?"

"No."

"Why am I not surprised?"

"I'll see you tomorrow afternoon, Karina." He hung up.

God, he was infuriating. I couldn't imagine James ever jerking me around like that. If James said he was giving me two weeks, I would bet my phone wouldn't ring even one minute early. And if I told him I didn't have time for something, he wouldn't wheedle me into doing it anyway. James respected limits and knew how to take no for an answer. Damon . . . well, Vanette had told me, he would try to get away with whatever he could without outright breaking the rules.

Michel poked his head out from behind the machine. "Everything all right, Karina?"

"Oh, fine. An artist wants me to pose in the nude."

"Ah, hence your emphatic statement of your boundaries. Good girl." He grinned. "Did I ever tell you that Paul and I met in art school?"

"No, but I kind of assumed it had to be something like that."

"She was in painting, I was in sculpture, and we each ended up needing to pose for the other when either models or references didn't pan out. Amusingly, I needed a male model, she needed a female model, so that was the first time we changed for each other."

I'd been wanting to ask about that but hadn't known how to. I sat down at the marble bar, where there was one creaky stool. "Is that how the portrait of you wearing each other's clothes came to be?"

"Exactly. She makes for a handsome man. I, unfortunately, make a very frumpy woman, but she loves me anyway." He shrugged with a smile. "James, when he first learned to work with glass, was part of a coterie of students who would come to hang around our studio."

"How old was he then?" It was still thrilling to have someone to talk with about him.

"Oh, still in university, maybe twenty or twenty-one. He was the quietest of all of them, if you can believe that."

"Oh, definitely."

"Always let someone else take the spotlight. He stayed in the background. Of course, he was such a good-looking chap he had no shortage of the others throwing themselves at him. Oh, but you don't want to hear about that."

I shrugged. "I assume as a famous rock star he has people throwing themselves at him all day every day."

"Which is perhaps one reason he is so secretive. He can walk down the street to buy a newspaper without hordes of fans trampling him. Many at his level of fame cannot do so. They are literally captives of their own fame."

"Is that why he retired from performing? Was it becoming too hard to maintain the secret?"

"I don't know. Perhaps you'll get a chance to ask him."

The next day, as promised, Damon picked me up at the museum. He drove a very cute, very small Italian sports car. I think I was supposed to be impressed by it. He was all business as he took the car along the Thames and then across it. He told me he had been painting for years but had been throwing away every canvas as "unworthy."

This was a side of him I hadn't seen before. I was used to him being a rich playboy, a tycoon, confident and smooth. Seeing him as a neurotic artist was new.

His hands shook as he tried to get the keys into the lock on his studio. He took me up to a loft where the wide windows bathed the entire space in natural light.

In the center of the room stood something seven or eight feet tall and draped with black cloth so large that it covered the floor for three or four feet in all directions surrounding it. Cameras were stationed on tripods and stands all around the covered thing, whatever it was.

"Go on and get your clothes off," he said, "and I'll get mine on." He went into another room.

I took off my clothes and folded them in a pile on the workbench against one wall. Here I got an inkling of what painting he was working on. Color laser prints of the three Burne-Jones paintings about Perseus and Andromeda were sitting there. I remember him saying they should be read backward from the traditional myth. Instead of rescuing Andromeda, Perseus chains her to the pillar of rock and then, in what would be the next frame of the story, has his way with her.

"You never give up, do you?" I said to myself, shaking my head. Well, he had promised.

Damon emerged from the next room wearing head-to-toe leather armor, his hair artfully tousled. He was sexy—I admit it—but I shut down all feelings I might have had. There was no way I was going to be tempted by him, when James, the real James, was so close to being in my grasp.

He approached me at the workbench, the leather creaking. "Do you remember what I told you about Perseus?"

"I do. You didn't tell me *you* were the painter you had in mind, though."

"We all have our secrets." He gestured to the set. "If you would join me?"

So the covered thing represented the black pillar of stone that Andromeda was chained to in the Burne-Jones painting. I was not surprised at all when he produced chains and manacles and attached them to my wrists. These were of worked metal of some kind, not like the comfortable fur-lined cuffs at the club.

"Let's test the light." He adjusted my position so I had my hands over my head, my wrists crossed, my back to the pillar. He had a small remote in his hand. He stepped back and I heard the cameras clicking. He walked over to something and said, "Can you see that?"

If I craned my neck and stretched my arms a little I could see the sixty-inch screen behind me and to the right. A slide show of the photos just taken, running through the various angles, showed in a loop.

"Perfect," he said. He settled the leather helm onto his head and stepped up next to me. "Try this."

He took hold of my chin in his hand, tilting my face away from his. "Close your eyes. Relax. Andromeda wants this," he said. The cameras clicked.

"Does she?" I asked, though I did as I was told.

"Of course she does. He's her hero and he's everything that is sexy about the sea serpent as well." He changed pose. "Breasts out, head back, like you cannot wait to be ravished."

The cameras continued to click and whirr. "Andromeda knows there is no escaping destiny. She is not devoured by the sea serpent, because Perseus's snake will have her instead."

Whatever. I moved as he told me to, trying not to be affected by the heat of his body so close to mine and the suggestiveness of the positions.

"Lift your leg, knee to one side," he said.

That showed my vagina quite clearly to the cameras, a graphic pose that one would never find in pre-Raphaelite or any other fine art. I gasped as I felt something cold touch my stomach. The flat of his sword.

"Look into my eyes, Karina," he said, as he slid the metal prop lower, then spread my labia with the dull edge of the sword. "That's perfect."

The metal was cold and hard as it was brushing against my clit. My breathing sped up and I knew my skin must have been flushed.

"Perfect," he repeated.

Next he hitched one of my knees alongside his hip, turning so that the space between my legs was still visible to the cameras. Now he dug between my labia with the handle of the sword.

"You said no penetration," I gasped.

"And there will be none," he said, "even if you beg for it."

"Why would I b—" I broke off and gasped as he slid the smooth, slick knob of the handle against my clit.

"Because sometimes you need something inside you to come. Isn't that right, Karina? You don't even know why, but that's the truth, isn't it?"

I trembled under the rising pleasure from his touch and the distress from his words. "Sometimes." I was wet now and getting wetter by the second.

"I know what happened to you, you know," he whispered. "Some dom shaped you to his will, shaped your body to fit his cock, and shaped your responses to his whims."

I sobbed as he began to move the slick pommel faster against me. Every word he had said was true. James had literally shaped my insides with dildo training, and from the very first time he'd made me come had rewired the way I experienced pleasure.

"That's the only reason you crave so very much to be with him," Damon whispered in my ear. "You think you need him like a drug. You'll rationalize your addiction any way you can."

I whimpered, my hips jerking as I tried to rub myself against the smooth metal in a way that would actually get me off. But it was never the right amount of pressure or the right amount of friction.

"I'm telling you, Karina, I can be your methadone. I can be your rehab. I can make you a whole woman again. I can fill the space inside you. I can. I know I can."

I groaned and moaned, angry at him for provoking me like this but almost wishing he'd break his promise and shove the thing inside me because at that point I thought that would trigger the orgasm I was so close, yet so far, from achieving. Almost.

Instead, I ground my teeth together, promising myself that the next thing I'd have inside me would be James's glass and nothing else. Nothing else.

And then the way to end this came to me. It wouldn't work if Damon really knew me as well as he claimed to. But if it did, well, then I would be scot-free. With a deep breath and a *here goes nothing*, I started to fake an orgasm.

For a moment he was startled, and nearly pulled away, but I cried out, "Don't stop, please!" and he took pity on me, or thought he did, grinding the handle against me harder. That really hurt, but cries of pain sound exactly like cries of ec-stasy sometimes, and I kept it up until it seemed reasonable to go limp.

He threw the sword to the floor. I heard it clatter. Then he leaned in and kissed me, his tongue delving into my mouth while I held my breath. He thrust me away then.

"You still resist me," he said, pulling off the helm and shak-ing his head in disbelief. He really had thought that was all it would take to get me to give in. He was so wrong.

"My two weeks are not up yet," I said. "Now let me go."

He said nothing more. He undid the manacles, rubbed my wrists a little to warm them up again, and then left the room. When he came back a few minutes later, he was casually dressed in a pullover and slacks, his feet still bare. With my clothes held to my chest, I investigated the room he had come out of and found a small bedroom and attached bathroom. I cleaned myself up and got dressed again.

When I emerged, he shut off the video screen quickly and picked up the car keys.

He drove me home without saying anything. His silence was unnerving, but I wasn't going to rise to the bait and be the first one to say something. When I moved to get out of the car, he finally spoke.

"Five days," he said. "Five days."

"Yup," I agreed, and slammed the door.

Thirteen

Love Is My Bet

Peter and Linae arrived the next day with several huge crates and a third helper in tow: Helen. She hugged me when she saw me, and then they set to work on moving, assembling, and whatever else was necessary to construct the installation as specified by "J. B. L." I went off to the museum as usual.

As lunchtime approached, Tristan surprised me by sneaking up on me. I was sketching some notes for the dance choreography in my notebook and he caught a glimpse. The shapes on the page didn't look anything like a person dancing. They were more indicators of arm and leg movements, combinations that I thought would work and wanted to try later.

"What's that?" he asked. "Butterflies? Hieroglyphs?"

I hadn't told him about the performance. I had been hoping I might get him to come on the Saturday of the opening weekend and miss the actual dance, so I hadn't mentioned anything about it. I was keeping to my promise not to lie and

I knew once I started to explain this, it would be too late. "It's dance choreography. This is how my old dance teacher used to notate things."

"Dance! Karina, I didn't know you danced!" He put his finger on top of his head and did a joking pirouette, then stumbled, dizzy. When he recovered, he said, "This dance is for you? Or someone else?"

"For me. The dancers who were supposed to perform at the opening of the ArtiWorks had to cancel and I volunteered to fill in."

"Oh, that's fantastic! I must come to see it!"

I knew you were going to say that. I gave him the details on when it would be and the address.

"This Friday, how perfect," he said, though he didn't explain what was perfect about it and I didn't press him for details.

That evening, Michel and I worked on my costume. We had settled on something sheer for the bodysuit, close to the color of my skin, so from a distance I might appear nude except for the deep red chips of glass sewn into the fabric and the petal-like skirt made of a diaphanous fabric with frothy white swirls on it. The outfit reminded me of something a figure skater might wear, though Michel said it was much like what he would do for a ballerina. The bodysuit had three tiny snaps at the crotch just like a ballet suit, he said. He also offered to make wings to match the skirt, for a sort of Tinker Bell effect, but I felt that was too much, and kind of off topic.

The mask was still a question, but we had a few days to figure that out.

Meanwhile, downstairs the art was beginning to take shape. The next day I watched for a while as Peter painstakingly measured the space, placing various pieces where they belonged.

"It's a giant mouth, isn't it?" he asked me as he knelt on the floor to affix one piece in place, the main curve of the sculpture hanging over him. "I mean, these bits here are the molars."

I grinned. Yes, there were some blocky bits that could be seen as teeth, but the two that mattered most to me were obviously shoes, weren't they? Not to Peter, apparently.

Later that night, after everyone else had gone to bed, I had an attack of worry. What if he didn't like the dance? What if I looked ridiculous? Well, it was too late to back out. Besides, what if I was wrong? What if James really wasn't thinking about me when he designed the piece? I slipped down to the gallery, using my phone as a flashlight, and slid my feet into the shoe-shaped pieces.

They fit perfectly. I stepped aside carefully, my heart pounding with excitement. So much for the thought that he didn't have me in mind. That didn't mean, of course, that he wanted me back. All great works of art could have multiple interpretations. But I couldn't think about him rejecting me now. I had to think positive.

The phallus had not been installed yet, and I wondered if James was bringing that with him. I was sure he was.

The thought struck me that other than the slender plugs I'd worn with the chastity belt, I hadn't had anything sizable in me in quite a while. I snuck back up to my room and took out the glass dildoes. I still had a few days to go. One each day to work up to the biggest size was probably the best plan. I masturbated to make myself slippery, and I slid the smallest one into my body, imagining that his hand moved it in and out of me instead of my own. But I didn't allow myself to come, thinking about what Vanette had said about self-discipline being as important as discipline.

Three days before the event, I convinced Linae and Helen to be part of my performance. "Just at the beginning," I told them. "We're to represent the three Muses, you see." I'd gotten the idea while surfing art websites the night before, researching the Burne-Jones Perseus cycle.

I had been right all along. He had painted the three paintings with Andromeda in sequence, from the rescue at the rock, to the defeat of the sea monster, to showing her Medusa's head in the garden. Then again, he had begun another where *Perseus* was the nude instead of the female figure in 1877 and didn't finish it until almost twenty years later, more than ten years after Andromeda. So maybe the dates proved nothing other than there was a whole lot going on in the artist's head regarding Perseus.

One of the other Perseus paintings, not in the Tate exhibit, had been of the three Muses giving him his helmet, and that's where I had gotten the idea.

For masks, we would each be wearing an actual reproduction of a Muse's face from a famous painting. The entire dance, for the audience, could represent the ways in which art itself can devour us, and how the artist can be devoured by it. I was very satisfied that would be the main interpretation people would come away with.

Paulina made the masks, while Michel made diaphanous gowns for us to wear. Mine went over my other costume and would be shed when appropriate. I listened to the music I'd chosen over and over again, walking through the movements and steps in my mind even when I wasn't actually rehearsing.

It was exhausting. It was thrilling. Every night I fell into bed with the next larger dildo and prepared myself as best I could.

Everything was speeding along like a train out of King's Cross. Then, the morning of the performance, my phone rang.

It was my sister, Jill. "Jill, are you all right?" It was four in the morning for her.

"I got word that Mom fell," she said.

"What do you mean, Mom fell? Is she okay?"

"She's in surgery now. They gave me the name of some guy I've never heard of who's there with her. I'm guessing her boyfriend of the moment. I tried to make sure they know I'm the next of kin and they have to call me for any kind of medical decisions, but... but he's there and I'm not."

"Did they give you any idea of how serious it is?"

Jill let out a long breath. "I was pretty shocked when they called. I don't even know if I was hearing everything right. Let me see. I tried to write it down, but I can barely read my writing. Fractured kneecap, torn ligaments, broken elbow, and she hit her head, to boot."

"Wait, all that from one fall?"

"I think she fell down a flight of stairs. Wait, and a broken neck. Oh no, wait, that was what they told me she *didn't* have. Neck and spine okay. Sorry, sis. I was pretty shaken up by the news."

"Understandably. Holy shit, Jill!"

"Anyway, I wanted you to know as soon as possible. I only got the call a little while ago. I'll call you back as soon as I hear anything else, I guess. I'm looking at flights. The soonest

I can get something under a thousand dollars one way might be Monday, though. By which time she'll probably be in rehab and good and cranky." Jill chuckled a little. "Okay, I must be calming down if I'm making jokes about it."

"Well, keep me informed. The bones I'm sure she can heal. Hitting her head is a little more serious."

"I know. I'll keep you posted. Should have an update in another hour or so, after she gets out of surgery. So how's London? I haven't heard from you except for a couple of e-mails, you know."

"London's good. My God, I've been so busy here. I told you I'm living with this couple who are building an art gallery in the café on the ground floor of their building, right?"

"Yeah, you e-mailed that."

"Well, I've been helping with the renovation, and doing a ton of stuff for that, plus working at the museum, plus working as an artist's model," which was true. "Tonight's the big grand opening of the gallery!"

"That's great," Jill said. Then more soberly, "I don't know how long I can stay with Mom. I mean, I know I'm the oldest. It's my responsibility. But I can't stay for a month. If she needs someone there—someone other than boyfriend of the day—you might have to pick up the baton next, Karina."

"I'm already booked on a flight to New York ten days from now," I said. "I'm sure I can get another academic leave if I need it. It's not like I need to take more classes."

"Okay. Yeah. Good to know."

"You really think she's going to be okay?"

"They didn't say get on a plane now. If someone's got a chance of dying, they usually say that. So I'm hanging on to that," Jill said. "I wish I knew how to get in touch with Troy."

The last either of us had heard of our brother had been several months ago when he'd hitchhiked his way from Colorado to California. "Can't help you there. Talk to you later, Jill. Try not to stress."

"I'll try. Love you, sis."

"Love you, too." Somehow that was easier to say when I was thousands of miles away, hadn't talked to her in nearly two months, and wasn't currently angry or annoyed at her for any reason. Also I was relieved that I didn't have to fly to Ohio immediately. For a moment there I had feared that all my careful planning would be wasted if I had to jump on the next flight out of Heathrow. But no. Jill would go first. I was grateful for that.

The phone call merely meant my already high state of anxiety over the performance was ratcheted up even more. So much so that when Tristan, the poor guy, mentioned at work that all the other docents from the museum and Mr. Martindale were planning to come to the opening tonight, I nearly bit his head off.

"What do you mean Martindale's coming?"

"You didn't think he'd want to see a new work of J. B. Lester? He's a huge fan."

"The work will be there for a month, maybe more!"

"Karina, are you all right? Usually people are happy when they find out people are coming to their gallery."

"I'm worried over my performance is all," I said, trying to hide my embarrassment. Well, the job was nice while I'd had it, and I was going home very soon anyway. Might as well confess partly. "I'm self-conscious about my dancing. I didn't really want you to see it either."

"Oh, Karina, I'm sure it's going to be perfectly lovely," he assured me. He bought me lunch, but I was too nervous to eat more than half of it. As we sat there in the café, I noticed Tristan was starting to seem nervous, too. He was always fidgety and awkward, but this was more than usual.

"Are you all right?" I finally asked. "You're acting like the nervous one."

He gave a weak laugh. "I have a confession to make."

"What kind of confession?"

"The kind of confession that makes blokes like me nervous to talk to women like you," he said. "See, the thing is . . . I'm bringing my mum to the soiree tonight."

"Your mother?" Oh no.

"Well, yes. You see, she's arriving by train shortly, and she's been haranguing me all summer about how I'm doing, how I'm getting on, you know . . ." He grimaced and forced himself to spit the rest out. "So, you see, I told her about you."

"What did you tell her about me?"

"That I met this American girl who works at the museum also, and about how I take you to lunch and everything . . ." He trailed off and looked at me helplessly.

"You let her think we're dating."

"Yeah."

Goodness knows I had been guilty of the exact same kind of partial truth to my own mother in the past. I had stopped, but Jill still did it. I could hardly blame him for that, and if I did, I was a hypocrite. But I had to make sure he knew what he was getting himself into, then. "Tristan, you're a really nice guy and all—"

"Please don't take it the wrong way! I mean, I would have loved to be dating you, Karina. But as the expression goes, you're out of my league."

"Okay, first of all, the only thing that makes me out of your league is that you think of yourself in a lower league, but let me finish what I was saying. Tristan, I think tonight's performance might be a bit more edgy than I've let on. Meaning, I don't know that it will be, well, *mom appropriate*."

"Oh." He bit his lip and stared at me while he worked through my possible reasons for being self-conscious. "Oh my." But then he brightened. "Perhaps it's for the best, though. She'll be scandalized and tell me I must have nothing further to do with you, and I'll say 'All right, Mother; you know best,' and we'll carry on from there!"

I couldn't help but laugh a little. "So long as she isn't so scandalized that she makes you go home."

"Oh, did I tell you? They said yes to my transfer to CUNY. So I might really and truly be headed for New York. Oh dear, you don't think my mother would try to stop me, do you?"

"You tell me. Was she against you going to London? New York isn't any worse. It's about the same."

"Now that you mention it, she was all for my coming to the city. Though I don't know that she pictured me getting mixed up with a . . . controversial performance art crowd. Well, nothing for it. If she begs off attending tonight I'll let her, but she says she's been looking forward to it. In fact, I ought to go off now to meet her train." He stood up, nearly knocking over his chair. "Karina, thanks. You've been a really good friend to me."

"Likewise," I said, and shook his hand. "See you tonight, *boyfriend*."

We had a little laugh about that and then off he went.

I called Michel before heading back to the ArtiWorks. "Is he there?" I asked. "What should I do to stay out of his sight?"

"He's at the bed-and-breakfast down the street right now,"

he told me. "The glass is fully installed, there's only one painting waiting to be hung, the chairs and tables are done, and
the espresso machine is working. Everything is ready, Karina.
Hurry home and you can hide in your room until it's time to
get into costume."

I had on a hat and sunglasses just in case, which was probably silly and useless, but I didn't want to take unnecessary
chances. I paused for a moment to look at the front of the
gallery café now that the paper had been taken out of all
the windows. The letters THE ARTIWORKS were carved into the
wooden sign and filled with gold.

I turned to go to the door to the flat, though, and nearly
ran into a man in a stained white undershirt.

"Karina," he said.

It was Damon George, looking like he hadn't slept or
shaved in several days. "Damon, are you all right?"

"I will be. Had to make sure this was delivered on time."
Behind him two men were carefully carrying a large, square,
paper-wrapped parcel. I assumed it was a painting. "I'm going to go have a shower and a nap now."

"You don't look well." I could see dark circles under his
eyes, and one of his eyelids twitched.

"I'll be all right. See you tonight." He gave me a weak wave
and wandered back to the truck he had arrived in. The two
deliverymen helped him up into the passenger seat, and then
away they went.

Odd. I wondered if he had spent every waking moment
since I'd last seen him working on the painting. Up until that
moment, I'd half-wondered if he actually painted, or if the
photo shoot had all been an excuse to push me.

I went upstairs, not wanting to get caught in the gallery, and told Paulina what I had just seen. She was in the kitchen, glazing the tops of a hundred tiny éclairs with chocolate. She called Michel downstairs, who assured her the painting was fine and he was hanging it.

My stomach was starting to fill up with butterflies, so much that I couldn't even sneak an éclair off the tray when Paulina urged me to. How many hours until the performance? What was I going to do?

I went up to my room and checked my e-mail. There was one from Jill saying she had run her phone battery down and was on her way to the airport. Mom was out of surgery and doing well. At least that was one less thing to worry about at the moment.

Then I caught Becky on video chat. "Ahh, Becks! I have so much to tell you!"

She grabbed her laptop with urgency, and her face grew huge on my screen. "Oh my God, Rina! I got a message from Paul saying she thought maybe you might meet him, and then I've heard nothing since! What is going on over there?"

"Where to start? The short version is the gallery is opening tonight, and through the people I met in York we got him to agree to do a glass installation for it, and he's here in London right this second, just down the street, actually."

The image on my screen went blurry as she bounced herself onto her bed from her desk chair. She lay sideways facing her computer as she talked. "And so you're going to, what, go talk to him? Right?"

I bit my lip, trying to figure out how to explain my plan.

"Wait, no, let me guess. It always has to be more complicated than that," she said, as her cat came into the frame and lay down in front of her. She petted him.

"Yeah, it's complicated. See, the art installation that he did? I'm convinced it's about me, that it's an expression of how obsessed he is with me. I think if I try to talk to him, he'll run away again. But if I show him? I'm planning to do an interpretive dance as one of the three Muses, and then, um, interact with the sculpture."

"Is interact a euphemism?"

"Maybe?" I cringed a little. "It's hard to put it all into words." I needed to show him I belonged in his world and in his vision. I would show him how well I knew him and his art, too. And I would show how willing I was to be the target, the recipient, of all that primal male sexual energy, violent as it might be. And the fact that the shoes fit me...Could it be that he was that obsessed with me, down to my shoe size? Or was it a kind of wishful-thinking invitation on his part? Or both?

The more I thought about it the more certain I was that he pictured me in the midst of that glass, in the negative space created by the great wave.

I explained as much of it to Becky as I could. The Hokusai reference intrigued her. "Hey, listen to this," she said, as she pulled up biographical information on Hokusai on her screen and read it to me. "*Hokusai was known by at least thirty names during his lifetime. Although the use of multiple names was a common practice of Japanese artists of the time, the number of names he used far exceeds that of any other major Japanese artist.*" She grinned. "Sound like someone we know? Also there's this. *His father never made Hokusai an heir, so it is possible that his mother was a concubine.*"

James had never mentioned his father to me once, though he'd told me about his mother a few times. "Interesting. Well, with any luck, I'll get to ask him soon whether the reference is real or if I just imagined it. Here, let me e-mail you the photos we got for the setup."

"So what gave you the idea to do a dance?"

"I always liked dancing. The only reason I quit was I didn't really have time. And I wasn't as good as a lot of the dancers who were serious about it."

"Is that really true? Or is this another one of those Karina-doesn't-know-what-she-wants situations?"

"I don't know. It's hard to tell how good you are or not." I shrugged. "Like I said, I always liked doing it. I've been practicing and practicing. I'm so sore! I forgot how to use half those muscles."

"Please tell me someone will be taking video. I want to see this!"

"Even the, uh, interactive part?"

"Oh. Is it going to be really graphic? Will I be embarrassed to watch it?"

"I'm not sure, honestly. My skirt will hide what's going on, I think. I mean, it might look worse than it actually is, but I'm going to do my best to make it look very erotic."

"Good to know. Okay."

"I mean, my boss from the museum and my coworkers are all going to be there. One of them is even bringing his mother, but I can't really think about that. The only person in the audience who matters is James." I blinked and sat back suddenly.

"What? What did you just realize?"

"Another guy I know, Damon George, showed up today

with a painting. But I never told him about the gallery open-ing. How did he find out about it?" Clearly he had known for a while if he'd had time to plan the photo shoot with me and create a painting.

"That's the guy you said was the rich donor, right?"

"Yeah."

"I'm sure he heard through the art world, then. Paul and Misha are blasting it all over the place, you know. It's not like the show is a secret."

"I'm sure you're right."

I kept her distracting me for as long as I could, listening to her tell me about how her class was going, and taking Milo to the vet, and how hot a summer it had been in New York, until Michel knocked on my door because it was time to get into costume.

He himself was already in his garb for the evening, which was a flower-print housedress, complete with frilled apron. He had curled his hair and was wearing large cat-eye glasses. If not for the spot where he had a bit of razor burn on his neck, he could have easily been mistaken for a happy, thick-armed, middle-aged housewife.

We put Helen and Linae into their gowns first and gave them their masks, and they went downstairs to hang around and mingle. Linae also said she was going to quickly check that Peter wasn't being stupid. Apparently he had cut himself on a piece of glass while they were working on the installa-tion. The edges were truly sharp. My plan was to stay upstairs until Michel called me at the last minute before my perfor-mance.

"How do you know Damon George?" I asked him, as he stitched a loose glass chip into place.

"He's well known for his art philanthropy," Michel said. "Some of the funds for the renovation are from him."

"Really? Out of the blue? Or did you know him before?"

"We knew him before, but when he found out you were living with us, he called up and demanded to know the details. Checking your references, I believe, but he was very intrigued by the gallery project."

I flashed back suddenly to a conversation James and I had about whether donors could be taken seriously as artists themselves. "And he convinced you to hang a painting of his?"

"I didn't need much convincing, chérie. Did you ever look at the signature on the painting of Paul and me? It's a bit messy, but it says *Georgiades*."

"So Damon was in that crowd of twentysomethings who followed you and Paul around?"

"It's not uncommon for the children of the very rich to end up in art school. They can indulge in an impractical education," he said.

"So he knows James, too."

"They met, at least. They might have been rivals if James had not left for other pursuits shortly thereafter." He sat back and handed me the gown to pull on over the bodysuit.

"Damon didn't tell me any of this."

"Of course he didn't."

I put on the gown and Michel fussed over it, making sure it hung properly. "Is Damon any good at painting?"

"Did you think we would commission a portrait from a man who was not?" Michel asked, somewhat amused. "Very strong technically, also very good with oils. His only drawback is his lack of a subject. He used to paint himself most of the time. Nothing else held equal interest. As you can imagine, the art world was less interested in the self-portraits of an unknown than Damon's ego could handle."

I held in a laugh. Poor Damon. "Well, I'm glad he chipped in."

"When you go downstairs you will see what he painted. I think it is by far his best painting yet, but I must say, Karina, it is recognizably you there with him."

"Is it? I did model for the reference photos."

"It is an outstanding painting. All right, chérie. I must go. I will call you when it is time for your grand entrance."

He bustled off then to play host. Out his window I could hear people on the sidewalk, chatting and buzzing. I snuck a look. A short line of people had formed waiting to get in.

I went back up to my room. I had at least an hour to wait, probably more like two.

Becky was offline now, probably out for the afternoon. There was nothing new from Jill. I sent e-mails to all the last-known addresses I had for Troy, all but one of which bounced immediately.

And then, because I couldn't think of anything else to do with myself, I checked how comments were going on the story I had posted to that LL fan site. I had disabled the e-mail notifications a while ago because I'd gotten such a deluge.

Comments were still coming in. They were mostly more of the same, praising either how hot the story was, the writing, or expressing how much they missed him, too.

Am I special? I wondered. *He made an entire world love him and left them. Do I deserve to be the one who gets him back?*

I had to stop thinking that way. To keep myself positive,

I tried to imagine sitting down and talking with him later, maybe over breakfast or tea. Yes, tea at a fancy restaurant here in London, a long, leisurely meal where everyone's re-laxed. What would I ask him?

I started to write down a list of questions, which grew quite long.

Why did you abandon me at the party?

Why didn't you tell me not only your name, but who you were, sooner?

When had you planned to tell me, if not then?

Is there some reason you're so hung up on secrecy?

What's the story with Lucinda?

What was art school like?

How did you meet Paulina and Michel?

Were you rivals with Damon Georgiades?

Why don't you ever talk about your father? Did you know him?

When can I meet your mother?

How did you become Lord Lightning?

Why did you keep your artist identity a secret, too?

What drew you to glass art?

How did you get into the society?

How did you know you were into BDSM in the first place?

Why do you love sex in public places so much?

Are you proud of me for turning in Renault?

Why didn't you shut off my phone?

Have you had your heart broken (before)?

My phone rang and I jumped, I was so deep in thought. It was Michel.

"Showtime, chérie," he said. "Your music is cued."

Fourteen

Love Dares You to Care

Paulina had helped me pick the music. I wanted something instrumental that started slow and then got faster toward the end, something with lots of drums, preferably, and that wasn't too long. We'd found the perfect thing on a soundtrack album she had, which she said James had worked on in Japan under another name, but which the deeply devoted fans had found out about. The song used Japanese taiko drums, beginning with the small ones, played lightly, and ending with the huge ones, sounding like thunder. That matched my interpretation of the glass crest as Hokusai's great wave.

My other two "Muses" were waiting at the bottom of the stairs to the flat. We adjusted each other's masks and they giggled a little as Michel opened the door to check on us.

"Ready?"

"As we'll ever be," I said, swallowing hard. The butterflies were gone now, replaced by a lump in my stomach, but at least I was calm. It was time to go through with it and then see what would happen.

Michel signaled someone inside the café, the lights went down, and we entered through the ArtiWorks front door, the first tappings and beats of the music beginning.

The other two had flowers in their hands, and they scattered them into the audience as we made our way to the cleared area that was our stage at the foot of the huge red and white glass sculpture. This was the first time I had seen the art lit properly, with some of the lights glowing from underneath it, including one tiny LED right at the tip of the phallic part. Intense.

We moved through the steps we had rehearsed, holding hands and dancing in a circle the way the Muses are sometimes shown in paintings, and then the other two faded off to the sides as I shed my gown and one of them took it with her. Maybe fairy wings wouldn't have been bad after all, I thought, since it was like I was emerging from a chrysalis.

The music got faster and I began to spin in place, the petal pieces of my skirt flaring up to expose the bottom of the bodysuit, then a quick run to stage left, then back to stage right, a leg lift and scissor kick at each. Now I was the wave, the water, and what I did with one little toe rippled through my body to break like a wave out one arm or the other or up my spine, throwing my head back. The dance was as sensual as I could make it.

I moved toward the glass then, repeating many of the same motions I had done at the edge of the audience, but now my arms unfurled between the stalactites of red glass hanging down like teeth. Peter had cut himself on one of these pieces, some of them sheared and broken. I was careful not to touch the edges. Bleeding would definitely put a damper on my plan.

I then focused my movements on the phallic piece. Unlike the jagged parts, it was utterly smooth, and I ran my palm in a circle over the bulbous end, both as part of the sensuality of the dance and to check that it was as smooth as it looked. It was. I rubbed against it with one hip, then the other, then did a long slide into a crouch, running my pubic bone down the nearly waist-high shaft, then back up again, teasing it the way I would had it been a cock, teasing the audience the same way. I was teasing myself, too, making myself wet and aroused. I ground my clit against the hard tip, my hips moving in an obscene circle. I heard a gasp over the sound of the drums growing louder. Almost time.

As the music came to a crescendo, the drums thundering and the cymbals crashing, I turned around. The angle of the phallic part was such that it would work better from behind. I slid my feet into the shoes, unsnapping the crotch of the bodysuit with one hand and easing the glass tip into me with the other. Let the audience think I was miming it; I wasn't. The sculpture had mounted me. My mouth fell open and fresh sweat broke out across my face as I pushed myself back, forcing it deeper. It was large enough to be a challenge, large enough that some of those watching would probably be certain I was faking taking it in. Wouldn't they?

I pushed back once more, an involuntary sound breaking from my throat as the final cymbal crashed and I flung my arms forward into my final pose. The lights went black and the audience erupted into applause.

I held the pose, my chest heaving and my heart pounding, as the lights gradually came up inside the sculpture, only enough so that a stagehand in coveralls and heavy gloves could help me free of the art. I eased myself off of the glass inside me, and then he took me by my hands. I tried to step out of the shoes, avoiding the spiky "teeth" jutting up, but he picked me up and carried me free of the sculpture, around the espresso bar, and into the back room. I clung to his neck, my heart in my throat, hardly daring to hope that the reason his arms felt so familiar was something other than my wishful thinking.

By the time he was carrying me up the narrow stairs into the flat, I knew it was James. He set me on my feet when we reached the sitting room, kissing me as if his life depended on it. I sank my fingers into his hair, which was black today, and kissed him back. He threw off the gloves and fitted his hands around the curve of my ass, grinding me against the erection inside his coveralls. The portrait of Paulina and Michel that Damon had painted looked down on us like a pair of benevolent saints.

"My bedroom is upstairs," I said.

"Take me there." His voice was husky, barely controlled. I had a feeling if I didn't hurry, he might change his mind and take me right there on the carpet of the sitting room.

I ran quickly up the stairs and he chased me, the work boots he was wearing thumping on the steps.

He caught up to me at the door of the room and we tumbled together onto the bed, knocking the phone onto the floor. He was struggling to kiss me again, while I was trying to get his coveralls open. His tongue plunged into my mouth as my hand made it inside and wrapped around his thick shaft.

I heard the sound of Velcro ripping as he shed most of the coveralls like a snake, baring himself down to his waist. I kept stroking him, milking a clear droplet of fluid at the tip.

He took my hands then and flattened them against the bed above my head with his own, pushing his way between my knees.

I gasped against his mouth as I felt the hot tip of his cock rubbing the slick inside of my thigh.

"Any demands this time?" he whispered, sliding it closer and closer to my center with each rock of his hips, until the head was gliding over my clit again and again.

"None," I answered. "None but you."

He continued to rock his hips, smearing my wetness up and down his shaft. "Do you have any idea what you do to me, Karina?" he breathed.

"Didn't I just prove that I do?"

His answer was a growl, and the first few inches of him plunged into me. My breath caught, though, as he cruelly jerked it back again, leaving me empty. "You—!"

"Shhhh," he whispered. "You've brought me to this point. You've set the demon loose. From here, I'm in control. Your only choice is surrender."

"Yes, God yes. I surrender!"

"Good, good." He buried his nose behind my ear and pushed my knees toward my shoulders, spreading me wide. He ran his cock slowly up and down my wet seam again, and I held as still as I could to let him. But I wanted to wrap my legs around him and pull him in!

He gave me the tip again, a few short, quick thrusts and pulled out, his head bent and watching the place where his cock tormented me. Then he put it in and thrust to the hilt, making me cry out, punishing me with the thrust and giving me everything I wanted at the same time.

He held still, pressing against me, all the way inside me,

and looked into my eyes. "It would be very cruel of you to stop me now."

"I was going to say the same thing to you."

"So long as we understand each other."

"I understand that you're going to fuck the living daylights out of me." I couldn't catch my breath, so my words came out less suave than I was trying for. "Do you want me to beg? Is that it?"

"That won't be necessary," he murmured, brushing his cheek against mine and nuzzling my neck, one last tender moment before he clamped his hands atop my shoulders and thrust hard into me again. I was glad I had stretched both inside and out in training for the dance. Instead of pain, I felt only a deep electric pleasure, again and again as he settled into a rhythm of pulling free and then plunging into me again, his penetrations rough but regular.

It was everything I'd remembered from that perfect night before it had gone un-perfect, and everything I imagined tonight could be. I dug my hands into the futon, pressing my head back against it, trying to meet the force of his fucking.

When I realized I was growing close, I nearly hyperventilated, begging him silently in my mind to keep going, just like that, squeezing as hard as I could inside, trying to get more friction, more force, more of everything. He shifted position then, pushing himself upward so my face was against his breastbone as his cock ran roughly through my lower lips as he drove it downward, smacking my clit on each thrust. I cried out, an animal cry, as my whole lower body seemed to melt into pleasure, this orgasm boiling over and flowing like heat from my center.

As soon as the waves of pleasure began to ebb, he took

one of my legs in his arms, turning me almost on my side, my other leg crooked. This angle was much harder to take, his cock burying itself in me sideways and feeling huge for it. But he was right. I would not ask him to stop. I had most certainly wanted this and I surrendered to it, to whatever he needed of me, whatever he could take from me. I cried out in both pain and ecstasy, abandoning myself to the unstoppable force that was James's desire.

He was gorgeous, looming above me, his face suffused with passion and need, his muscles taut. He was a force of nature plowing into me.

He forced himself to slow, though, to draw it out, lifting my leg as if he could get his cock to go even deeper.

"On your stomach," he whispered, as if he couldn't quite catch his breath.

I rolled over, wondering if this meant he was going to avail himself of the tighter hole there. But no, he continued to plunge his cock into my core, tickling my anus with a slick finger but not penetrating me.

He looked around then. I saw over my shoulder that his gaze came to rest on the dildo case. "You brought it with you?"

"Of course I did," I said.

"Stay still. Don't move." He disengaged himself from me and went to the case and opened it.

I was expecting him to take out a glass dildo to torment me with, but instead he held up the string of pearls he'd once used. I'd nearly sold them to get the money together for the plane ticket, before Martindale had explained that he'd buy it. I was glad I hadn't.

James wrapped the pearls around his cock, crisscrossing it

and holding them in place so that his turgid flesh bulged under the beads when he closed the clasp with a click.

"On your back," he said.

I complied hurriedly.

"Spread yourself. Show me you're ready for this. Show me you want this."

I reached between my legs and showed him everything. "Please, James."

"Look me in the eyes, Karina. Look at me while I do this."

He held my gaze as he rubbed his cock, now ribbed by the string of pearls, up and down along my slick seam and over my clit.

Then the head of his cock pressed inward, right into my center, stretching me as he slowly increased the pressure, as he forced his way inside bit by bit.

I couldn't keep my hands where they were. I had to grab on to him, one shoulder, one arm, holding my breath as he pushed in. I know the pearls couldn't have made him that much larger, but he felt huge, and as he began to fuck me with short jerks of his hips, I felt my arousal spike again. I was going to come if he kept that up.

He seemed to know it, continuing to stare into my eyes as he brought me closer and closer, his own lips trembling in a snarl of lust, holding himself back to keep control of me, too.

"Touch your clit," he rasped.

"I don't think I'll need to—"

"That wasn't a question!" His whisper was urgent.

"Yes, James!" I reached down with two fingers and massaged my clit, rocking my hips and driving his cock deeper into me. "Oh God!" It wasn't painful, but I could feel I was being stretched. "Oh God, I've missed you."

"I've missed you, too," he whispered into my ear. "Now, I want you to come again. Touch yourself, Karina. Show me that passion. Show me the wanton desire that makes you do what you did tonight."

He held himself still while I lifted my hips and forced myself up and down on his pearl-wrapped shaft. I closed my eyes then, losing myself in that sensation, my fingers sliding in time with the pump of my hips until I began to cry out, a deep wail of satisfaction coming from deep in my core. Oh God, I felt it in the soles of my feet and in the blood pumping through all my veins.

He could not hold back. I slid my palms down the toned plane of his bare back and over his buttocks and marveled at the feeling of his muscles bunching each time he thrust. He lost control then, fucking me wildly, and I heard a sound like raindrops, as the string of pearls broke and they were scattered onto the wooden floor.

He pulled free suddenly, scattering more pearls, and I sat partway up. He was already spurting onto me, shuddering and gasping, painting my thighs with his come. Was he afraid I had gone off the Pill?

He collapsed forward onto his hands, shaking all over, his head hanging.

"James? Are you all right?"

He cleared his throat and sat back, blinking. Then his eyes focused on me and his expression hardened. "Was that what you wanted, Karina?"

"What are you talking about? What I want is you."

He made a dismissive noise and tried to climb off the bed. His legs were wobbly, and the coveralls were bunched around his ankles, tucked into his still fully laced work boots, which ruined that plan. Good. I grabbed hold of the sleeve of the coveralls. "Uh-uh," I said. "You're not running off this time."

He glanced around the small bedroom. Since escape seemed impossible at that moment, he relented. "Here. Clean yourself up." He could reach the bath towel that was hanging on the doorknob to the closet. He used one corner of it himself and then handed it to me. I wiped myself up and then sat up cross-legged on the bed, the petals of the skirt making me look almost respectable. He shifted until he was sitting beside me, some space between us, the coveralls pulled around his waist. Loose pearls rolled across the bedsheets.

I was starting to get my breath back. "Where did you watch the performance from?"

He looked at me with guarded eyes. "Michel hinted that there was something in store regarding the art. I told him I had always planned it as an interactive exhibit, but I didn't expect it would ever be used the way I intended." He looked away, his cheeks flushed.

"Let me guess. I came pretty close to what you had in mind."

He nodded, then put a hand across his eyes. "We should go back to the gallery now."

"You're crazy if you think I'm going to let you go anywhere before I get some answers, James." I reached toward his chest, where the chips of glass sewn into my bodysuit had left red scratches on his skin. He let me touch him and didn't protest. I took a deep breath, trying to keep my cool. I was not going to fall apart merely because my dream reunion wasn't going perfectly. Not yet, anyway. "You at least owe me a decent explanation about what happened between us."

"Is that what you want? Closure?" He tried to shift away from me on the bed, but I held fast to that sleeve with both hands. "Now that you've moved on, what does it matter?"

So much for staying calm. I felt my eyes go hot and prickly with tears as I shouted, "Closure! Are you kidding? I want you, James. You! What the fuck do you mean, moved on? I haven't moved on at all! I've spent this entire summer trying to track you down!" I wanted to hit him, but I didn't dare let go.

He made a dismissive *tch* sound. "It certainly looked to me like you'd moved on when you let Damon and the men at the club have their way with you."

"You're a fucking idiot! You don't know anything about it!" I threw a shoe at him I was so angry. It was one thing if he didn't want me anymore. It was entirely another thing to blame me for things that weren't true. He deflected the shoe and it struck the door. "The only reason I was at that damned club was to look for you!"

He gave me a cold glare. "And what made you think I'd be there?"

"I'm not stupid, James! When I realized the society Damon was talking about was the same one you'd mentioned to me, the same one that hosts the balls in New York, I grabbed at the lead. You had completely disappeared. I had to pursue any connection I could find!"

He stared at me, his expression moving from angry to puzzled to annoyed. His voice was still skeptical. "Damon wouldn't have known about New York. And you didn't know about the society."

"I wouldn't have known about the society except Renault got drunk and ranted about how he'd been barred from it," I hissed.

His eyes widened and his mouth softened. "You turned him in? You did it?"

"Yes . . . I did."

He looked proud for a moment, a caring expression flickering across his face as one of his hands settled on the back of mine. "We . . . we clearly have a lot to talk about."

"That's what I've been saying!" Inside I felt a pang of relief, as I started to believe that he wasn't about to flee the scene. I still didn't let go of the sleeve in my hands, though. "I have so many questions. And you owe me answers." A spike of anger made me ball my fists. "In fact, you'd owe me those answers even if I had slept with Damon George or anyone else at that damned club."

"I'm still not convinced you didn't." His eyes flared with anger.

"Did you forget I was wearing a chastity belt when you saw me there?" I couldn't help it. I raised my voice. "That was my dictum. No sex. You can ask Damon. You can ask Vanette! The belt was her idea to keep me safe from club members who might forget and get carried away!"

James got to his feet in front of me and jerked his head toward the door. "He's down there, you know. Mooning over that painting of you." His jaw clenched.

"Imagine that, a man who couldn't have me turning me into a muse!" I smacked him in the thigh with both hands, letting go of the sleeve and pushing him back.

He went pale as he stumbled back a step. He pulled the coveralls up the rest of the way and fastened them, keeping his eyes off of me.

"Tell me you don't love me. Tell me you have nothing more to say to me. If it's true, go on and say it."

"It's not that I don't love you..." He trailed off, struggling to find words.

"It's that you don't trust me," I spat.

He broke off and stood still for several seconds, drawing deep breaths. When he finally spoke, he was calm. "There is more going on than you know."

"Ha! Yes, James, that's one of the problems. You've kept too much hidden from me."

He ran his hands through his blackened hair. "I haven't just been hiding from you. I—"

I reached down from the low bed and picked up the phone where it was lying amid the strayed pearls. "I've been texting you, you know. Why didn't you shut this phone off?"

"I don't know." He didn't meet my eyes.

"Who has the matching one now? Stefan?"

He nodded.

I pulled up the log of texts. "You want to know how loyal I've tried to be? I texted you every time I told a lie."

He looked up and swallowed, his expression both hopeful and taken aback. I thrust the phone at him.

I got called a slut and a whore for reporting sexual harassment at the hands of my thesis advisor. Yet when I rode naked in the back of a limousine and screamed from orgasm as we drove through the streets, I was cherished and praised. I know which world I'd rather live in.

He handed it back after reading the last text I had sent, his hands shaking a little. "What about Damon?"

"What about him?" I shook my head.

"Have you seen the painting?" His voice was bitter with venom.

"No, I haven't," I said. "I wanted nothing to do with Damon and his painting. He delivered it earlier today when I was busy getting ready to perform. For *you*."

He put his hand over his eyes. "You were amazing," he whispered.

I stood and pulled on the bathrobe Paulina had given me. It was Turkish, she had said, "fit for a pasha." I belted it and held my head high. "What is amazing is that everything I've done to try to stay true to you means nothing."

"That's not true," he said.

"It is. If you don't believe me, then none of it means anything." I felt my eyes prickle hotly again, but I drew a deep breath and did not cry. "Let's go ask Damon what he thinks, hmm?"

James scrubbed his face with his hands. "You know there are people downstairs waiting for us."

"You're not going to hide from them?" I chided.

He winced as if stung. "I have my reasons for hiding when I do."

"That line is getting old."

This time he bristled. "All right. Let's go back to the party. It'll be down to friends and family now, all people who know I'm the artist. Are you up to it, though, Karina? Can you put on a public face for appearances?"

"They've already seen everything there is to see of me," I said angrily as I slipped the phone into my robe pocket. "I will be fine. After all, I only have to be *one* person."

I marched ahead of him, down the stairs, my mind whirling. A voice in the back of my head was pleading with me not to scare him off again, but that voice was tiny compared to how angry I was at him. But maybe it was time to be angry. Maybe if we were going to start fresh, it was necessary to get it all out now.

I wasn't sure. What I *was* sure of was that he stuck right behind me, never letting me get too far ahead, and he was at my elbow as we entered the gallery again, to sudden applause.

Fifteen

I'll Place the Moon Within Your Heart

In the gallery, the coffee and wine were flowing freely. Fifty or sixty people remained out of the crowd that Michel said was close to two hundred at the peak. "Packed to the rafters!" he enthused, "and then you brought the place down! Karina, that was amazing!"

As we moved through the crowd, James stayed right at my side. I watched him, sharing a smile or a handshake with this or that person, accepting their congratulations and listening to their praise. He was used to this, I realized, this sailing through the public eye while churning with angst underneath.

Well, if he could do it, so could I. And I admit, it was very nice to hear the compliments from people who had enjoyed my dancing. A friend of Michel's gave me his card and said he could introduce me to Richard Alston, a choreographer of high repute. As James had said, Damon was there. He was standing beside his canvas, talking animatedly to a few onlookers and yet with only a hint of his usual cocky edge. Vanette was hanging back from the group, watching him. James and I stood just beyond her, where I could get a look at the painting and hear what Damon was saying.

"I would be paralyzed for days, looking at the great works. Then I'd walk up to the canvas with a brush in my hand and freeze, thinking I can't do this. It's not even worth trying. I'll never be that good."

The painting, though, was grand. It wasn't quite Burne-Jones, but it was luminously done. Damon had chosen one of the side camera angles, and one of the poses where my legs were together, my head back, and his expression of longing was almost one of helplessness. My skin seemed to glow in the sunset light, which suffused the dark rock and the shine of his leather armor with warmth. The way James had re-acted, I thought for sure Damon must have picked one of the pornographic poses. If anything, it was the emotional content that was too raw and naked in the painting, not my skin.

The man Damon was talking to was a skinny fellow with a patchy beard wearing a red "patron" ribbon, meaning he had donated more than a thousand pounds to the ArtiWorks. "And you go through this every time you paint?"

"Well, truth be told, every time I've tried to paint for the past ten years, and I've never broken through it. Until now. And I thought I would be rusty, but no, once I started putting paint to canvas, I felt as if I had been working on my craft all those years! All those canvases I had worked on endlessly in my mind, it was as if I had trained myself with them. I can't explain it."

"You must be very pleased with the result."

"I am."

"How much for the painting, then?"

"Aheh. I'm not sure yet if I'll offer it for sale. I hadn't thought beyond getting it finished by today."

Michel and Martindale accosted us then. "James and Karina are brilliant together, aren't they?" Michel was saying.

"Certainly," Martindale answered. "It was already a very powerful piece! But it took Karina to bring it to life. I'll never be able to look at this sculpture without imagining her there."

"Was it that obvious it was made for her?" James asked.

"Far from it," Martindale said. "I don't know that any of us would have wrung your intended interpretation from it, as we're on this side of the looking glass. But Karina saw it from the inside, from your side. Karina, you are brilliant."

"I agree," Michel said. "And the brilliance of the piece is that it lends itself to so many interpretations, and yet all of them lend themselves to a facet of the vision her performance crystallized."

"Oho, crystallized. Was that a pun?" Martindale said.

"Perhaps!" Michel said and poured more wine into Martindale's glass. "Karina, chérie, have some wine." He handed me a glass from the tray by the wall.

"Thank you." Martindale clinked his glass against mine. "Oh, by the way, Karina, I have a message for you from Tristan."

"Oh?" I swallowed the wine quickly. "Er, he told me he was going to bring his mother tonight."

"I believe that he did. He told me to tell you thank you for a fantastic performance and, I don't quite understand the message, but he said *his* went swimmingly as well?"

I laughed. "Long story. But all's well that ends well. I can't thank you enough, Mr. Martindale. You've been really awesome to me all summer. I wouldn't be here at all if it weren't for you."

He smiled and blushed a little. "Art is my call of duty," he said. "And look what's come of it." He gestured around. "We'll be sorry to see you go. I was going to suggest that this week you ought to hand back all the tour duties and do some sightseeing." He raised an eyebrow at James, as if hinting at who should be playing tour guide for *me*. James merely raised his glass with a small smile.

Another well-wisher took James's attention at that moment, and I took the opportunity to finally sample one of Paulina's mini-éclairs from the tray on the sideboard. Delicious. Paulina hadn't skimped on the chocolate at all, and she'd made the custard intensely vanilla.

I was just licking the chocolate from my fingers when I got a hug from Helen, who called the performance "Brilliant!" and then motioned at me to turn and look at something.

Peter and Linae Simpson were locked in a movie-pose kiss, with her bent back, one toe pointed and one hand keeping the hat on her head. He had a bandage on his cheek and one on the hand I could see, but neither one seemed to be hampering him. When the two came up for air, they began saying their good nights.

"What's the story with them, really?" I asked Helen as they waved good-bye on the way out the door.

"They're mad, I tell you. You know how he gets so jealous? But if he doesn't get jealous, it's like the spark goes out of their relationship. It's why she and I go out. We don't even talk to men, but the fact that Peter thinks we do, that's what gets him all hot and bothered." Helen grinned. "I'm not sure which of the blokes here talked to Linae and set him off, but there you go. They're on their way back to the bed-and-breakfast to make mad, passionate love. I best wait a while before I head back myself or I won't get any peace."

"When are you going back to York?" I asked.

"If I can manage it, I think I'll stay until Monday. I met the nicest boy here tonight. You must know him, says he works at the Tate, too."

I smiled. "I'm sure I do."

"Yeah, his mother and I got to chatting about York while he was in the loo, and then when he came back we were talking art, you know, like you do, and I ended up talking him into showing me around the sights. His mum seemed all right with it, so that's out of the way, and he's such a cute fellow. I'll give him the time of day and see what happens, you know?"

"Yeah. You can only try and see."

"Cute though. Very cute. That helps." She giggled.

"That it does. Come on. Let's get more éclairs before they're gone."

I put a few onto a small plate and carried one over to James. I wondered if I could see the real James under his public veneer.

I held up the pastry without saying anything. He took it gently with his teeth and licked my finger as he pulled back, chewing it thoughtfully.

"Hmm, that's twice," he said, licking his lips.

"What's twice?"

"Twice we've had éclairs after you had a public art performance involving glass."

"Involving my *ass*, you mean."

That made him break character. He made a silent laugh and shook his head. "I've missed you." He glanced toward the others as if wondering if it was safe to say more.

I looked around the room. The crowd was beginning to thin a little. Over by his painting, Damon was listening attentively to Vanette. She was wearing an almost military-style jacket, which may have added to how severe she looked.

Then Damon got down on his knees and kissed the pointed toe of her well-polished boots. I stared. I couldn't help myself. James turned to see what I was staring at and then looked away quickly, pretending he hadn't seen.

"What do you suppose is going on there?" I asked.

He had an impeccable public mask, but I couldn't miss that he blushed. "I'm sure I can't guess." He looked at me instead of at them, his expression darkening.

"Let's go find out," I said.

"Karina—"

I marched up to them. Vanette smiled when she saw me and gave me a kiss on the cheek. "That was an inspiring performance," she told me. Her eyes flicked back and forth between me and James.

"Thank you," I said. "And thanks for your help. I was wondering if I could ask Damon a few questions, though."

She snapped her fingers and Damon got to his feet, his hands folded in front of him and his head slightly bowed. "Actually, I have a few questions for you, too," she said. "Can we go somewhere private to speak? All four of us?"

There were still too many people in the gallery to do it here. James cleared his throat. "Stefan is driving one of the larger cars tonight."

"Excellent. That would do perfectly," Vanette said coolly.

James took a phone out of one of the many pockets in the coveralls and texted a message. A car in front of the gallery flashed its headlights. "Ah, he's there already."

Stefan tried hard to contain his excitement and happiness at seeing me, keeping his stoic and professional demeanor as he opened the back door for us. But his eyes were alight and his eyebrows twitched at me. I couldn't help but give him a little smile back, squeezing him on the arm as I climbed into the car.

He closed the door behind James and then stayed on the curb, as if keeping watch. I suppose he was.

James and I sat on one side of the spacious limo. Vanette sat across from us with Damon on the floor at her feet. Other than earlier, I had never seen him dressed so casually. He was in worn-looking black jeans and a plain white T-shirt. His hair was tousled and glossy, as if he'd gotten out of the shower with it wet and it still hadn't dried. His eyes were on the floor.

Vanette looked back and forth between the two men like a dog trainer trying to figure out which puppy had peed on the carpet. "I think there's been enough miscommunication between the three of you to fill a couple of plays of Shakespeare and a Russian saga." She crossed her arms. "Frankly, I've had enough of it. Karina, what did you wish to ask him?"

"I wanted him to explain some things to James."

Damon looked up.

"Like first of all, my dictum."

Vanette smiled. "Go on, Damon."

"Penile penetration," Damon said in a low voice, like a schoolboy being chastised by a teacher.

"Louder, please."

"Penile penetration," he said with a huff, looking up and meeting James's eyes.

"And what about before she joined the society?" James pressed. "What about then?"

"As you know, she refused me when we met. Her sole motivation for getting into the society was to search for *you*."

Vanette took up the questions then. "And do you remember what I said when we interviewed her as a trainee candidate?"

"You said you feared she wouldn't make a good trainee because the real reason she didn't allow sex was that she was saving herself for someone."

"And was I right?"

"Yes."

"And did we take her as a trainee anyway?"

"Yes, though now I have to wonder why we bloody bothered," Damon snarled.

"Language," she snapped. "Tell us why you agreed to help her reunite with James."

"Because James is a coldhearted fucker who would never give her a second chance, and I knew she'd fall into my lap once he turned her away," Damon said, then, "Ow!" because Vanette had seized him by the chin and slapped him across the face.

"I warned you to watch your language," she said, then released him. "Again, please."

"I hoped she'd come to me after he rejected her," Damon said.

"And would you say you did your absolute best to be sure they met under fair and neutral circumstances?"

"Oh, come on, Vanette. Now you're being—" he huffed. "Of course I didn't. I did everything in my power to make her look bad in his eyes and I engineered every possible opportunity for her to choose me. All right? I didn't expect to fall for her. Of course I pressed her as hard as I could."

"And did she crack?"

"No." He sounded quite bitter. "She isn't interested in me in the slightest. Nor any other man. Only *that* one."

Vanette looked at me then. "Karina, what would you say was the most valuable thing you learned in your short time as a trainee in the society?"

I ran through possible answers in my mind. *Even the most complicated lusts still boil down to the same thing. Sometimes people can't ask for what they want.* "I'm not sure what you mean."

"Then I will be more specific. Did you learn anything about yourself?"

"Oh. Well, I definitely learned that I get turned on by kinky things, but that getting turned on, fantastic as it is, isn't that big a deal to me."

She looked surprised at that answer. "Truly?"

"I guess what I'm trying to say is that although I discovered I liked being flogged and I was excited by all the blindfolds and tests and things, they didn't *mean* anything. All I did was obey. It was a practice run for submission, but it could never be surrender. And it wasn't love."

I dared a look at James. He was staring at Damon and shaking his head slowly.

"James taught me that I had to be honest, about my desires and my feelings, and with the people around me," I said. "Isn't that kind of what the society is about, too? I mean, I understand why it has to be a secret, but isn't that why people have to be honest about everything else? Isn't it kind of an unwritten rule?"

"Yes," she answered simply. "Anything else you'd like to know?"

It was too good a chance to pass up. "Oh yes, actually...Damon, when did you first meet James?"

"When I was still in art school," he said. "He was sort of in
and out. I met him through Paul and Misha's crowd."

"And how did you get hooked up with the society?"

"I don't know about James. In my case, well, my father
passed me his membership."

So that was something people did, it seemed. I didn't want
to know more about that. "James?" I asked. "What about you?"

"I was brought in by a member I was in a relationship
with," he said quietly.

"Okay." That sounded simple enough. But something still
didn't quite add up. "Damon, when I asked you for help finding someone who went by 'Jules,' did you already know who
I meant?"

Damon swallowed and looked down. "I did."

I looked back and forth between them, and James shifted
in his seat. James spoke then, surprising me. "Karina. You
have to understand how careful I had to be."

I bristled, trying to listen to what he was saying, but already on guard at his defensive tone.

"When I left you in New York, I was...I thought I was in
danger."

"From me?"

"From people who might be trying to find me." He faced
me. "I told you I haven't been hiding from you alone. I re-
gretted leaving you like that. But I had to know."

"Had to know what?"

"If you were really what you seemed. I'm the one who encouraged Martindale to bring you over here. And I'm the one
who set up the meeting between you and Damon."

Damon was hanging his head so that I couldn't see his face. James looked rather stoic, like he was holding a lot in.

I, on the other hand, wasn't holding anything in. "You *what*? You mean you're the one who sent this lech to try to test me?" I nudged Damon with my foot. "And now *you're* upset that I *let* him?" I was so angry I could barely see. "What the fuck gives you the right—?"

James's phone suddenly chirped. He looked at it with alarm. "I think we had better—"

I wasn't about to let him distract me.

"How the fuck does that make sense? I think I passed your little fucking test then, didn't I?"

"Karina," he said in a mollifying voice, reaching for me.

It was too much. I'd worked so hard to get him back, or so I thought, and it turned out he was testing me the whole time? And now he was angry? He didn't know angry, I decided. I'd show him angry.

I burst out of the car, nearly hitting Stefan on the ass with the door and instead running headlong into a woman I didn't know.

"Excuse me," she said, trying to get past me as if to get into the car, like I was exiting a taxi she wanted. She was extravagantly dressed for a London street after midnight, in a diamond choker and Chanel-style skirt suit, the edges trimmed with fur.

Instinctively I blocked her. "Oh, that car's not for hire," I tried to explain.

But behind me Stefan had run around to the driver's side, and I turned to see Vanette closing the door and stepping back from the car as the tires squealed and it sped away.

"No!" The woman took a few steps toward the car, her

heels clicking. She turned to me. "My husband is in that car!"

"Damon is married?" I said, looking at Vanette incredulously.

Before Vanette could answer, the woman turned to me and hissed, "I'm Ferrara LeStrange. Who are you?"

Vanette put an arm around me protectively. "She's a club trainee," she said. "Nice to see you, Ferrara. I didn't realize that you and James had actually married."

James, *married*?

"Last year," the woman said, waving her hand as if throwing away a piece of trash. "In the States. He's been dodging me for months though."

"Oh, truly? He has visited our London location a few times recently."

"I didn't think he did that sort of thing anymore," the woman said. She snapped her fingers, and a man standing behind her handed her a clutch purse. She took a business card out of it and handed it to Vanette. "I would appreciate it if you would let me know if he returns. I can't believe the bastard slipped through my fingers!"

"I'll be certain to let you know," Vanette said to her, then to me, "Come. It's time we were going."

"Yes, Vanette," I said automatically, trying to keep my expression as blank as possible as she led me away from the scene.

The anger that made me bolt from the car was still boiling. James had a lot more explaining to do than I'd even guessed. He sent Damon to test me? And then got bent out of shape about it? He was the one who needed a fucking test: he needed his head examined. And now I find out I'm not the only woman he's hiding from?

"Who the fuck is Ferrara LeStrange?" I burst out, as Vanette turned a corner.

"She is the very definition of trouble." Vanette looked behind us, as if checking that the woman was no longer in sight. "More than that, I cannot say. I cannot break the confidence of a club member."

"Oh come on, Vanette!" I had to suck in a breath to keep angry tears from spilling over my face. "I spend the entire summer trying to find the bastard and then she shows up and . . . poof! He's gone! Who is she? What's her problem? For that matter, what's his problem? No one's giving me any answers! He's married?"

"Well, so she claims."

"Claims? What's her story?"

But it was no use. Vanette just shook her head and clammed up again.

She didn't deserve the brunt of my anger, but I couldn't stop it. "I thought you would help me!"

She was very calm and didn't answer with words. Instead, she gently steered me back toward the gallery, where it appeared Ferrara and her accomplice had left. I resisted for a moment but then went.

I repeated more weakly, now that I had vented some, "I really thought you would help me."

She stopped us outside the door to the gallery. "I don't know if I can help, Karina. There's only so much I can do. Here." She handed me her card and emphasized once more, "I can't violate the privacy of society members. But for anything else . . ."

I took the card and went inside.

Epilogue

I lugged my carry-on bag through the crowded duty-free area, looking for a seat. I was exhausted. I had barely slept last night, crying over tea to Paul and Misha, who were very sympathetic but who couldn't help me any more than Vanette did, really. I was too upset to really absorb the fine details or wild speculations they had about the woman they called Ferrara *Huntington*. They were just telling me they knew her as the wife of a record company executive when my phone had rung again. Jill had arrived in Ohio to find my mom's house robbed. Normally my sister is pretty hard to shake, but the thought that it might have been my mom's supposed boyfriend who robbed the place while she was in the hospital was a scary one. And while Jill went to stay with a neighbor, I immediately searched for the next flight I could get there, which was first thing in the morning. I woke up poor Reginald Martindale to tell him the news, and he graciously agreed to pay for the astronomically expensive last-minute ticket. I told him he should charge James for it. Now that I think about it, maybe he planned to anyway.

So here I was, underslept, exhausted, still aching from the sex I'd had with James last night and feeling bruised in soul and heart over the turn of events. My bag was crammed full of gifts from Paul and Misha—some for Becky—and what souvenirs I could manage to pick up on my way to Heathrow, and I dragged it behind me tiredly. I found a place to settle at last, in front of a shop offering free scotch tasting. That was something you'd never see in an American airport, that was for sure. The whole duty-free area was like a huge shopping mall with a big central court that served as the waiting lounge, ringed with shops selling cosmetics, booze, souvenirs, and more. Passengers stayed in that central lounge until their flight number and gate were announced for boarding.

Maybe a free shot of whiskey wasn't such a bad idea. I couldn't stop the thoughts running around and around in my head. I'd never been so anxious in my life. My mother was in the hospital, her house in disarray, and it might have been her own boyfriend who did it. Was love worth it? Were men worth this much pain?

Ferrara certainly believed so, I thought, if she was fighting that hard to get him back.

A little voice of doubt nagged at me. Vanette had acted skeptical of Ferrara's claims, and Paul and Misha seemed to think she was married to someone else. But if there was no marriage, then why was James hiding from her? Was she just a crazy fan? And if the marriage was real, why keep it a secret?

For that matter, why was everything with James a secret? I

felt angry and disgusted all over again. I still loved him, and my body ached for him, but I couldn't do this. I couldn't live a life where everything was about hiding and keeping things from people. How many times had he asked me what I really wanted in life? Who was the real Karina? Now it struck me as terribly ironic that he'd asked me those things. What about you, James? Is there a real you under there, or am I in love with a phantom? Am I in love with the man you wish you could be, but *aren't?*

I was angry with him, and I was angry with myself for being so hung up on him.

I was so deep in my turmoil of thoughts that I nearly missed it when they called my flight. I finally heard it on the last call. The distance to the gate was so hugely long, it felt like I was walking forever, and I finally broke into a run, fearing I was going to miss it. When I got there, though, they didn't act like it was at all odd that a flustered American was the last one to board the plane. Thank goodness. If they'd been snarky or judgmental I think I would have lost it.

I made it to my seat. I took out my phone to turn it off and then jumped as it rang in my hand.

The caller ID showed it was James. I silenced the ringer. A flight attendant was coming down the row, checking that we were ready for takeoff. I turned it off and stowed it before she could scold me about it. I could not answer the phone now, even if I had wanted to.

And you know what? I wasn't sure I wanted to. Yes, I was full of questions, but I was done with chasing and digging and piecing things together. When he couldn't reach me he'd call Paul and Misha and find out I was on an emergency trip back to the States, but right then I wanted him to stew in it.

It was his turn to wonder what was going through *my* head for a change. It was his turn to wonder what he did wrong to drive *me* away. If he really loved me, if he was sorry, he wouldn't let a little thing like the Atlantic Ocean get in his way. After all, I hadn't.

If he wanted to give me some big explanation about why he ran away and why he was hiding, if he felt I deserved that much, he'd follow me.

It was his turn to prove there was something there. It was his turn to chase me.

Karina and James's steamy adventure continues...

Please see the next page for a preview of

Slow Satisfaction.

A Preview of *Slow Satisfaction*

Dearest Karina,

I have no idea if you'll read this. I hope you will. I decided to sit down and write it because it seems whenever I try to explain myself to you in person, either my passions get the most of me, or my fears do. Perhaps sitting down in a quiet place to compose this, without the distraction of your presence, I can put my feelings into words.

First, an apology. I regret many things, but none more than how much I hurt you. I have no excuse. My past is my past. My baggage is heavy, and perhaps now you can see why I wanted a fresh start with you, as if I had no past, no attachments, no burdens. You gave me the freedom to be myself and to love you without reservations. I wish I had been able to keep my past and my demons at bay for one more day back in April, and I wish it again now. I'm sorry. I let my fears get the better of me that night at the ball, my suspicions and my paranoias blinding me to what I had right in front of me.

The love of my life.

I'm a fool. Maybe that means I don't deserve you. Stefan, who has never said a word out of line in all the time he has worked for me, even told me I had made a mistake that night.

I hope you will let me apologize in person. I have so much more to tell you, so much that I dare not put in a letter. I want to tell you everything. Everything you want to know, anyway. It might take years. But I want to spend years with you. I want to share my life with you. Whatever life I'm going to have going forward from this moment, I can't imagine it without you.

That life is about to get very complicated again.

I thought I had put a whole chapter of my life behind me when we met. I thought my contractual obligations to my record company had been fulfilled and I thought various other obligations had been invalidated, but I see now that the book is not closed as I had thought. I cannot say more in a letter, but please let me tell you in person.

I do not know what will happen from this point. I would disappear completely, into anonymity in some distant country, perhaps, except for you. There is no other woman like you in the world, and I was a fool not to love you as you deserve.

Please let me try.

Yours, heart, body, and soul,
James Byron LeStrange